BÉSAME MUCHO

Ex Libris

H. S. Satterla

NEW GAY LATINO FICTION

BÉSAME MUCHO

Edited by
JAIME MANRIQUE with **JESSE DORRIS**

Painted Leaf Press
www.PaintedLeaf.com

Copyright ©1999 by Jaime Manrique and Jesse Dorris

Cover design by James Maszle
Book design by Brian Brunius

"What's Up, Father Infante?" 5 Concurso de cuento Carlos Pastro Saavedra, Fondo de publicoeiones. Transempaques: Medillín, Colombia, 1994.

"Awakened from Their Dreams" courtesy El Corazon.

Library of Congress Cataloging-in-Publication Data

Bésame Mucho/edited by Jaime Manrique with Jesse Dorris
    ISBN 1-891305-06-9 (alk. paper)
    1. Hispanic American gays—Social life and customs—Fiction.
    2. Short stories, Hispanic American (Spanish)—Translations into English.
    3. Hispanic American men—Social life and customs—Fiction.
    4. Gay men—United States—Social life and customs—Fiction.
    5. American fiction—Hispanic American authors.
    6. American Fiction—Male authors.
    7. Short stories, American. I. Manrique, Jaime, 1949– II. Dorris, Jesse.
        PS648.H57 B43 1999
        813'.54080920664—dc21
                                                              98-50721
                                                                   CIP

CONTENTS

INTRODUCTION

Jaime Manrique

A few years ago, for Gay Pride Month, A Different Light Bookstore organized an evening of gay and lesbian Latino/a writers. It turned out to be standing room only. The effervescence in the room was contagious. The readers received not just applause but ovations, and I sensed that something daringly new was being celebrated. Sitting in that packed room, I thought, "A significant event is taking place right here; it's time to start chronicling it and to let the world in on this novel and delicious writing." Thus, *Bésame Mucho* was born.

For the purposes of this anthology, I've defined Latino as any fiction writer of Latin descent who has lived a significant portion of his life in the United States. The aim of this anthology is to present a sampling of contemporary, living, Latino writers. That's why the great forerunners—Lorca, Cernuda, Manuel Puig, Reinaldo Arenas, Manuel Ramos Otero, Gil Cuadros—are not here. My hope is that some day in the not too distant future the not too distant future such an important and much needed volume will appear.

Readers may note some glaring absences in this volume. Several important contemporary Latino writers who were invited to participate could not contribute to this enterprise. Nonetheless, I suspect that what there is here will enthrall and surprise many readers. This is a generation of Latino writers who write openly and defiantly about their sexuality, a taboo subject in Latino culture. These men are among the writers who will help transform American writing in the twenty-first century.

And why the title *Bésame Mucho*? After the stories began to come in, it struck me that despite the wide range of themes explored in these pieces—homophobia, the sinister influence of the Catholic Church on homosexual culture, magic realism, the constraints imposed by Latino families on their gay children, history, rock, santería—the underlying force propelling and infusing these works was a romantic and passionate view of life. Many of the stories deal with the oldest and most universal theme in literature: the need human beings have to love at all costs, and to romance the heart.

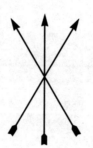

Photo: Debra St. John

GUILLERMO REYES' stories have appeared in the *American Review, Caffeine, New Mexico Humanities Review, Crazy Quilt, Magic Realism, Christopher Street*, the *Evergreen Chronicles*, and the Alyson anthologies *Shadows of Love* and *Certain Voices*. Better known as a playwright, his play *Men on the Verge of a His-panic Breakdown* was produced off-Broadway and in regional theaters across the country, along with *Deporting the Divas, Chilean Holiday, A Southern Christmas*, and others. He is the head of the playwriting program at Arizona State University in Tempe.

The Straight Friend Who Came to Dinner

Guillermo Reyes

I wouldn't normally apologize for my well-developed sense of lust. It wouldn't be like me to belittle the one drive that has kept me yearning for another day, way in the future, when it would be fulfilled. Lust as hope, lust as the struggle for self-realization, lust as a zest for living, I won't apologize for this, but I will make amends (one day) for trying to fulfill my lust by impersonating a Catholic: I will shamefully admit that only lust led me to attend Sunday services at St. Matthew's. Hesus Sang had become president of Catholic Youth and whether or not he remembers it, he touched my hand, or rather scraped it, when he passed a flyer to me after school and the edges of it scratched the surface of my skin so lightly that I nearly bled through the sensation alone.

My first, second, and third services were quiet affairs, spent in reticent observation of Hesus Sang's firm posterior as he sat in the front pews of the well-lit glass church on Wilshire. I then walked away alone, fearful of my desire. I didn't know how long

I could continue to attend services before they began to suspect genuine piousness on my part and start inviting me to First Communions. When I finally made my move on that fourth Sunday, I introduced myself not to the youth leader himself but to Father George, the parish priest, who led me like a guiding spirit to him. I shook his hand, firmly and as macho-like as I imagined a same-sex shake of hands must be.

I must clarify that I am not, and never have been Catholic. I am instead Jewish, or culturally Jewish and religiously apathetic with a mother who is militantly atheist. But born in Santiago, Chile, and brought up there until my early teens, I'd been around Catholics long enough to know how to pass for one, if and when necessary. In Santiago, I succeeded in my attempts to blend in, although, due to the vociferousness of my mother's beliefs, we were expelled from Chile anyway. Not because we were atheist or Jewish, but because mother was a Socialist. Personally, I was never much of a leftist convert, but I did learn to please my mother and pass for a socially concerned activist. I was born to don disguises, and therefore I had no qualms about attending Sunday services at St. Matthew's with the single motive of—let's say—sodomizing the president of Catholic Youth or, given my real inclinations, to be sodomized by him instead.

"This is Hesus," said the priest. The youthful leader wore a gray two-piece suit and a tie long enough to administer an execution by hanging. "He'll be your mentor," he said, "should you need one, of course," he added not having meant to read neediness on my gaunt, famished face.

"Anything I can do," said Hesus, "that's what I'm here for."

He was fantasy, and at seventeen, already a man in the flesh, fully formed, with a glint of eagerness in his eyes. I knew already that his Salvadoran mother had gained fame baking her notorious fresh pupusas laced with kimchi in honor of his Korean father (they'd been "Pick of the Week" in the *LA Weekly* earlier that spring). Like one of his mother's culinary creations, he was the best of both worlds, with his wiry black hair partly covering his almond-shaped eyes. A light orange tinge spread through his skin, but his lips bore a bright red seal as if they would stain if they were to kiss one. His nose lowered from his forehead into a pointed tip, and his nostrils often spread out as if flaring in anger. He shook my hand. I felt a softness and boyishness in his weak (or perhaps uncommitted) grasp which was otherwise betrayed by a severity and seriousness of purpose in his expression.

But that was only the beginning of a long process of mere insignificant acquaintanceship. His mentoring left a lot to be desired. It consisted mostly of playing basketball with me and with other members of Catholic Youth, followed by Father George's brief after-game "Scriptural follow-ups." Silence ensued between us the rest of the time. An occasional pat on the back made things physical, but the same pats went elsewhere, generously distributed to the rest of the members of Catholic Youth. During the showers after each game, I felt compelled (by the paucity of opportunities, one must understand) to develop a method of looking at my Catholic playmates without ogling. I learned that a brief glimpse of some aspect of flesh went a long way to stir my imagination. I had a practical reason for training my mind not to dwell on the look of naked playmates: I feared getting an erection at a Catholic gym. I was at least grateful to discover that most Catholic boys in the U.S. are circumcised, and here I did not have to fear any cultural disclosures from that angle. My penis remained mercilessly silent throughout the ordeal.

That day, I decided that I would finally make a declaration of some kind, a disclosure, anything that might break the silence. I waited until Hesus Sang had draped the towel around his waist and he stood shaving in front of a mirror. His face was too smooth for shaving, but I wasn't about to shatter his illusions. I was dressed in my jeans and Catholic Youth T-shirt and matching cap and windbreaker. "Can I, like, speak to you about something really serious?" I asked. He was headed toward his locker by then, feeling shaven and brazen, eager to get dressed. He walked with his arms arched, as if he'd been some buffed-up Asian-Latin cowboy.

"Can it wait?" he asked. "How about dinner?"

I fidgeted in discomfort. "I can't afford that."

"I own a restaurant," he said.

"Oh," I looked on perplexed. "That's right, the Salvadoran-Korean Express."

"Got it!" he said. "Hope it won't take long—I got physics homework. Could you help me?"

"I'm failing history," I answered. "And math," I added, as if adding to a list of youthful failures. I didn't have much else to say for myself. I had nothing to offer him except this belief that my feelings, for some reason, mattered and needed to be reciprocated lest I fall into a state of depression that would endure to old age and I'd die a tragic hero of unrequited love (so many of my Chilean aunts had).

I followed him through the doors of the standard mini-mall store with its confining hole-in-the-wall look and was surprised to feel comfortable inside. The restaurant was furnished by modest foldout (but padded) chairs and patio tables. Pictures of both Salvadoran and South Korean landscapes decorated the walls and green plants hung from the ceiling. I was introduced first to Mr. Sang, a short thin-faced man who surprised me by bowing. Mrs. Sang (maiden name Leticia Contreras) greeted me in reticent English, as if fearing her pronunciation. Mr. Sang asked her to bring us sodas using broken Spanish. She answered in spartan Korean, telling him what I took to mean, "Get it yourself." Neither spoke English well. But perhaps silence was required between them to get on with the matter of survival and prosperity and the simultaneous multiplication of the Salvadoran-Korean communities. The couple had spent some twenty years working at their restaurant while giving birth to their five sons. I met only two of them that night, the two brothers who worked for the Salvadoran-Korean Express. Hwan-Jose was the youngest, the shortest, and the most prepubescent-looking, practically a child at sixteen. He wore a busboy apron that tightened into his small frame and made him disappear behind it. Kyong Javier, the older brother, was more to my demanding taste. Kyong Javier resembled Hesus and bore the same arrogant stride of manner, although he was shorter and, again for my taste, not as enticing as the president of the Catholic Youth. "He never finished school," said Hesus with surprising disdain as if to warn me to avoid him like radiation.

Mrs. Sang served us tamales with bi bim bap and an assortment of other dishes I could hardly name. She smiled at us with a cocky reassurance as if to suggest she rated the best, if only, Korean-Salvadoran cook in the world. The aromas arising from the table, pickled cabbages and green corn tamales, entranced me, and, one might even say, seduced me.

"I—I love all of this," I told Hesus, uncertain of what else to say.

His red lips looked stained in kimchi. "Yeah, little hole in the wall, keeps the family going. Want more pulgogi with your chile relleno?"

"No, thank you. I think the sulong tang with albóndigas was rather filling. But you know what I really want to talk about..."

"Yeah, what?"

"These last couple of months have been very special for me."

"Me, too," he said. "The faith grows within us."

"Uh, yeah, that too, what I really mean is..."

"Yes? What?" He tore the leg of some poultry-like animal soaking in some inscrutable sauce.

"I feel very close to you."

"You should. We go to the same youth group, we're in the same school, even though it's too secular, my parents don't want to pay for Catholic prep."

"I prefer it that way—you get to meet different people."

"But we didn't meet *because* of school. You're in the slow courses, they segregate us too much, maybe I should tutor you to get you going in your senior year. I'm your mentor, anyway. What are mentors for?"

I sat crumpling the paper napkin. I didn't like that the conversation was headed in an academic direction.

"Are you a virgin?" I finally asked.

He looked unaffected. "Oh, you want to talk about sex."

"Not really talk."

"I know, who needs talk?" His mother walked by like an attentive waitress and smiled. We waved. "Better not get me started on that subject," he said. "Not here."

"Do you masturbate at least?"

"Look…" He stared around him. Kyong Javier could be seen busing an empty table, pocketing the tip. He wore a green apron and stopped to light a cigarette. He took a few puffs before continuing to clean the table and giving us both a smile of complicity, as if he'd heard us.

I pressed on. "Have you ever masturbated in public?"

"What? What type of question is that?"

"I read it in Arthur Miller's biography."

"Who?"

"Famous Jewish playwright," I answered and almost added "like I myself would like to be," but I did not want to explain either my theatrical ambitions or my actual heritage. "I read it in his biography that he once caught the entire football team in his school masturbating in the locker room, not each other of course—each to his own, you know, but together like a good team. And he wouldn't join because he was too shy. I would have been too shy too, but I probably would have looked. What about you?"

I thought I'd dropped enough hints. He looked by now rather perplexed. Mrs. Sang walked by wiping her hands on a white cloth. "¿Todo está bien?"

"Oh, sí, sí, ¡exquisito!" I said, giving myself away as a Spanish speaker. I didn't feel I had time for her and I hadn't bothered to make an effort to speak much to her in any language. Mrs. Sang looked as if she would leap at me and embrace me, which mercifully she didn't.

"Muy bien, habla español," she said. "Casi nunca hablo mi propia lengua, a estos estúpidos les da miedo, fíjese."

"Mom, stop calling us stupid," said Hesus. "I'll study Spanish and Korean in college, OK? Right now I got to concentrate on pre-med, remember?"

I decided not to get involved in this cross-cultural, intergenerational, opportunistic debate.

By then, Hesus had thrown down his napkin. "I think I should drive you home now."

Two weeks went by, and I did not hear from Hesus. My mentor missed two weeks of after-school church activities. Father George announced to his flock of young basketball players that their president was preparing college applications and couldn't be bothered with the game. He encouraged us to make our own collegiate plans—I resented Hesus for this already. At best I rated as one of the more promising students in remedial math but hoped that in the arts—probably in the crass entertainment wing—I'd rise above the norm. That was my highest form of ambition, but my audition as King Lear did not impress the prominent members of the Drama Club, so I had already been rejected in the only field of endeavor I found. I decided the judges didn't know intentional overacting when they saw it and hoped I'd be better understood by future vanguards of culture.

A few nights before Halloween, I opened the door of our one-bedroom apartment to answer an unnecessarily loud thump and found Hesus standing on the welcome mat. He held a six-pack of O.B. Korean beer he'd lifted from the restaurant. I was alone. He had missed my mother by a few minutes. She'd slipped into her red Partido-Socialista-de-Chile-en-el-Exilio T-shirt and gone to meet her friends at a Nueva Canción concert, leaving me some Afghani take-out for dinner. Hesus Sang found me in a thermal set of pajamas that sealed my body from neck to toe as if to hide it from the lust of strangers. He walked by me without at all commenting on my appearance. He had no words on the shoddiness of the apartment, with my single bed in the middle of the living room where a coffee table might have fared better. He couldn't have failed to notice the Che Guevara poster, but instead plopped down on the couch, eager to talk about himself.

"Finished the applications, man," he said. "I'm ready to party." He was about to hand me over a can of beer when we heard the keys jiggling outside. Hesus managed to throw the beer beneath my mattress, then sat up to witness the entrance of my mother, a woman in her late thirties with long reddish hair that curled up into U's on the side. Sabina Sverloff, daughter of purged Soviet Marxists who ended up in South America from where we were equally exiled, cut a striking figure, a presence, an intensity of epic proportions. One could imagine her posing for Delacroix holding a revolutionary flag as her breasts broke through her blouse to hover over the battlefield. She looked irked about forgetting the tickets to the concert, a benefit for Chilean human rights organizations, but when she saw Hesus, she appeared to change into softness and sweetness uncharacteristic of her.

"So he has a friend," she said, surprised. "One friend."

"From Catholic Youth," said Hesus Sang, shaking her hand. She thought nothing of it; she herself associated with gentiles in greater proportion than Jews. "I'm his mentor," he added as I rolled my eyes.

"Yes, please be his mentor," she said as she found her tickets beneath a flyer for an anti-nuclear proliferation rally. "Be a good one—I'm his mother, by the way."

"And he's told me so much about you."

"No, he hasn't. He's ashamed of me. We had to leave Chile

because of me. I'm a subversive, he'll never forgive me, sometimes I think he just disdains me... I have to go now." She swung her bag on a thin leather string and was gone.

Hesus sat down hitting his knee with the palm of his hand.

"She's a subversive," I reminded him. I was worried. I'd begun to imagine an attraction between them. Worse than mutual attraction, passion and consummation, I feared the two would wed and mate and I'd end up Hesus's stepson instead of his lover. I imagined I'd end up as a baby sitter to my stepbrothers as she and he attended South African anti-apartheid rallies. Sabina had a tendency to date men I found attractive and the message of Fate or the Life Force seemed clear: she attracted men, I didn't, and I was doomed to know the difference. "She's a Marxist, and very, very dangerous," I told him.

"And who am I supposed to be? General MacArthur landing at Inchon?" He popped his first beer open. "Pretty South American women—you can tame them, you know. Dad should know."

"Your mom is Central American," I corrected.

"You know what I mean. What's wrong with you today, man?"

"And why are you calling me 'man'? Why are you here?"

"Because," he said, breaking into a pout full of playful boyishness that was, to my eyes, irresistible although I never would have let him know this. "Because I've missed you."

"Missed me?" I looked up suspiciously. "Why?"

"I've been thinking about what you said, and I guess I am kinda shy, like that writer, Arthur Mills."

"Miller, Arthur Miller."

"I guess I couldn't whack off in public either."

I reached out for my own beer can. "Well, why not?"

"Because it's gotta be private. Just me and the thoughts of that special someone."

"Someone?"

"You know...a babe."

"A babe?"

"Make that a hot momma!"

"What? Stop that, stop right now!"

"I should, but hey, this is my fifth beer tonight."

"Fifth beer?"

"Yeah, and after a couple more beers, I think I'll go home and do what the football team did, but alone."

"All alone?"

"I won't get into trouble that way, I have pre-med to think about—hell, it's all I've got."

"How sad...if that's all you've got."

"I don't want to get anyone pregnant."

"That shouldn't be a problem."

"You mean condoms."

"They've become necessary."

"No, I don't want to blow my chances. It's pre-med or nothing, I don't wanna be like my brothers, bunch of nobodies. Whacking off is all I've got."

I felt my face flushing in anger. I finished my first beer, placed the can on a stack of anti-Pinochet flyers and stood up. I felt responsible for all this. I'd been the one to bring up the subject, and all I'd done with it is confirm his celibacy. I felt like a failure.

"You have to go now," I told him. "I have to, uh, do homework."

"You don't like homework, you said you're not academically inclined."

I opened the door for him. He noticed for once that I was serious.

"Oh yeah, right! What's wrong with you...I come here, everything's fine, your mother's awfully pretty."

"Out!"

"I like her a lot!"

"No!"

"Man! I don't believe this!"

He left clutching the four remaining cans of beer and heading for his father's pickup truck parked off Sunset Boulevard. The evening traffic had become loud and festive with weekend cruisers crowding into pickup trucks and shaking their vehicles back and forth to crawl through the 10-mph traffic.

I shut the door and bolted it. I threw the weight of my featherlight body on the bed and began to suffocate myself with the synthetic pillow. But then I felt my stomach turn as my first beer ever had its effect. I lifted my head and threw up on my mother's bookshelf, straight onto the leather-bound collected speeches of Fidel Castro.

For an entire week afterward, I found myself sitting at home at night by the kitchen table that was my desk, attempting to bury any thoughts of my future in wasted subjects like math and history, wasted at least as taught by uninspiring teachers. I was an underprivileged student from a Third World country, a poor Jew posing as a Catholic, a repressed homosexual incapable of attracting the president of the Youth Club, and living in fear that in order to compete for Hesus's affection I would have to fend off not only the female gender but my mother, an obstacle of gargantuan proportions.

Sabina came home eager to peel out of her sweaty deli uniform and to soak her contact lenses. "I saw your friend tonight at the Fairfax," she said, squinting.

"What friend?" I asked. My stomach felt bloated, full of gas and resentment. Sabina on the other hand looked healthy, hair flowing down to her shoulders, rosy cheeks full of vigor, legs exposed to the evening air as she gave them a sponge bath in front of the radio that was playing marimba classics. Her fingers squeezed through the yellowish sponge. The water came gushing out and running down the smooth trail of her legs into the tin basin she'd bought once in the artisan town of Pomaire near Santiago.

"What do you mean what friend?" she answered. "The only one you've got. Havier something."

"Hesus."

"He's cute. What is he? Filipino?"

"Too complicated to explain, Sabina. Go to your room."

"Hah, hah, hah, that's really funny." She was rubbing lotion on her legs. "Let me tell you this—this friend of yours. He just sat there all night sipping on a cup of coffee and nibbling on a hamantasch. He was staring right at me, and when I asked him if he wanted a coffee refill, he bit his knuckles."

"He's a stalker. He's deadly. Like one of those men that go after stars and strangle them. You should have called the police."

"I can take care of myself," she said, then sighed. "Ah, the president of Catholic Youth's after a deli waitress, an exile, a nobody in the scheme of things—rather flattering."

I thought I'd gotten used to the attention Sabina got. There was the Alabama gas attendant who used to follow her home at night until she made it clear she was a Jew, the Armenian owner of a shoe repair store who offered to make her a partner, the Spanish professor at UCLA who claimed to be studying South American accents, the lesbian supervisor at the deli who quit her job after mother declared her heterosexuality in kind but firm words. My father himself had been a gentile she never married. He left her to wed an upper-class young Catholic woman in Santiago, daughter of a fascist politician. He ended up joining the National Party, which he used as a forum to promote not so much his politics but his wine bottle cork exports. When the Revolution failed, he was at least enough of a gentleman to find us a safe way out of the country. He got rid of us without killing us, and that was in fact quite civilized for a National Party member.

"Hesus left me his number written on a napkin," she said. "Should I call him?"

I sat up, shut the textbook. "Call him? As in to ask him to come tutor me? To help me with school and all?"

"Oh, hasn't he mentored you enough? He's paid his dues, I'm sure, trying to teach you math and stuff. He is infatuated with an older woman—I like that in a boy."

"He's young enough to be your son," I reminded her.

"I didn't get kicked out of Chile to be told who to date," she said.

"Date?" The word became threatening and alarming. "He's seventeen, you'll be arrested."

"Look, Hesus looks serious, looks older and mature, knows where he's going, he's going to be pre-med. But all right," she compromised, "I won't call him until he turns eighteen."

I sat staring at her as she continued to wash. We'd come to a standstill in the conversation. She was whistling. I was for the first time ever trying furiously to finish my homework.

The truce lasted a week. The following Thursday she came home with an announcement: "He's coming next Thursday, to help you with your homework. He's really generous with his time." She went into the freezer and unloaded a pound of fresh salmon into the refrigerator.

I knocked on Father George's door that afternoon and he yelled for me to come in. I found him with his gym shorts slipping up past his knees, tightening into his crotch. "Why haven't you changed?" he asked. I had gone to the church gym seeking neither inspiration nor exercise, but I had trouble explaining all that to him. "Ready for a mean game of basketball?" he asked.

"Has Hesus talked to you recently?" I asked.

"Why? What's going on? Anything I should know about?"

"Call his house," I said. "Better yet, call the restaurant, talk to his parents. Stand in the way, do something, call the cops, do anything to stop him. Bye now."

"Wait a sec—"

I rushed out the door, leaving him standing with the basketball beneath his arms, looking puzzled, calling after me.

My next move was to head over to Koreatown on the bus and get off on the Vermont exit within walking distance to the Salvadoran-Korean Express. The Sangs had installed a neon light that flashed the colors and logos of both the Korean and the Salvadoran flags. Kyong Javier walked out of the restaurant, cigarette between his lips, leather jacket over a torn T-shirt as his shift had just ended.

"Looking for my brother again?" he asked. He offered a cigarette and I looked at it with disgust.

"I just thought I'd leave a message if he's not here," I said, although I knew where Hesus could be found. But my only intention that evening was to warn Mrs. Sang that Hesus had begun drinking beer and to express concern for her son's future and get her to call Father George if he hadn't called her already. But Kyong Javier had his own surprises for me.

"He's not gay," he said. I stood, feeling my throat roughen. I tried to sidestep him to get into the restaurant, but he stood in my way. "I'm off now," he said. "Why don't you come to my apartment and we'll talk about it?" On his face, I noticed a softening, a hint of vulnerability. He appeared, however subtly, to implore, "Please come…"

I found myself that evening in Kyong's apartment with his lips buried in my neck and one of my hands wrapped around a bottle of Korean beer and the other clutching at something firm between his legs. I did not like Kyong at the time, with the residue of nicotine and beer in his bitter mouth, and his roundish face resembling nothing but a failed replica of the original masterpiece breathing on me. Unkind of me to say so, but my body sensed the difference. His face was smooth like his brother's, and equally unable to grow a beard, and his eyes as black and intense, his eyebrows as lightly hairy, lips thin and red, but all the same he was no Hesus Sang.

"Relax," he said, pulling my neck back with his lips exploring it. His shirt unbuttoned, his chest stood exposed revealing firm nipples and smooth hairless skin. "You relax. Forget the asshole. He's as straight as his A's in Physics."

It had gotten to be nine already and we'd been in his apartment two hours. My clothes—uncomfortable acrylic though they were—were still on me and this frustrated him. "Hopelessly straight. Why can't you just forget all about him?"

Kyong Javier's apartment was a one-bedroom space in a converted turn-of-the-century hotel populated mostly by Central American families crowding into equally small units. I could hear children above us riding tricycles. Photography books and action cartoons littered the floor of Kyong's apartment along with empty beer bottles, mostly imported, and, for some reason, towels, workout towels perhaps, looking unwashed and used for many curious purposes. We sat on the couch, the only furniture in the room except for a rolled-up futon. I didn't understand the purpose of the futon. He had a one-bedroom with an actual bed to which he was trying to get me to transfer, but I continued to refuse. I pulled my hand away and his penis dangled back and forth, coming at me like a boomerang.

"I am in school, you know. I have a curfew," I said. "I have to get home."

"You don't really want to do that."

"Oh, really? Why not?" I asked defiantly.

"Because you're disappointed in him. If he's going to lose his virginity to your mother, you might as well lose it to his brother."

"Good one," I said. "But who says I'm a virgin."

"Don't give me any of that shit. What's so special about the Altar Boy anyway?"

"I don't know. I'm in love, that's all."

"Besides, he'll go off to some university. He won't need you. He won't need us. He'll meet some sorority girl from

Connecticut. He ain't never gonna come back and talk to us, we're losers, we ain't going to college. We're destined to remain here...Koreatown. It's kinda nice, ain't it? It's good enough for folks like us."

"I have my ambitions, you know," I said not wanting to reveal my King Lear audition. I stood up, seeking even more distance from him. But Kyong's hand followed me, soothing one of my shoulders until his other hand was grasped firmly around my waist. He stood behind me, his entire body pressed against mine. I withdrew, he pulled me back toward him and I could feel his breath on my neck. I pulled away again and I saw the anger on his blushing face. "You are gorgeous," he said, "but he's blind to that. He's handicapped...I say we belong in Koreatown, you and me, forever, and God help us, we'll never mention college! It'll be you and me against them." For the first time, my lips complied, rising up to kiss his. Mesmerized under the sway of his strange words, seduced by the poverty of his outlook, convinced we would feed, as they say, on love, for a brief instant, I imagined I could love Kyong Javier Sang.

But it was then that the door opened. Kyong zipped up his pants and I discovered the reason for the rolled-up futon. Hesus's younger brother, Hwan Jose, walked in with a Vietnamese male friend, both about sixteen, both with their arms around each other. Kyong Javier gave me a disparaging, all-knowing look.

"I know what you're thinking—two gay brothers?"

Hwan Jose and his boyfriend unrolled their futon and sat on it to accommodate the sodas and chips they had put on the floor.

"It's not just two gay brothers," Hwan Jose explained. "Martin Bo Soo moved in with Hank, his Anglo truck driver, just last month in Reseda. Miguel Pyong has been living with his Cuban boyfriend Lalo since they met working as gas attendants for the Thrifty gas. They have a lesbian friend who's pregnant by Lalo and then she's going to give birth to one of Miguel's sperms— Dad's happy about that."

"Wait, you mean…" I grew silent.

Kyong Javier read my troubled face out loud. "It's true," he said. "There's five brothers and you're in love with the only straight one."

"He's in love with the pre-med jerk?" Hwan Jose said as he and his Vietnamese friend joined Kyong Javier in a good laugh at my expense.

I reached for my bottle of beer and Kyong Javier reached for my lips with his aching, thirsty mouth. Hwan Jose and his boyfriend went into a passionate embrace after taking over the futon. I endured Kyong's bitter lips as I imagined the Sang brothers and their male lovers in one passionate embrace together in a family of universally imposed inverted love. If only the stray member would join in.

It was 7 A.M. when I woke up. Kyong Javier slept on the couch, I on a pillow on the rug. I was horrified to find myself naked, as if I'd never seen myself that way. I got myself dressed and dashed out without even brushing my hair. I had to go to school avoiding my house altogether. Knowing the troubles ahead well enough I let school provide me with the refuge and the time needed to think about what had just occurred. There was no sign of Hesus Sang. The entire morning went by without any indication that the world around me had visibly changed. I sat on my seat eyeing the Cliff Notes for *Native Son* that I was expected to write a book report with. It was then that the door opened and a student aide walked in bearing a note.

"You have a lot of explaining to do," said Father George as he shut the blinds at the Salvadoran-Korean Express and put up the closed sign. Mrs. Sang sat with a cloth napkin to her face, daintily drying her tears. Mr. Sang held her hand as if wringing more moisture from it. Hesus sat beside them staring at the floor. Father George had summoned me to the Express after school. Hesus had not been in school at all that day. Eyes turned to me as I entered.

"Tell us what happened," the priest told me.

I shrugged, not quite able to respond. But before I could bring myself to begin any type of explanation, Kyong Javier ran in, carrying his white shirt and black pants in a dry cleaner's plastic-wrapped hanger. "What's going on?" His mother would not answer, and instead buried her face in the cloth napkin. His father was just as reticent. Kyong turned to me. "What's he doing here?" he asked. The priest wouldn't answer. "Does this have anything to do with me—or my sexuality?"

"This is not the time for that," the priest told him, looking irked.

"Then what?" Kyong stared at Hesus. "Did little brother lose his virginity?"

"I said please," the priest responded.

"Then?"

The priest handed him a piece of paper. The scandal that had broken had nothing to do with Kyong's nor Hesus's, let alone my, sexuality. Hesus had been rejected from Stanford, Harvard, Yale, U.C. Berkeley, and Johns Hopkins all in one week. He would have to settle for his one acceptance to the much unheralded U.C. San Diego. "Not U.C. San Diego!" cried Mrs. Sang.

"So that's it?" cried Kyong Javier. "He gets accepted to U.C. San Diego and we're supposed to feel sorry for him?"

"Well, there's something else going on," said Father George, turning to look at me. "His mother called."

"My mother?" I asked.

"The two of them, those boys...they stayed out all night. Something's going on between them, and they're not talking."

Kyong Javier pulled out his pack of cigarettes, and even though Mrs. Sang reminded him it was a no-smoking restaurant, lit one all the same. "I could tell you all in a word or two!"

"Look, we're trying to figure out your brother's collegiate future."

"Let him go to San Diego, for god's sake! San Diego is fine! It'll do! Now you want to know what's going on, and where the boys were last night, you really want to have a little talk? Because I—"

"Let's not talk about it," I said, not feeling comfortable.

"There's nothing to talk about!" cried Hesus, breaking his silence. It was then that he bid us all look behind us. "She's here," he said. We turned around. Sabina Sverloff stood there, imposing in her Fairfax Deli uniform. Her striking face, all jagged, sharp, and severe, created quite a stir even in the cheapest of diner uniforms.

"I've been worried about you both," she said, staring at me and at Hesus. "I'm glad to see you're all right."

Father George looked quite in awe. "You must be Mrs.—"

"I've never been a Mrs., I am Sabina Sverloff, activist and waitress."

Hesus got up and nervously walked up to her. "That's her," he said, looking at his parents. "That's the woman I've told you about: that's the woman I love." A murmur of shock rose among us. Kyong Javier blew smoke in the brother's direction. Father George decided to have a smoke himself. "I told you I'd rather devote some time to learning about my feelings than school."

His feelings, I thought. This period in my life was supposed to be about me, my foolishness, my isolation, my despair. I felt as though I'd been upstaged by Hesus Sang's own bout of madness. At least I could empathize with him a little better, except that I would have been the first to tell him to choose U.C. San Diego over my mother.

Mr. Sang attempted some fatherly advice in a rather bitter and not at all convincing tone of voice. "You young, you premed!"

"*¡Sí, mijo!*" cried his mother. "You pre-med, *¡y quítate esas cosas románticas de la cabeza!*"

"If I may," said Sabina, approaching Hesus. "Look, last night was very special."

"Special?" asked Father George.

"Let's not talk about it here!" cried Hesus.

"Did he lose it?" asked Kyong Javier. "Do tell!"

"Hesus and I had a wonderful chat while waiting for my son to come home—which he never did, by the way, but we'll get to that soon enough…. While we waited, we…we made a commitment to be friends. Isn't that right, Hesus?"

"No! I don't want your friendship, Sabina!"

"I know," she added. "He wanted more, yes, but I can assure you, I've already been exiled once, I don't need a second run-in with the law. I behaved, he tried not to, and eventually I had to ask him to leave. I thank you for the attention, for making me feel wanted. Most men don't seem to think I'm special, and what can I say…. Now if you would just return the blouse you took—"

"Blouse?" Our voices went up in unison.

Hesus admitted that before leaving that night, after she had finally slapped him for insisting on staying and shut herself in the bathroom, he had rummaged through her drawers and found a satin blouse that he used to rub over his neck and chest. He took it with him and he'd slept with it in his car and had, in a sense, molested it. "I will return it," he said, "after I take it to the dry cleaner, if you know what I mean."

"Got ya," she said.

With this cleared up, it was time for everyone in the room to suddenly find themselves with the irresistible urge to turn to me. It's as if, hungry for more scandal, their eyes searched and landed on their likeliest target, the kid. If Hesus had been at my apartment alone with my mother, where had I been? Why was there an air of suspicion hovering over me?

Father George seemed to come to my rescue. "Perhaps this is something for Catholic Youth services to take care of," he said, smiling.

Sabina smiled too. "It's fine by me. I encourage my son to build bridges with the other denominations."

"Bridges?" asked the priest.

"Other denominations?" asked Hesus.

That did it. The pieces began to fall into place. Other denominations? Then what was I doing joining Catholic Youth?

Why? Why? *¿Y por qué?* What were my intentions? What was I
hiding other than my Semitism? Who was I? Why did I look
suspicious to all of them except Kyong Javier who sat smoking
by the corner enjoying every minute of it? Mrs. Sang had thought
we were Catholic—weren't all Latinos Catholic? Father George
stared at my mother, such an attractive woman, underprivileged
and struggling through life—but weren't all Jews, shall we say,
"better connected"? Hesus stared at Kyong Javier who'd been
staring and hinting by constantly adding references to all he
knew about us—had I possibly spent time with his brother?
Which meant that I was— But weren't all his friends, as they had
to be in the gym shower, straight?

So there I stood surrounded by the aura of suspicion, the
doubt, the supplication, the recognition that I was other than
what I appeared to be, the straight Latino Catholic boy in need of
a basketball game and a Scriptural follow-up. I wrapped my arms
tightly around my chest, feeling a chill run through my body at
having to confront these questions not just then, but from then on
in life…Jewish, atheist, socialist, homosexual, frightened of sex
and of life, a foreigner, an immigrant, not a citizen, not a goyim,
illegitimate son, poor and failing student—all these issues of
identity hit me at once demanding definition, a label, something
to cling to, something to go by, a name, a statement, a declaration, who are you, who really, really are you, voices mixing with
the sneering laughter of brother Kyong Javier, who would never
go to college nor stop smoking, intimidating me, knowing too
well the answers but never saying them on my behalf as I crawled
into a chair and held my head down as if headed for the crash
landing in that long uncleared path called Adulthood.

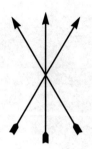

JAMES CAÑÓN was born and raised in Ibagué, Colombia. He is the author of short stories such as "My Lessons with Felipe" and "I Was Born That Way." He is currently working on a novel set in Queens, New York, where he has lived since 1992.

THE TWO MIRACLES
OF THE GRINGOS' VIRGIN

■━━━━━▶

James Cañón

My grandmother never goes to bed without drinking a shot of *aguardiente* and saying her prayers to a small replica of the Statue of Liberty. I've told her many times that it isn't a virgin, just a symbol of freedom, but she is stubborn, and a little crazy, too. She insists that the Statue of Liberty is *la virgen de los gringos;* and that one of these days the gringos' virgin is going to work her two miracles: making my penis disappear and reuniting me with my mother.

I know that faith is all we need to make things happen; however, since I learned that the Statue of Liberty has never been a virgin, I've been trying hard to dissuade Grandma of lighting candles and praying with such devotion to the rigid image. My first try was to send a *peon* into town to buy a few virgins of different shapes, hoping my *abuela* would get attached to any of them. He brought La Virgen de Chiquinquirá, La Virgen de Las Lajas, La Virgen del Carmen, and a few others from different places of our country, but I had no luck. All those virgins ended up on an old shelf with San Antonio, El Divino Niño Jesús, San Lázaro, and some other "second-class" saints to whom Abuela only lights candles once a month.

"This is the gringos' virgin. She lives in Los Estados Unidos, where your mother is. Only she can reunite the two of you." She tells me this while gracing the altar with fresh-picked flowers, avocados, oranges, papayas, coffee, and everything else she thinks the Statue of Liberty craves.

Once I tried what I thought would be the perfect argument to convince her that she was wrong.

"Abuela, tell me why the gringos' virgin is not holding a baby Jesus like all virgins do?"

"Well…" she stammered, "the gringos, you know. They took the baby out of her hands; they don't hold babies like we do, God forbid. They pay someone to take care of their babies so they can go out and make more money." She learned all this from letters that my mother used to send us from New York.

"What about the book she's holding?" I asked, trying to sound smart.

"That's the book of the Sacred Scriptures." She answered confidently while grabbing the small statue with two of her shaky fingers.

"And what about the torch? What's that for?" I didn't want to give up.

"That's to light the way for those disbelievers like yourself. And now leave me alone because I have to start making dinner for sixty starving *peones*.

This madness may have started when my mother disappeared in Ibagué, the big city, two months before I was born. I was rooted out of her belly when she was only twenty-six weeks pregnant. Then I was put inside an incubator until I was ready to face the world, ten weeks later. My mother never went back to Fresno, the town where she and my father had lived; on the contrary, she ran away as soon as she was freed from the horrible pain that I was causing her. She didn't wait to see what she and my father had created: a hermaphrodite.

The doctors in Ibagué told my father that only one child in ten million was born a hermaphrodite, and that they couldn't explain the reason. My father took me back to Fresno where *el doctor* Ramírez, the only doctor in town, said out of ignorance that I was meant to be a girl, but that Mamá had eaten too much *caldo de aquel*, a soup made with the penis and the testicles of a bull, and that the bull had been so sexually powerful that it affected my reproductive organs.

The rumor spread in town that Don Francisco Medina, my father, had a little monster hidden in his house, and that Doña Carmenza de Medina, my mother, had disappeared. Therefore, all the nosy people in Fresno started paying unannounced visits to my father and my grandmother, just to see the amazing human being with both penis and vagina.

The first one to visit my father's house was the Mayor; then the sheriff; then *el padre* Rafael, and then everyone else who thought they had authority in town to put their nose in father's house. Not only did they visit him, but they all felt they had the right to ask indiscreet questions that never got an answer, and so they made up their own explanation of my astounding condition, agreeing among themselves that it was a castigation. The mayor, for instance, said, "This is God's punishment because they have been evading taxes for over five years." He also refused to register me as a newborn since my sex wasn't defined. "It is a punishment coming straight from heaven," affirmed *el padre* Rafael, the town's priest. The reason, he explained afterward, was that my father, among other people in Fresno, wasn't paying the right tithe to church, and so the clergy had ended up full of fat hens, eggs, yuccas, and plantains, but no cash. He also refused to bless me with the holy sacraments. Nevertheless, it was Doña Melba, a neighbor, who went further than anyone else when she proclaimed, "That kid is the Antichrist. We should burn it alive in the public plaza before it's too late."

My father, however, made sure nobody else would see me by sending me along with my *abuela* to his farm. It was a smart decision. At least for himself. He avoided the unpleasant situation of having to show his anomalous child, and he punished my grandmother, whom he had always hated for being an alcoholic, by making her cook three daily meals for about fifty *peones* who worked on his farm.

In regard to my mother there were a few versions. Doña Romelia, another neighbor, said her son had seen my mother working in a whorehouse in Ibagué. Don Raimundo, Fresno's self-made dentist, assured he had seen, "with my own two eyes," my mother begging for money on the streets of the big city. Someone else said Mamá had killed herself by jumping down the bridge that connects Flandes and Girardot over the Magdalena River. Abuela, though, defended my mother by saying, "My daughter joined the convent of Las Carmelitas Descalzas," a bunch of crazed nuns who renounced the use of anything to cover their feet but their callosities, and were not allowed to show their faces to anyone on earth. Grandma even said mother wrote her letters from the convent every now and then; but Don Miguel, the mail clerk, denied the version. "That old woman hasn't gotten anything in the mail since her husband died, about ten years ago. I remembered she received one hundred and thirty-seven condolence cards. No one has beaten that record."

Maybe all this madness began with the bitter taste of Pancha's herbal infusions on my father's farm, where I've spent twenty-three years hidden between the smell of fresh milk and the stench of cow dung.

I was only five years old when Abuela and I met with Pancha, the witch. Grandma thought I looked exactly like my mother when she was a little girl, and so she wanted me to lose, as if by magic, my penis and become a girl. Pancha, who took pride in having witnessed the most bizarre things, became horrified when she saw what I had between my legs: my penis was four inches down from my navel; a prominence the size of a growing silkworm, always pointing down like a boneless finger vanquished by gravitational force. The outgrowth was completely covered by soft skin contracted into folds, except for a little hole at the end from which urine sluggishly sprinkled. Right below it, two tiny little protuberances timidly appeared through the thick and wrinkled skin: those were my balls. And just because this wasn't enough to make me a hermaphrodite, one inch down from my balls I had a slitty cut. A straight narrow incision from which urine also came out sporadically. "This is a very special case," Pancha said after a close scrutiny. "But there's nothing in this world I can't cure. If God gives us the disease, he gives us the remedy." From that day on I started drinking her "miraculous" potions that were supposed to help the gringos' virgin in making my little penis disappear.

My father, who didn't know anything about Pancha's sorcery, nor Grandma's wishes, decided to ignore the mistake of Mother Nature and started calling me Francisco, just like himself. He also ordered Abuela to make sure I was always dressed as a little cowboy: a pair of jeans, a shirt, a pair of boots, and, of course, a sombrero. He used to drive his red truck every morning from Fresno to help the *peones* milk the cows. He was a master. He taught me how to approach a cow so it wouldn't kick me. "Remember this, son," he told me once. "Cows are like women, you can never trust them; so make sure you tie their legs before you start milking them." Father also taught me how to press out the cow's udder so that more milk came out of it in a single squeeze; and once we were finished, we would drink together a full cup of warm, foamy milk sweetened with honey. After two or three hours, he would go back to Fresno with about one hundred gallons of fresh milk that he would sell to food stores, cheese makers and, if any was left, door to door to his big clientele. Then he would go back to his house in town, where his second wife and my two younger half sisters were waiting for him. They were not allowed to come to the farm, and I was forbidden to step off the eighty acres.

As soon as my father disappeared in clouds of dust, I was under the tutelage of my grandmother. My name was no longer Francisco but Carmencita, just like my mother. Abuela taught me, while drinking her shots of *aguardiente*, how to brew coffee. "Coffee should be like a good husband, not too strong, but not too weak." She also taught me how to scale, clean, and cook fish; how to kill a chicken without letting the blood ruin the meat; how to wash and iron clothes, how to sew hems. She also taught me to please men, "But don't let them touch your body." To be obedient, to always say, "*Sí, señor,*" just like she had taught my mother. And when the night came, she made me repeat one hundred times, "*Soy una niña, soy una niña*"—I'm a little girl— while drinking Pancha's bitter concoction.

For my tenth birthday Father brought me a cake with my male name written on it; and just like every year he also brought his guitar to sing to me the *feliz cumpleaños* song. He was just about to start singing when Grandma walked into the room.

"She's got to go to school," she said timidly in her anise-flavored voice. "I don't want my granddaughter to be *bruta* like me."

"It's not a she, damn it. It's a he," my father yelled. "And he's not leaving this farm unless I say so."

"But that isn't fair to her. She's got to learn to write and read." Father got up and grabbed Abuela by her shoulders as he repeated loudly, "It's a boy. Don't you understand, drunk bitch? It's a boy." Grandma must have said something else that I didn't hear, because all of a sudden he knocked her down on the floor and struck her with everything that was on the table. I saw the white frosting of the cake mixing with Grandma's white hair, and the guitar breaking against her head. I saw flying in the air the vase with the flowers, dishes, cups, and two of Abuela's yellowish teeth. I saw red blood squirting out of her mouth, and still I heard her repeating softly, "It's a girl, it's a girl." Father grabbed the only thing left on the table, a knife, and threatened her: "Don't make me kill you, *puta borracha*. I don't want to go to prison for slaying an old crap like you."

I couldn't hold it in any longer and began to cry. Father looked at me with compassion, stabbed the knife on the wooden table and walked out of the house. As he was leaving, Abuela managed to drag herself toward the door, and from there she repeated as loud as her almost toothless mouth allowed her to do: "It's a girl, it's a girl."

This madness, perhaps, started a few days after my tenth birthday, on a rainy day in October, when a plump, bleached-haired woman came to the farm looking for Grandma.

"I have news about your daughter," she told her, and even though they had never seen each other before, they locked themselves in Abuela's room and talked for hours. After the woman left, Grandma started dancing, singing, and screaming "Your mother's alive, I knew it. Carmencita's alive." I thought she was drunk again; and she was, but this time with happiness. "Come to my room, *hijita*. I'm going to show you some pictures that your mother sent me." In the first picture mother was surrounded by two men and another woman; they were wearing strange outfits and seemed to be very happy. In the second picture she was alone standing in front of the Statue of Liberty, the same symbol that would later become, in my grandma's drunken mind, the gringos' virgin. Mother looked totally different from the sepia pictures of her that I had seen before. She was another person and I didn't like her. I just couldn't think of a mother wearing bell-bottom jeans, polyester flowery blouses, rolled-up handkerchiefs tied around her head, and dozens of necklaces and bracelets. But my grandma was so happy to hear about her daughter being alive, that she didn't care if mother had become a hippie.

In addition to the color pictures, mother sent a box taped all around, and a short letter that the plump lady must have read aloud, since Grandma was, and still is, illiterate.

"The letter said she is working hard, taking care of people's kids and cleaning houses. And guess what else she sent me inside the envelope?" she asked me with half a smile.

"I don't know. More pictures?

"No, *hijita*," she whispered. "She sent me these green bills. They're worth a lot of money." She rolled up the bills and hid them in her bosom.

"Did she send me anything?" I asked with anticipation.

"No, Carmencita. Not this time. She doesn't know you're alive." Mother never expected me to survive the incubator, the abnormality, or the rejection.

The box contained oversized clothes for Grandma, all with the textures and colors of the unknown and the distinctive smell of freedom; shoes, silver jewelry, a blond afro wig, key rings, and a small replica of the Statue of Liberty. As soon as Abuela saw the statue, she lifted it with both her hands, looked up at the ceiling and said, "*Gracias, Virgencita.*" Then she moved down all the saints she had on the shelf in her room, and replaced them with her new, most-powerful virgin ever.

From that day on, Abuela became the most devoted and loyal disciple the Statue of Liberty ever had. For more than twelve years she never skipped a night without lighting a candle and saying prayers to the green piece of plaster. In addition to that, every Sunday she showed respect to the gringos' virgin by offering her typical dishes that she served on fine porcelain and placed right on the shelf next to the statue. "She was hungry today," Grandma would tell me while taking the empty tray back to the kitchen. The truth is that the strong smell of garlic, cumin, and cilantro invited mice, roaches, and ants to celebrate every Sunday over *sancocho, cuchuco* or whatever dish Abuela chose to offer.

It's not unusual to find chicken bones under Grandma's bed, or rotten pieces of food under her pillow. "She made a mess," Grandma would whisper in my ear blaming the statue. "But this is all part of my sacrifice. The more I suffer, the sooner you'll lose your penis and the sooner you'll be with your mother."

And she suffered plenty without giving up her faith or giving in to my father; because even though Father ended up paying *la maestra* Cleotilde, the school's teacher, to come to the farm and teach me how to write and read, he and Grandma continued fighting over my sex every time they met for about two years. Most of the time they just raised their voices and insulted each other, but a few other times my father lost control of himself, and it was in those few times that Grandma lost, one by one, all the teeth she had left in her mouth.

All this madness may have begun when my body decided to please both my father and Abuela by merging his dream with her wish.

A few months before my twelfth birthday, my body began to suffer drastic changes: my arms got strong and my hands grew big; a bulky Adam's apple sprouted out of my throat; my nipples began to hurt, itch, and finally grow into two protuberances the size of small oranges; thin hair began to show on my face and my chest; and the upper bulge of my odd private parts became more noticeable. My voice, however, remained soft and delicate.

It was at around this same time that I started taking pleasure from the strong smell of the sweaty *peones* that worked on the farm, and paying them night visits at the shelter where they slept.

As my body started defying nature with its unusual changes, my father stopped coming to the farm to train me on how to be a man. His dream of making a man out of me was being sabotaged by destiny, and he couldn't put up with it. He never came back, but he hired Don Luis as a tenant farmer, and it was through him that father made sure Grandma and I had everything we needed to survive physically, because emotionally we were both dying slowly.

I remember sitting on the bench at the porch of the house in the peaceful mornings, hoping to see father's red truck coming in raising clouds of dust, hear my male name pronounced in his hoarse voice, or feel the warmth of his embrace. I remember sitting on the same bench in the silent nights, watching the man he wanted me to be fade away with the years.

Learning how to write and read was a lot easier for me than it was for the children that went to school in town. At least that's what *la maestra* Cleotilde said to Abuela. She also said I was brilliant but obscure, lucid but enigmatic. She would have taught me mathematics, sciences, and geography, if Grandma hadn't hit her with a fat yucca when they got into an argument about the pureness of the Statue of Liberty. *La maestra* never came back either, but though she left me half-learned, I started writing, in embroidered calligraphy, long letters to my mother that Abuela dictated; then, the first Monday of each month, we would secretly go into Fresno to mail them.

Before going into town, we would disguise ourselves so that my father wouldn't recognize us if he saw us. Grandma would wear the blond afro wig that mother had sent her, sunglasses, and as if that wasn't enough, she'd put colorful makeup on her wrinkled face. Once she had transformed herself into what she called "a distinguished lady" she'd make me wear one of her oversized dresses aromatized with mothballs, and her old, torn mantilla. The first Monday of every month was the happiest day for me. On that day I had the opportunity of seeing, from afar, the handsome men that gathered in the café by the public plaza. They all wore pressed shirts and their hair was neatly combed; and they seemed very happy eating flavored ice in tall glasses, or drinking hot coffee in beautiful cups.

In our first letter, Abuela complained to Mother about how my father hit her and made her work like a slave, despite her old age. She thanked mother for sending us *la Virgen de los Gringos*, and she also updated her with the very little town gossip she knew. Finally, when she had nothing else to add, Abuela told Mother about me. She started by saying that I had survived, and that although the priest had refused to baptize me she had decided to name me after her, Carmencita. She also explained that "she's not a complete girl quite yet, but I teamed up with Pancha, the witch, and she's vanishing Carmencita's little penis with a magic concoction." Grandma was lying. In defiance of Pancha's potions my penis only grew bigger and thicker. Abuela knew so, because checking my private parts was then, and still is, our every-morning routine. As soon as I wake up, I rub my erect penis with one hand, and my sticky vagina with the other, while thinking of the strong, sweaty bodies of the *peones* or the good-looking men of the café. After a few minutes, I rush to stand in front of the vertical mirror on the old wardrobe, and inspect closely between my legs, wishing to see my penis magically replaced with another navel or a bigger vagina, or at least hoping to notice any reduction in its size. Then Grandma comes into my room with a cup of coffee for me, a shot of *aguardiente* for herself, and a measuring tape, which she can't read, to verify the actual size of my penis. The tape is all marked in red ink with the growing length and width of my upper sexual organ.

About three months after we mailed our first letter, we received a small package from my mother. They held it for us at the post office until we picked it up. She sent us new pictures in her eccentric outfits, and a long letter that I read for Grandma. In it she wrote about things the meaning of which I didn't know, like love, peace, and harmony, and how she was fighting to make this world into a more tranquil place to live. She also wrote about the importance of affection, devotion, and kindliness in a friendship. She wrote about the many friends she had, the many places she had visited, the many people she had shared soul-thoughts with. She wrote about everything and everyone but me. And so Grandma excused her one more time. "They must have lost the page where she wrote to you. You know how careless they are at the post office." We would patiently wait for the next letter to come. One hundred and thirteen letters were mailed by us after that, and seventy-nine came back from Mother, and still my existence was never even alluded to in any of them. Mamá was so preoccupied changing the world that she didn't have time to care about me.

Perhaps this madness started after the rainy season of 1976, when I came down with what el doctor Ramírez said was malaria.

I was nineteen years old and we had already lost contact with my mother. The last two letters we got from her came from different cities; after that we never heard from her again, and with her silence ended our Mondays' cheerful visits to Fresno. Grandma was getting old and I could see the nineteen years of suffering on her flabby wrinkled skin, her shaking arthritic hands, her dilated, swollen veins, and her deranged mind. She said there was no reason worth the risk to go into town; and though I wished I could see again the handsome men of the café, I was terrified by them and other normal human beings.

Some boys had made fun of me before, some girls had called me names, some men had insulted me thinking I was a man dressed as a woman, some old ladies had made the sign of the cross upon themselves as Grandma and I walked by them with our heads down.

And it was due to my fear of people and Grandma's ignorance that we waited three days before sending a *peon* to get *el doctor* Ramírez. I began feeling ill on a Tuesday night. It's easy to remember, because that's the night of the week when Grandma and I say together a rosary to the "second-class" saints that she keeps apart from the gringos' virgin. I couldn't sleep that night, feeling hot and cold, and the next morning, when grandma came into my room for the penis-measurement routine, she found me shivering. It didn't stop her from measuring it, but right after she marked the tape with the new size, she sent a field hand for Pancha.

The witch came in the afternoon with a basket filled with herbs that she boiled in purple chicken's blood. Once ready I drank from the coagulated potion three or four times, and every time my stomach rejected it. Since magic didn't work, Abuela tried religion. She improvised a little altar in my room, and placed the Statue of Liberty on it. Then she spent the whole night saying prayers to it, alternating rosaries with shots of *aguardiente* until dawn, and when the sun started rising, she was completely drunk but still repeating, "Amén, amén, amén…"

Pancha came back again in the afternoon, with more herbs and a wild rabbit that she killed with a knife right in front of my eyes. Then she forced me to open my mouth and drink the warm blood directly from the gash she had made on the rabbit's neck. I couldn't hold the blood for more than five seconds in my stomach, and so I threw up again until there was nothing left inside of me.

My temperature kept on rising and my body sweating. My eyelids felt heavy and my mind slowly got lost in a feverish dream. I saw myself completely nude, standing erect, like a naked version of the Statue of Liberty; only instead of a book I was gripping my penis with one hand, and instead of a torch, my other hand was holding upright a sharp blade. Without losing the straightness of my posture, I saw my right hand coming down furiously and chopping off my penis from its root in one single cut. There was no pain, nor blood, just relief. Then I saw myself running up the hills, my arms widespread as if I were ready to fly, running away from my past, taking nothing with me but my mutilated nude body. When my past was behind me, I saw myself running away from my present, fast, faster so that not even my future could reach me. I saw myself running for hours, days, years without stopping, without looking back, until I saw my mother.

She looked exactly like the sepia pictures I had seen of her when I was a little child. She was standing in the middle of a crystalline lagoon, surrounded by trees of green leaves and yellow flowers, and colorful birds serenading her. I walked slowly toward her, and I saw her singing lullabies to a baby girl she was holding in her arms. I walked a few more steps in her direction and I saw myself again. I was the baby girl mother was singing lullabies to, and for the first time in my life I understood the meaning of love, peace, and harmony. I thought about Abuela's sacrifices, and I thanked her gringos' virgin, because even though it was in a dream, I had finally lost my penis, and mother and I were together in the only place where we could enjoy love, peace, and harmony. We were together in heaven.

Maybe all this madness didn't start after the rainy season of 1976, either. Maybe it all started before that, maybe after. Maybe I'll never find out how it all started, or maybe I don't want to find out. But I know how I'll end it. I dreamt about it.

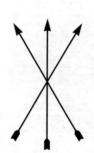

ALBERT E. COTA: I am a native New Mexican, sort of, living most of my life there. I was actually born in the Deep South. My parents' early careers had the family travelling all over the country for awhile. Mother's family was from New Mexico and Father's from Arizona. I have a bachelor's degree in English, with some graduate work under my belt. Past writing has been mostly in the technical field, but things have changed allowing me to get back to my creative pursuits. Currently I work in the computer field as a systems administrator. I am proud to call the Bay Area of California my third home.

DOWN BELOW

————▶

Albert E. Cota

I woke to the sound of water nearby in a place called Down Below. Late mountain spring morning tendrils of sharp, cold air grabbed the top of my head. Birds greeted the morning sun with plaintive cries. I heard another sound, a snigger and the splashing of someone taking a leak and opened my eyes. "Watcha doing?" I said to my cousin Jeff through thick, pasty lips. He stood there, all of five foot four, wrapped in a sleeping bag, all zippers down, crusty eyes and thick lashes. His tight muscled body swayed unsteady while his hands fumbled to close the zipper of his pants. Then I smelled piñon smoke, burning piss, and wet leather.

Faintly I heard Jeff's brother Paul yell, "What the hell are you doing?" from deep within his sleeping bag near the fire. Jeff snorted again and then loudly guffawed as Paul pulled his head out to take a peek, focus, and yell, "Hey, *tonto pendejo*! What are you doing?" Jeff was peeing into my old Hush Puppy shoes and laughed even louder as he saw my smoldering sleeping bag where I'd pushed it in my sleep into the fire to warm my feet. The warmth that spread up across my face did not come from the fire. Hazily I registered the two most important obstacles in front of me: my shoes and my uncle's burnt sleeping bag.

The shoes and the bag were my immediate concerns, but somewhere in the back of my mind I registered the eternal shame I'd felt since I was a young boy, the difference I felt among peers like the damp, smoldering sleeping bag, encasing my body. I struggled with my own zipper to release myself. I had still not quite realized, or quite accepted, and maybe didn't want to accept, that I was gay. The smoke from the fire hovered over our small campsite, leaned like a toadstool against the early morning inversion. The significance of that evening into morning would take years to settle into what it really meant to be a man—something I'd struggled with for years. The zipper finally broke on the bag and I kicked my way out to stand and stare down at my ruined shoes.

The night before, my cousins and I had embarked on yet another of our self-created rituals, celebrating our passage into the world outside of our small rural community of Suenio. Jeff and I could hardly wait to get out of that town. School was over and we would be graduating later in the week. Special permission had been given to spend the night in Down Below, a place of my DeVeaux cousins' family legend. A couple of centuries before, Jeff and Paul's great-great grandfather, Maximiliano, had traded for this land with the Pueblo people. His trapping skills brought him through the mountains and valleys of the Sangre de Cristos. The pelts he harvested were highly prized by the native people. Hidden, tucked way, Down Below was one of the choicest pieces of property, practically stolen from the Native Americans.

Max had convinced them the land was worthless because of the annual flooding, when in reality, decades later, it was prime pasture for livestock. Miles of fence hid the small canyon within a canyon. Here the Rio Chiquito worked its way west to join the Rio Grande. Its own small canyon and bow shape twisted and turned the landscape as it made its way to join its parent's flow south. I had felt it a great honor to be invited by my cousins to spend the night there, willing to endure any humiliation for a night out with Jeff and Paul. The humiliation was a common occurrence and I never was quite sure when I'd have to demonstrate my lack of knowledge of chopping wood, hunting, or weight-lifting. Jeff was more like a brother to me than the two I actually had, and every time Paul challenged me to do any of those types of things, he'd patiently come to my defense, albeit in private. "Don't worry about Paul," he'd say, "he's just got his shorts all twisted up around his *cojones* because he didn't get laid last night." I'd stand there with my deer-in-the-headlights look and just nod, inside swearing and tearing myself apart, anxious for the time and place where I would no longer need to prove that I was something I was not.

Jeff's older brother Paul once again had to chaperone us on the camp-out. He hated having to take us along and had hated it ever since we were younger, living at our grandparents' house off the plaza in Suenio. Maybe Paul was still mad that we'd told his parents about the chemistry set he used to make pipe bombs, the ones that had mysteriously blown many small craters in our grandfather's driveway. Bouncing along in the old Chevy pickup on our way to the campsite Paul asked, "Hey, Ernest, got any money?" I nodded my head, counting to myself how much I had in my wallet. Paul always shook us down for money. He was the king of the shakedowns. He had enough information on me and Jeff's escapades to last us well into adulthood, like the time he'd caught us burning our Uncle Eloy's girlie magazines out behind our grandfather's house, picture by picture, or stealing money from some passed-out winos in an alley off the plaza. "Well, if you and Jeff here expect to have a great campout, you're going to need beer." It was always "you" with him. As I gave him a five, Paul quickly pulled over. "Get out of the truck and hide over there in the bushes," he said. We quickly jumped out and heard him speed off to the liquor store.

We waited, hiding, already well past nine in the evening. As usual, whenever Paul was in charge, we'd gotten off to a late start. Jeff and I pulled back deep into the shadows of the trees near the side of the road as a car approached and went around the curve. "Hey, Ernest, this is going to be fun." Jeff chuckled. I looked at him and slowly smiled. I had not wanted to miss being here tonight. I had planned all week, getting special permission for one last sleepover at my cousins'. This was the last time we would be seeing each other for a long time. The following Monday, Jeff would leave to join the Army Special Forces, and two months later I'd be going to Yale, my years of books and studying providing my escape. "Later, we'll do maneuvers," Jeff had said, his eyes sparkling with their trademark gleam. What did Jeff know about maneuvers? I asked myself. As long as I could remember, Jeff had wanted to join the Army, to follow his father's example. Myself, the child of two parents who had met in the Navy, I wanted nothing more to do with that sort of life. I couldn't understand Jeff's fascination to pursue such a career. Since my parents' divorce, I'd had no plans for my own future other than waiting for the next cataclysmic change to happen in my young life. Without a father, my identity was suspect—a bad seed, unwanted, troubled youth from a single parent family. Every time my mother took us to visit Jeff's family, I'd beg to spend the night. Maybe by spending time with him I would get to be like him, popular in school and adept at doing all the things other boys our age were doing, sports, cars, dating girls. My only escape was reading. Now we would go no further together from this point. Joining the military was where I drew the line. I could make out Jeff's silhouette staring up at the star-littered sky, the Milky Way swirling above our heads.

Paul returned half an hour later to our hiding spot and flashed his lights once to signal us to get back in the truck. On the way to Down Below, Jeff and I sucked eagerly at our Schlitz malt liquor, a blue bull on the can, another part of the passage we sought to manhood, drinking beer with a thirst that would take years to quench. If I drank as much as my cousins and kept up with them, I thought, I could be like them. This was a way I could match them. Paul laughed at our attempts to inhale the joints he gave us, his special generosity not unnoticed. We slowly transformed as the pot coursed through our blood. We laughed and poked at each other, causing Paul to jostle the steering wheel a bit. "Knock it off, you two," he yelled, eyes bugging out, as we laughed at him now, wanting that night to be a night to remember.

The truck, loaded with borrowed sleeping bags and light provisions, turned left onto yet another of the many dirt roads that crisscrossed the Suenio Valley. Up ahead the road dropped away from the mesa. We dipped down and made our way to the meadows of Down Below. A small herd of cows watched us warily and moved closer to the river, swollen with the spring run off of melting snow. Jeff and I jumped from the truck simultaneously, my skinny body pushing past him, impatient to set up camp and drink another beer. Stolen firewood soon crackled and a sheet of plastic was draped like a net to a pole set up to keep the evening breeze out and the heat in. Another tall beer was popped open, spray shooting the three of us. "Hey, you guys, slow down," Paul commanded. "Leave some for me." Jeff and I smirked, knowing he had probably stashed another six-pack somewhere behind the seat of the truck, and made our way into the salt cedar and Russian olive stands near the banks of the Rio Chiquito. Before I knew it, Jeff grabbed a long pole of driftwood from the ground and charged the startled herd of cows, which quickly waded across the water to a small island.

"Ernest," he yelled from the edge of the brush near the swollen river, "get over here. We got some serious military operations to perform here." I grabbed a stick of my own and ran over to him. "Let's cross the river and bring those lost troops on back home," he drawled. I stood there, my drunkenness giving way to wariness. We approached the river slowly, hearing the sounds of large bodies splashing into water, branches breaking and the sucking sound of feet being pulled out of the thick viscous mud. The river moved fast. Swirling dark eddies and whirls gleamed in an almost full-moon light. Before I knew it, Jeff had plunged in and was halfway across the Rio Chiquito. "Come on, you chickenshit! Don't be a sissy!" I hesitated, grabbed my own stick before entering the water, and made my way across. The cold sucked my balls into my body as I fought to make my way across, realizing halfway there that I could not turn back.

Shivering on the island, Jeff's transformation was complete. Brandishing the stick, he charged the dark shapes in the spindly twisted brush. "Heyah, yah!" he yelled. I joined in, stealthily moving to flank the small herd of bewildered animals. I stopped and looked up at the sky littered with stars and heard Jeff cry out some sort of warning—drunken slurs mixed with military commands. "Ten o'clock, ten o'clock, points moving east!" I heard the sound of whacking, a stick striking thick skin. Lumbering shapes rushed me, parted around where I stood, and made their way back through the water to the other shore. The branches snapped around me as Jeff appeared out of nowhere. "Time to get back," he said, and before I could stop him he was back in the water. A swirling current sucked him under and he jumped back up, his small body fighting the movement of the water. "Help," he cried, and without thinking I jumped into the river and made my way toward him, the stick held high over my head.

The water pushed and pulled at me as I fought the current and slipping sand beneath my shoes. I had to readjust my course a few times before I got to Jeff. I knew I couldn't get close enough to grab and pull him back to the other side. I handed him the end of my stick and fought the force of the river that could drag him back to the other side. "You got to promise," he gasped, "not to tell anyone about this." He stared directly into my eyes, but I looked away. "Sure," I replied. Yet another undercurrent of the secrets we held between us, caught up in so many others we had picked up along the way in our separate lives.

Somehow, pulling him from the river evened the score between us. I demonstrated my physical strength and purpose in saving him from being swept away to an almost sure drowning. Back at the campsite, Paul glared at us. "Why are you guys out there yelling like a bunch of girls and scaring Tío's cows?" Jeff just laughed and shook his head at him while I pulled my sleeping bag close to the fire and took off my shoes so that they could dry.

Pissing into my cracked pigskin shoes was one way for Jeff to be superior and seal the pact. Here was this outstanding specimen of maleness off to fight some battle or other, whereas I was off to study for four more years. Years later I answered an early morning telephone call, its ring louder than the words I'd hear when I picked up the phone. Jeff hadn't moved fast enough as a building he and his troops were in exploded and crumbled down around them. He'd been trying to get his troops out of the building after he heard the planes overhead. I pictured him holding up one of his own men, wounded earlier in the building-turned-hospital, and dragging him to the door. Our United States military, in yet another of their Third World practice rounds, once again would get to practice hush-hush cover-ups and condolences to grieving parents and siblings. Medals of honor all the way round. Two men in full military dress knocking softly on your door.

All the unexpressed words crashed through my mind, how I had loved him and never said the words, how I'd never said how much I cared about him, his need, and the passion he felt for all things military. Words coming from me, the certified sissy. I put the phone down. I'd never told him I'd finally accepted that I was "different," gay, a fag, *maricón*, or whatever the going lexicon was at the time. We'd stayed in touch all those years, driving cross-country once at night, both on our way back to obligations, he to a new army post and I to school. All we did was catch up on all the ordinary day-to-day chatter of our lives. I would never get to tell him some of my own maudlin, cliché-ridden, too-tired-to-care-anymore, self-hating experiences of holding men in their own hospital beds, stateside, as they died in a war back here. Their own bodies imploding in on themselves.

That night as I drove home for Jeff's funeral, I remembered Down Below, where I had thrown my uncle's burned sleeping bag weighted down with rocks into the middle of the gushing Rio Chiquito and watched it swirl downward into the water. I made up some story to my mother about my shoes being stolen by animals in the night when I came home in just my stocking feet. I remembered the frightened look on Jeff's face the day he boarded the bus for Fort Bragg. And I remembered the last time we'd seen each other, the trip Jeff and I had taken cross-country, the look of fear in his face, which was then replaced by some grim determination to see through his military plans. My own face staring straight ahead, nodding in agreement to everything he'd said. He had explained to me what I'd kept seeing along the road, the shapes of turtles' shells and the bodies of other dead animals that had died trying to cross the desert highway, long shadows thrown up against the concrete dividers that blocked their way to the other side of the road and safety. The night of the rosary, Paul sought me out and handed me a wrapped box. His eyes, red from crying and years of smoking pot, wrinkled with the years, looked past and through me. "Here, this is for you," he muttered softly. Scribbled across the top was "Elysian Fields Bound" and, wrapped inside, was an undelivered gift from Jeff, a pair of shoes and set of dog tags: preparation for the next river crossing.

LAWRENCE LA FOUNTAIN-STOKES (1968) is a Puerto Rican writer, academic, and activist. Larry (as he is known to his friends) is presently an assistant professor of Latino/a Studies and Latin American Theater and Performance at Ohio State University in Columbus. He received his Ph.D. in 1999 from Columbia University in New York; the title of his dissertation is "Culture, Representation, and the Puerto Rican Queer Diaspora." His book of short stories, *Uñas pintadas de azul*, will be published soon.

My Name, Multitudinous Mass

→

Larry La Fountain-Stokes

My name, Manuel Ramos Otero, my parents called me but I respond to other secrets, other voices from within as well as to your name, the greatest mystery of all times. Today's sign, Pisces or divine fishies of the golden profession of the sea, you thread my destiny and don't even know it, you sinful owner of everything worth having, of that which has been said and is about to be said, fisher of lost souls. Your fleecy chest comforts me and I lose myself for you, I am nobody, my life is a void. By profession I tell, I am a teller of stories preserved in the memory of a black goddess, associated with those discreet practices of my followers. A water sign, of split identities (yes! I like that!), I write myself, I write my body on many pages as if an indelible tattoo on your buttocks. Yesterday's sign, your name; tomorrow's, the small space between your eyebrows and the illusion of a demented circus that goes by every so often, on its way from Bangladesh to Lima, from Rome to Islamabad, from my head to infinity.

Sometimes, when I walk down the street, I become other people: William Burroughs, Truman Capote, René Marqués. Like saying hustler, flaneur, drug addict, artist, writer, genius, pornographer, homosexual (I almost forgot this last part!) and other things that it would take me years to enumerate. Oh, and criminal, let's not neglect that. America needed its Genet, the tropics their Wojnarowicz, at your service, someone who could embody Arenas or Sarduy or Lezama in a novel way, without any of those excesses so common in certain cinematographic adaptations that we from the underdeveloped world like so much. With a body ravaged by AIDS, of course, but what does that matter.

And I write and think, what is there left to say that my many divine incarnations have not already said? I once went to a small bar in the East Village for a reading of my last book, *The Waterfront Journals*, so unfortunately posthumous, where many of my friends spoke and blurted out everything, all the stories, the many incarnations of a Hindu god that multiplied itself through rivers as if he were a relative of Oshun, a multifarious octopus, the anecdotes from my diary, of my trips through America, that perverse America of *Blue Velvet* and Nan Goldin and Walt Whitman, of those bars for black men and sailors where Lorca drank, of those gas stations in the middle of the countryside, of a countryside so abandoned, so full of wheat and corn and trucks and truckers who go from here to there and back and hang out in those distant rest stops, so that someone can suck their cocks. Someone like me, of course, someone who wanders down the roads of America, that abandoned continent north of the Rio Grande, full of pale faces with half-smoked cigarettes.

If it is a question of names, I have also been called Borinquen, Flor de Loto, Flamboyán, Alelí, Tulip (which always saves me from death), America, Cuba, Cardo, Clavellina, Carnation, Azucena of my hopes, beside you the reddest Rose, Daisy, Lily, Amapola, Azalea, Orange Blossom and a spate of other flowers, my many reincarnations, which I haven't mentioned because they are too expensive for my followers, the children of the divine orchid of Dorado and of a mystic dancer who sang love songs for me one evening in the sixties.

I am the flowered crown of the bride in *Blood Wedding*, a crown thrown to the floor with rage, a crown of spines, of wax orange blossoms, so that they would last longer and would be a remembrance of that groom whom I killed so cruelly and with such lack of pity, as I accustom to, as I have always done since the beginning of time. My mother, an inveterate bingo player, used to call me Nightingale, quoting names nonstop, Pitirre, Guaraguao, singing Hosanna in the skies!, Parrot from El Yunque, Reinita, Peacock, Pigeon from the Cajellón del Cristo, flying birds of delight, of Allah's garden, of worldly Paradise, of my dreams or of other nightmares, among the most nefarious being those of Central Park and Battery Park at night, of Coney Island full of urine and vomit, of my mysterious Sephardic Jewish cemetery in a place unknown to me. Paloma, a name which I like and which for a strange coincidence I never had. Names I would like to call myself, such as Sebregondi, Néstor Perlongher, Tulio Carela, John Rechy, Joe Orton, Osvaldo Lamborghini, but which I will have to leave for another story, another life, another series of unexpected occurrences and riddles, an exclamation point in the existence of so many people who cry and will cry my absence every day, for the rest of time, Amen.

And if my life is a movie called *Postcards from America* and if my story is told in thousands of poems dedicated to damned poets, dirty and perverse like me, and if my grave is close by Lorca's in a Jewish cemetery in Manhattan, and if Manhattan is a town in Puerto Rico, except that it's a couple of hours away by plane. And if my paintings lie buried around the planet, and if my face, with a cigarette in my lips, and if the covers of my books of poetry and short stories. And if I don't exist, what of you? Who saves you?

My name is Lawrence Martin La Fountain-Stokes but you can call me desert seashell, Gobi-plateau fermented yak milk that you drink with cinnamon to hallucinate, with regurgitated corn worms in Mexico, with chewed tobacco whose delectable juice you savor amid the smoke every time you light a Havana cigar to the goddesses I adore, my sweetest Yemayá, my patroness and savior of the seas. I write and I ask myself, with everything that has been said, with thousands and thousands of books with no readers, my flowered vintage and future magazines, Belgian lace and pirates and stories of slavery and rape, the cruelty of a people so miserly who do away with their island while you die of AIDS and crack cocaine and poverty, books in libraries that rot. If no one in Puerto Rico saves anything, there is always space for something new, your head, your nipples, your cock. The novelty, the lovely novelty. Among a people without libraries, who reads, if not the mold?

I write my name on my ass, in indelible ink, I spell the following word on my thigh with a tattoo needle: MANUEL. If my name is spelled DAVID WOJNAROWICZ, and said in a thousand ways, who am I then? Am I the son of my mother, the grandnephew of Martín de la Rosa, the one who saved her life as a child? Am I the yellowish skin of she who has survived pernicious malaria, the rotten teeth? Am I the tonic water that I pour in my gin, a vice that I breathe slowly, quinine that gives life? I am everything and nothing, I overflow my memory of transatlantic cruise ships, of migratory waves, of Hawaiian fields in which I am called mountain jíbaro, an old citizen of such illustrious cities, of snivelly and ragged dens of perdition where we learned to kiss each other on hot August nights. You are my beloved, never forget it, I carry you in my trashy heart and my rock songs are only for you, although I confess that I love and will only love the devil.

I smell the stench, it surprises me but I don't fear them, quite the contrary, I read them and quite enjoy their vagueness, they have already said everything. Those demons in your imagination, so critical, just as Klemente sang and Roy Brown repeated, those fools that buzz around our world and tear you apart, you, the most divine one! And in the fifth-floor bathroom of a library whose name I would rather not remember, where a man took me, the first one I dare to follow, you mean today, your life has been a long list of abandoned bathrooms among diverse continents of filth, which is why you could start with long lists of masculine-sounding names in thousands of languages that I do not know but interest me just the same. Lord knows what destiny, what inspiration made me follow him thinking of you, of those long desired days that I have not seen since Calcutta, Baghdad, Moscow, São Paulo, those paths we crossed until we ended up there, me breathless and trembling, my legs shaking like gelatin or tembleque or jelly or the leaves of a young tree, without memory, without knowledge of the cruelty of your past.

Tell me if the verdict of this road is nothing more than a chance encounter, what to think, why judge it any other way, my life becomes an instant and that is the point. I followed a guy among others in my life, through my life, my name is not known, his name much less, my heart on a silver platter in front of your chest. I was engaged as a projectionist in a movie theater on Eighth Avenue, like so many movie theaters of my life, over-flowing with color films and first- and second-class actors and actresses, a profession like any other, which nevertheless gave you life, your image reflected just the same in the eyes of beg-gars and millionaires, your Chinese satin and silk of Arab stories. And my life was the movies, me, devoted to films before I had the surgery of the thousand Katmandu hidden mysteries done, the nameless syrup, before I started to write or to sing in La Escuelita or in El Cotorrito or in El Danubio Azul, before I got breast cancer, before I died in a pilgrimage to the Tits of Cayey, before you saw that person who I am and am not and become again, the one I go through in my moments of glory and passion, that black goddess I know so closely even while I ignore her name, that I eat for breakfast with my mouth full of oregano and garlic and laurel. Life courses through my veins, salt of life, light of life. I am one and a thousand persons and no one knows who I am, except my sisters, who adore me.

I have been a john, bisexual, queen, man, woman, my name is desire and yours is hope. I know well that anyway, none of this matters, among thousands of practices, multitudinous, millenary nightmares and variations, I fuck whomever I want (or so the people say) and let whoever wants to fuck me do the same, we look like mysterious knots, tied one to the other in strange contor-tions that only wizards can undo. You unbalance my nostalgia, you leave me without a magnetic pole, you are my North, my horizon, even while you are always changing. I fear that you might hate me. "The more the merrier" I always heard but I think only of you and of all your faces, I am searching for yours and it is yours that I always find.

In the bathroom, yes, I followed him (but it wasn't me, it was the story of some authors who pursue me, or of thousands of people, of a movie house projectionist who walks out into the street and is blinded by the sunlight) and I stood next to him at the urinal (because it was you, just like all of them are, you being almighty and immanent), I who do not pee standing unless it is at the potty, I, trembling from the stairs and running, sweat covering my brow and my breathing made hard. He got it out and it was quite big, he was hairy and, most surprisingly, rather loving. He kissed me before going away, leaving me speechless, and I thought only of you. His kiss tasted like cock.

Mystic spiritual nothingness would serve to explain the mystery of the encounter if it weren't for one detail. What long list makes up for a passing kiss, a sincere good-bye, of the man whose name you don't even know? I would like to fill pages with the traces of transient dreams, whose sperm is the only memory, a certain smell that remained in my hands and that I discovered much later, causing me great impression, with your name.

I don't know if I should continue, a multilingual scrawl of many shapes follows me, the name I invoke of two (or a thousand) damned poets here sitting next to me, the bookcases in my house so overstuffed that at any moment they could fall, bury me alive, yes, that would be the dream, me with so many lists of names, all impressed on my forehead. I forswear this madness. The library of Babel of my forms is not human, it does not fit in Occidental philosophies nor theologies, it reclaims your past but your name is a mystery. Your name impressed in my memory, amid the indelible ink of those tattoos you left on my buttocks, with that face you had yesterday in the bathroom.

RIGOBERTO GONZÁLEZ was born in Bakersfield, California, and raised in Michoacán, Mexico, the son and grandson of migrant farm workers. He received an M.A. from the University of California at Davis and an M.F.A. from Arizona State University. He has been honored with an award from the Academy of American Poets and three Pushcart Prize nominations. His book of poems, *So Often the Pitcher Goes to Water Until It Breaks*, was a National Poetry Series selection and was published by the University of Illinois Press. He lives in New York City. "La Quebrada" is an excerpt from the novel *Crossing Vines*.

LA QUEBRADA

——➤——

Rigoberto González

The workers ate their lunches at the ends of the rows, beneath the vine canopies for shade, each group with its own colored ice chest. Still, a crowd gathered behind Merengue's truck to use the water tanks and to buy generic soft drinks for fifty cents a can. Aníbal had just squeezed in through the cluster of bodies to reach for his lunch when a violent tug forced him back.

"Check the weight on some of those boxes before the cargo truck hauls them off," Jesse demanded. "We've been getting complaints from the warehouse so make sure today's first shipment is perfect."

Jesse walked off with the static-ridden walkie-talkie bouncing against his hip. Flat-footed, he left behind a pair of parallel prints, like tire tracks.

Aníbal scowled, muttering under his breath but conscious about being heard by the pickers. The scaleboy earned a salary, the pickers worked for hourly wages and piecework; what was he complaining about?

"I'll have the piña colada, a piña coloda, bartender!" El Caraballo Uno yelled out to the amusement of those around him. He pushed his way to the front.

"Mexicans go first, *puertorriqueño*," Ninja said through his cigarette. Pifas, also annoyed, muttered, "*Pinche puertito.*"

"There's plenty for everyone. Back away. Don't crowd," Naro said. He and Amanda took charge of the soda sales for Merengue.

"Small bills only, Sebastián, this isn't a bank," Amanda said.

"Is this diet? I hate diet," someone among the crowd complained. Aníbal only saw the hand raised up, waving the can of soda in the air. He missed the soda rush. It was the same chaos and excitement as with the paycheck rush on Fridays—everyone pushed and shoved, but politely made way for the person exiting the mob. Minutes later the dust at the scene of the soda sale settled. The volume on a transistor radio went up.

When he bent down to lift a box from a low stack near group 15 Aníbal smelled chipotle sauce. His mouth watered. The scale read twenty-two pounds. Aníbal pressed his thumb down the plate to complete the minimum twenty-three-pound weight requirement.

"No lunch?" Don Nico asked.

Aníbal smiled back at the old man and shook his head. "I'm on a hunger strike," he said.

"He's trying to keep his weight down," Doña Ramona volunteered, biting into a crisp corn tortilla while using her free hand to blow into a miniature battery-powered *brasero*.

Doña Gertrudis removed her orange hard hat. The damp strands of hair stuck to her skin around the hairline. "Poor thing," she said, "working through the break. The union would never put up with this."

"Here we go," said Doña Ramona, tapping her finger against her temple. Around her neck hung a large stop-watch and a camera with its cap dangling from the lens. She broke a chip off the toasted tortilla to dip into her bowl of rice and sauce.

"Grape picking back in the seventies with Chávez," Doña Gertrudis began, staring out into space, "the union was so strong we could have had the gringo owners feed us with their own hands."

"Don't exaggerate, *comadre*," Doña Ramona said. "You sound like those women that come down from San Joaquín, telling us the grape pickers there get one-hour lunch breaks through the union. *¡Tonterías!*"

"One-hour lunch breaks?" Don Nico laughed.

Tamayamá, sitting just behind Don Nico, let out a quick, "*Aijodesutamayamá!*"

"We should be so lucky to get some decent hours working," Don Nico said.

"Well, we need the union," Doña Gertrudis said. "I heard talk about a strike down at Freeman's company. They'll show all of us how it's done."

"Strikes don't work anymore," said Don Nico. "Not like they used to."

"That's for sure," Doña Ramona said. "It's not the same nowadays, not down here in the Caliente Valley."

Aníbal walked farther down, the sun already pressing down hard on his back. He had been looking forward to getting out of the heat, at least for the short duration of the break since he spent the entire morning walking back and forth down the length of the block. As soon as one of Los Caraballos saw him coming, he elbowed the other.

"Well, well, look here, Demetrio," El Caraballo Uno said. "The scaleboy came to look at us. But I bet he likes me better than he likes you."

"That's because he thinks you have the bigger cock," El Caraballo Dos said. "But just wait until he gives me a chance."

Aníbal ignored them. Los Caraballos were loud and obnoxious. Mostly harmless but annoying just the same. From the corner of his eye he noticed Tinman observing from a distance. Tinman never ate. He only drank four of Merengue's cheap sodas, enough to let out a belch the entire crew could hear. During the break he read his book. His long hair brushing both sides of the open cover.

"The pretty boy's getting mad, Estanislaus," El Caraballo Dos said, making mock prissy gestures as he made his list. "Blowing up like the bullfrog. Glaring like the glass. He's going to break like the firecracker. Aim like the gun. He's—"

"He's scheming, Demetrio. Look at him. What's he thinking? What does he want and how bad does he want it?"

Aníbal checked the reading on the scale.

El Caraballo Uno kept goading in a whisper. "I bet that ass is real tight."

"It's this tight," El Caraballo Dos whispered, making a fist.

"Enough, already!" Aníbal said, hoping that an outburst would settle them down.

"Easy, easy," El Caraballo Uno said. "What do you think, Tinman? Should we let this pretty fish go?"

Tinman put his book down, pressed his hands together, and imitated a fishtail plunging back into an imaginary surface.

Afterward he released his belch.

"Tinman says you're not that good a catch," El Caraballo Uno said between chuckles.

"But at least an appetizer," El Caraballo Dos chimed in, puckering his lips and throwing Aníbal a kiss. "A nice sweet mouthful." He grabbed for his crotch.

"And we can net ourselves Tiki-Tiki for a main course," El Caraballo Uno said. "Where is that *jotete*?" Behind him, Tinman stood up and swayed his hips, wrists limp.

"Does anyone here have salt?" Eva came up behind Aníbal. Both Caraballos quickly scrambled for the lunch bag.

"I've got your salt here, Evita," El Caraballo Uno said. "Take your grimy hands away!"

"I brought the salt, *pinche boricua*. Let me see."

"I'll let you see it when I find it. Move!"

Aníbal seized the opportunity to sneak away, but was stopped by Doña Pepa with an offering of a piece of sandwich. "Take it," she said, bringing the slice of folded bread up to his face.

"No, thank you, Doña," Aníbal said with embarrassment.

"Take it, take it. You're going to thank me later."

Aníbal quickly stuffed the bread into his mouth. It soaked up the last traces of saliva, which nearly made him choke. He wasn't starving, but he wanted to please Doña Pepa, who reminded him of Nana back in Mexicali.

"If you get dizzy, suck on a lemon," Doña Pepa advised.

Doña Pepa sat on a box turned upside down. Grape boxes weren't made to withstand the weight of a human body, but Doña Pepa was petite, frail-looking, yet as strong as any other worker. Aníbal had seen her lift boxes of grapes that were twice the size as those her grandsons carried.

"Your grandsons?" Aníbal asked, to be polite.

"They're back there pissing," she answered. "*Cochinos*. I told them not to wear those propaganda shirts. What's Merengue going to think? That we're troublemakers? That we want to strike?"

Doña Pepa was the crew's *abuela*. Everyone knew she was beyond retirement age, but she came back to pick every year using her daughter's Social Security number. This year she brought with her two *poncho* grandsons who weren't very popular with the crew because they spoke broken Spanish.

"Tell your packers the boxes are a little heavy," Aníbal said. Doña Pepa chewed her food slowly. Los Pepitos, her grandsons, pelted grapes at each other farther down the row.

"Scaleboy!" Amanda yelled. Aníbal turned to meet his reflection on her sunglasses. "We've finally got the identification stamp," she said. She handed him the metal numeral stamp and ink pad. "The shippers will stamp what's already been loaded; you need to stamp what hasn't. Start at the other end."

Aníbal looked to the end of the block. The bright umbrellas stood out, adjusted against the sun. As he walked, he considered that this would be over for him in a few weeks. It was the heat that was killing him, not Amanda or Jesse or Los Caraballos. The heat was beating them up as well.

When he reached the end of the block, he bent down to begin stamping each box above the label. The ink pad was dry so he spat on it. In the absence of workers, the sandy avenue between the blocks widened, framed by the neat stacks of boxes and the litter of damaged covers and torn cushions. Aníbal knelt down in front of a stack. The vibrations of the electricity cables hummed from the end of the block. With his body pressed low to the ground, he imagined himself camouflaged, his eyes following the stamp, roving like the anxious horned toad.

"It's actually a lizard," Carmelo would clarify. Carmelo was fanatic about desert wildlife, especially birds. Aníbal could only point out the roadrunner from the quail; Carmelo knew shrike from mockingbird.

"It's all in the black bar along the head, see it?"

Carmelo had stood behind him that time, his arm propped over Aníbal's shoulder and pointing into the spindly mesquite. Aníbal's vision had blurred with excitement. Bird or no bird, the instant Carmelo's muscle touched Aníbal their entire bodies connected.

Aníbal caught the glare of the sun on the metal stamp each time he turned his wrist. He was careful not to make contact with the metal, or else it blistered his skin.

What Aníbal liked best about life in the fields was the privacy. Despite the occasional trouble from Los Caraballos, no one really cared who he was when he wasn't a grape picker. There was no prying. In Mexicali, he could never lose himself among the network of neighborhoods that knew him, his parents, and his parents' parents. Once a well-to-do family settled on its property it engraved itself on a map. There was little chance of escaping mention in the gossipy society columns. The unwritten rule was that if a man had roots on the border he maintained them. Only poor migrant campesinos from southern Mexico actually crossed it; if they lived on the border they did so in *ejidos*, the barren outskirts of the city, with no running water and no street names. They didn't live anywhere. But if a long-term border resident took that extra step into foreign soil then everyone would wonder: no money? no pride in Mexico? no place to hide?

Aníbal's parents were scandalized after he made his decision to become a field worker in the U.S. "A slave," quipped his father. They wanted him to stay and repair the damage he had done. For years he had worked as an assistant accountant for his father's construction business, saving up his money for Talina, the daughter of two lawyers. His mother anticipated the union, and the subsequent climb up the social ladder. And just when the engagement was about to be printed in the papers, Jorge came forward. Silly, romantic, and beautiful Jorge came forward, pleading with him to call off the engagement, to run away with him the way they fantasized after making love. Aníbal and Jorge. Forever. In an act of desperation, Jorge revealed everything to Talina, who revealed everything to his father.

"Who's Jorge?" his father had asked. And within minutes the room exploded into stutterings and incoherent explanations. Then the cover-up: *Talina had a change of heart; Talina's too young to marry, say parents; Young Pérez Ceballos needs to secure his future first.* Finally, the escape: the move out of his parents' household and into Nana's, the resignation from Industria Pérez, and the jump across the international border, without Jorge who had betrayed him. He was no longer Aníbal, but Scaleboy.

This afternoon Aníbal was going to tell Carmelo he was joining him on the grape route north, to Sonoma and San Joaquín. The understanding was clear, but left unspoken. Carmelo would keep his girl on that side of the border, and his male companion on this one. Last month Carmelo had Aníbal take pictures of him standing outside a house with a nicely kept lawn. Then more standing next to some stranger's Cadillac. The best ones Aníbal took were shot at the downtown shopping mall, where Carmelo asked the blonde from the ice-cream parlor to pose with him by the indoor fountain. Aníbal imagined the look of envy on the faces of those who saw the pictures across the border—a deception that probably compelled others to seek similar fortunes. Little did they suspect that it was the eye behind the camera that saw the truth, the whole truth, the necessarily hidden truth.

Aníbal kept one of those photographs with him at all times for comfort. Carmelo's smile was his. Only one side of his cheek perked up when he smiled, revealing the crooked canine. After his meal, Carmelo sat hunched on the hood of the car with a plastic case of dental floss. Aníbal followed the green string from the case to Carmelo's mouth to the ground. He studied the waves and loops of its design, attractive as chest hairs.

Down the block, one of the foreman honked the horn to signal the end of the break. Merengue yelled out "Merengue!" and Los Caraballos let loose a barrage of whistling. Bodies merged one last time at the path between the block, scrambling to steal one last drink of water before heading back into the sulfurous rows of vines. At his end, Aníbal felt like the solitary woodpecker that no one sees or hears but that everyone has been around because it pecks pecks pecks, leaving its mark behind. Peck peck peck. A distant knock so faint it remains unnoticed when it ceases, as if there had been no knock at all.

ADÁN GRIEGO grew up in the El Paso-Juárez area. He endured attacks of religiosity while attending college in San Antonio. He thought he was going for graduate studies at the University of Wisconsin-Madison, but he just wanted to prolong his adolescence, which he did for 6 years. Before reaching 30, he got a job and a life, saying he had entered the Twentieth Century when he bought a car, a TV, and a microwave after his first job as a librarian at the University of California-Santa Barbara. He now lives in San Francisco and works at the Stanford University Libraries.

Onions Are for Men

———▶

Adán Griego

A Virgin No More…

My sister had come back from work early. She had managed to leave early from the factory "on the other side." She used to get up at five every morning to get ready to cross the bridge. It had been five years since she had begun working at the jeans factory. Her company claimed their jeans were as famous as Levi's. But the strike and the boycott from the previous year had ruined the fame. "Now that we have a union we won't be getting a turkey this year for Thanksgiving," she came home complaining after the strike had been settled.

It was about three in the afternoon when she arrived. She had been suffering from headaches, stomachaches, and *cólicos*, all of which led her to scream and insult everyone in sight and horrify my mother. She would even excuse herself when referring to the *cantineras* as prostitutes even though what she really wanted to say was… But the only time I heard a derogatory word from my mother was when she referred to my father's *querida* as "*esa vieja*," and she did not mean old.

Just by coincidence, the traveling doctor, to whom the *ejido* paid a yearly fee, was due in town that afternoon. In the last few days there had been an epidemic of colds, vomiting, and other ailments. Following the monthly visit of the traveling doctor, the town's health magically returned to normalcy. Even the drunkards seemed to enjoy their hangovers on Sunday mornings with a plate of hot *menudo* as the acceptable remedy.

The pills prescribed by the traveling doctor seemed to possess some magic the local *boticario* and Doña Lola, the *curandera*, no longer possessed. The *boticario* lamented to Doña Lola, "they're a bunch of *pendejos*…all they got was aspirin…I could have given it to them for free." Doña Lola, in turn, complained to her nemesis, the *boticario*, the only one who listened to her these days, "If only they had taken the *estafiate*…" The town was surprised to see them both seated in the plaza together. They had not been on the same side since the local elections a few years ago when they both voted for the opposition, when the winner was, well, the same as always, of course. "There's nothing like the magic of aspirin," the *boticario* continued his lamentation as he drank a cup of *estafiate* prepared by Doña Lola, who added, "Or like the advances of modern science," both of them acknowledging the ingratitude of those who had been their patients up until a few days ago.

At about six in the afternoon my sister returned from the doctor. She was fuming. She had waited in line for two hours and the doctor had not even given her anything. "He touched me all over the place, at least three times," she complained. How I envied her. I had faked a cough for his last two visits. I enjoyed his soft hands caressing my chest, while he told me, "Say ah…" I would make a weak sound so he could touch me and say, "Again." This time I had started coughing earlier that morning, hoping to be taken to see the young doctor again and feel his soft hands on my skin. But my sister's ailments were more important, according to my mother. "At least Doña Lola would have given me some *pomada* and the *boticario* would have prescribed aspirin, that's what he does all the time," my sister continued, still struggling to contain her anger. As we were getting ready to have dinner, my father reminded her that now we at least had a traveling doctor and did not have to drive five miles to the neighboring town. And grades four through six were added. My father felt so proud, "Progress has finally reached the *ejido*," even if the priest would still come only once a month. But in only a few weeks the bishop was coming for the feast of Our Lady of Fátima. There would even be a procession with people from Zaragoza bringing the statue of Our Lady of the Pillar. On the twelfth of October, from our town we would carry the statue of the Virgin of Fátima to Zaragoza in the procession to celebrate the Fiesta del Pilar.

That night, while washing dishes, I heard my mother and my sister talking in the kitchen in low voices. The doctor had recommended that my sister get married to alleviate her "pains." As she talked, my sister still could turn red with anger, even as my mother encouraged her to calm down. At barely nineteen, my sister already considered herself a *solterona*. As they finished cleaning the kitchen, she made it very clear, if by the following month she did not get married, "I will not remain a virgin." The following week her boyfriend's parents came to ask for her hand. It would have been a festive occasion but my father forgot all about it and decided to fix a small leak in the roof by boiling tar in the kitchen. When the in-laws-to-be arrived, the house was full of smoke.

On April fifteenth she got married and ceased to be a virgin. She refused to listen to my mother who asked her to wait two more months and become a June bride. Even that joyful day, my father was so bored during the church ceremony that he took out a pack of gum—you can imagine my sister's anger.

Onions Are for Men

It couldn't be clearer than water. I was fourteen and that was too old to spend another summer reading in the public library. "He has to become a man." I heard my father's voice coming from the kitchen. Up to then my rugged experiences were limited to picking up chopped wood and playing with our neighbor's old tractor. Everyone knew I was a disaster feeding animals since the day I "liberated" my aunt's cows because they cried. Then there was the excursion into the cotton fields when I refused to continue picking cotton because it hurt my hands.

From then on, anytime someone in the family made fun of my "delicate hands," either my mother or my father would come to my defense. "Leave him alone." "Let him read." And I was saved again. But now, it was my father who insisted on me going to the onion fields, "because that's where men become men." I expected my mother to come to my defense, but she did not.

We had to get up at dawn; it was about four in the morning.

"It's time," I heard the same voice from the previous night. It came from the kitchen where my father was already drinking coffee and my mother was preparing something for us to eat. As I tried to wake up I could only think, "Time for what? To get up or to become a man?"

We had to hurry, to rent the tools: sacks, cans, and scissors. Then we ran to find a row of onions as close as possible to the loading truck. "At least these are nice, they look so pretty," I thought as we made our way through the morning dew that welcomed us. It was not even five when we started. I had barely put on my gloves—I was the only one wearing them—when I heard my father calling me: "Hurry up." Not too long after his call, he came to help me catch up. If it had been one of my other brothers, he would have cussed me out from beginning to end. But I had made it very clear, on the first insult, "I will leave."

I was a lost cause. Even with the gloves and my father's constant help, I did not get too far. Having received all A's in Mrs. Adams's spelling class or an "A+" in conduct did not count for much here, much less having read all of the A-L part in the bilingual dictionary. "This is work for men," I heard one of the boys who had started at the same time as me and was pulling ahead say. "What am I doing here?" I said to myself, but when I looked up, I saw his friend, who smiled at me.

At eight we took a short break. Finally, time to eat. They all took out their tacos and burritos. I unwrapped the specially made sandwich I had bought at Rogelio's store. I would save the fruit juice for later. After the break I fell even farther behind and my father gave up. The gloves did not seem to help much, I had blisters on my hands and was not making much progress.

We left the onion fields shortly before lunch. The temperature was about to reach 90 degrees. When we got home, I fell asleep right away, lulled by a *corrido*. I woke up two hours later, engulfed in sweat. In the distance, I heard the radio announce the weather. The temperature was approaching 100 degrees, and it was only the third week of May. Not quite awake yet, I wanted to return to my dream, where I had encountered the smiling boy from the onion fields.

In my hastiness to leave the fields behind, I had not even bothered to ask how much I had earned. That night my father announced that I did not have to go anymore. "You can stay home and continue reading the dictionary they gave you at the public library." I found out the real reason the following afternoon while I struggled to understand Mary Tyler Moore on television. I hadn't even earned enough to pay for renting the tools.

That evening I went to the public library. I sat in a corner by myself, not just because I smelled of onions. I had discovered a magazine with pictures of men in swimming suits.

The smell of onions surrounded me for what seemed like the rest of the summer. One more thing stayed with me, the realization that I was becoming a man…a different kind of man.

Still a *Padrecito*

We came in from the fields a little bit before four. Don José and the others, all in their sixties, working to supplement their Social Security benefits, had made it very clear: they had to be home by four. It was the beginning of their *telenovela* and they were not going to miss it for anything. I had suggested taking a one-hour lunch, so we could take a siesta. I was outvoted. "Don't you like *telenovelas*?" Don José asked one morning. "Do you think he loves her?" he asked another time, lamenting the *mal de amores* of the woman who ruled his life that summer.

They still called me *Padrecito*. I had not tried to explain to them that I had left the seminary. They still joked about priests. "Can you hear confessions yet?" Don José asked me. "Because Santos has not confessed in thirty years and he thinks you'll give him a light penance." But they were always careful not to break an unspoken agreement of respect for the Church—the same church they attended only for funerals and weddings. Their wives and daughters were the ones who went every Sunday to pray for them. That had been my father's excuse over the years for not attending Mass or going to confession. My father was even fond of telling the story of the last time—"the only time," corrected my mother—that he had been to confession. As penance, the priest had given him a rosary for a week. Since he did not know it, he enlisted my mother's help. When they were ready to start, my mother informed him that he had to kneel down. But my father didn't see why. "I'll sit here, you can kneel, if you want to." He would also tell of the first time he attended Mass after *saludo de paz* was introduced. When one of the men seated next to him extended his hand, my father, already bored and not knowing what he was supposed to do, warmly shook the other man's hand. "*Mucho gusto*, Mariano Griego," he introduced himself.

My mother was very quiet, then she mentioned I had received a letter from a university. But it was not the one in San Antonio. It was from a name she did not recognize. "It's north of Chicago," I told her. Her eyes were red, I knew she had been crying and they filled with tears again. "Are you leaving us?" How can I tell her I am suffocating here? I would be even if the temperature were not 100 degrees. I miss Paul. I hate working in the fields. I have worked here every summer for ten years. I dislike being here. But I do not want to hurt her. She has already been hurt enough. All she can see is her boy leaving her. The same boy whose hand she held and to whom she read. The same boy she took to the doctor, at sixteen, and refused to hear her brother, my *tío* Juan, as he tried to convince her that my headaches would be alleviated if he could take me to—she did not let him finish. No, not her boy, he would not be taken to the *Calle Mariscal* to see those…she could not bring herself to say that "p" word, no matter how angry she was. It was unlike her. But her boy has been a stranger since he returned from the seminary. He speaks differently now. He uses some words she has never heard. He's always reading books in English. She used to understand the titles of the ones in Spanish. "Who is Lorca?" she asked me one afternoon. Now her boy only wants to hear classical music and refuses to listen to *corridos* anymore. He used to send all those postcards signed, "With the love of God." Now he won't even fast on Good Friday. What happened at that seminary where he was? But she never asked. My sister finally did, years later when I was visiting from California and I stood way in the back while the priest said something about love and compassion.

Mother has been crying all week as the day of my departure approaches. "Why are you going so far?" I tell her I got a scholarship, but I would have gone anyway, even without it. I have to get out of here. I have not talked to anyone since I left the seminary. I wanted to talk to Paul but the last time I saw him, from afar, I did not have the courage to say good-bye to him. Now he is six hundred miles away and I will not see him again. If he were here, I could talk to someone. But he is no longer with me and I have nothing to take his place. I try to find him in Lorca and I finally find him, hidden in the leaves of Whitman.

Sometimes with one I love I feel myself with rage for fear I effuse unreturned love,
But now I think there is no unreturned love, the pay is certain one way or another,
(I loved a certain person ardently and my love was not return'd Yet out that I have written these songs.)

Sophisticate's Lifestyle

I have been prolonging my adolescence for six years. I am almost thirty. I have to get a life. How am I going to answer my niece's questions next year? I have to get out of here, it's getting colder and colder. "More snow is predicted for the weekend…"—I catch the last of the weather update on the radio. It's already April and I'm ruining the shoes I bought last week.

My niece is all excited today. It's New Year's Day and she's never seen an airplane before. She sees all the people coming out of planes, and immediately figures out that everyone around is waiting to get on the planes. She looks at me and asks me, "*Tío* Adán," I just cannot get used to the idea of being called uncle, "are you going to get on one of those planes?" She is very inquisitive, always asking questions about everything. Earlier in the day she asked, with such innocence, "Aren't you too old to be in school?" I tried to explain to her that there were people much older than I who were also in school. How could I get my point across to her? Her mother did not understand why I have been going to school all these years, neither did my father, nor my brothers, nor the neighbors. It's been ten years now, right? Even I forget how long it's been. "*Tío* Adán," she asks again, "do you have a car? My cousin Jimmy has a car and he's not as old as you are." Those are the same questions my father, and my sister and the neighbors would also like to ask me. "*Tío* Adán, do you have a girlfriend? Jimmy does and he says you…" There is complete silence at the table and she realizes she has asked something she was not supposed to after her mother gives her a fearfully penetrating look. I try to ignore her question and leave the kitchen. "I think we better get going." My father finished the sentence for me: "Better be there on time." Normally we would not have listened to him insisting that we leave two hours ahead of time. "You never know what's going to happen along the way, you might get a flat tire," continues my father. That's why we used to get up at five and leave at five forty-five in the morning every summer when we worked in the fields. "But, it's only three miles," I would protest, "and we don't start until seven." Today, however, my father's wise advice is followed with no questioning.

"I'm moving," I almost scream on the phone. Lately, I have to speak louder and louder. "What? You're what…where… California? Yes, I was there, to visit your uncle…" Then we talk about the weather. "It's rained again, second time in a week… Where in California? Santa what…?" He sounds excited, California is closer than Wisconsin. Even if he will not remember the exact name. He tells my sister I'm moving to Santa Monica; to our new neighbor he says it's Santa Ana, and to Don José and his other *compadres* he tells them it's Santa Cruz. When my brother asks him which one, he gives up, "It's one of those Santa something, in California." For him it's the beginning of a much awaited return, even if it's still far from El Paso. He knows where California is on the map, he can pronounce it, he can write it, he's been to California. He has never been to Wisconsin.

I look at the newspaper ad again to make sure I have the right address.

Great Ocean Views,
hardwood floors,
fireplace, your own room,
quiet area.
Sophisticate's lifestyle.

I guess I have a sophisticate's life now that I own a car, a television, and a microwave. I'll tell that to my niece next time I see her.

I park on one of the side streets close to the old church and walk up the hill a few blocks. I was here last week and the young man, he must be about eighteen, said they needed a roommate. They would prefer a professional, mature person. That's me. "The last guy left without paying his share of the rent, and he left us a phone bill…You'll have to install your own line." He's from Utah and studies architectural design; actually he's "just taking a few classes now, but I want to be an architect. My roommate is looking forward to meeting you. He works at the university also. Where can he be?" He moves toward the window, "He's here."

The man who comes in is in his thirties, slim and blond. He looks older, though. He speaks with a drawl. I tried to trace his twang and ask if he's from Texas. No, he's from Oklahoma. "Oh yes, there is that rivalry with the Texas Longhorns every year," I add, looking for a way out. "We have a couple of people interested," he says. The Utah young man had told me several people had looked at the room but it was too expensive for them. "We're looking for someone who travels a lot." His roommate mentioned how they wanted to have someone else around the house. "We entertain a lot. It'll be too noisy for you." What has made him change his mind? Over the phone he sounded quite amiable and very interested. "I thought you were from…you don't speak like…" He realizes he has said too much in so few words. "Yeah, well, that happens when you teach language, you lose your accent and it becomes harder to tell where I am from," I catch myself saying.

I want to get out. I leave the house. He now looks more familiar. Yes, he was at the bar the other night. He walked away from the counter when a group of young and boisterous Latinos stood next to him and asked for a margarita. He was the one drinking wine. He was with a group of young men, all blond. They were drinking wine, too. I heard one of them saying, "There are so many of them now." But the group of lively Latinos could not have cared less, even if they had heard the remarks. They were on their way to the dance floor as Los Lobos started to sing "La Bamba."

Our Secret

The plane has just landed and I feel the weight of returning— where I encounter a present that leads me to a past, a past I would like to forget, but that brings a feeling of nostalgia. A nostalgia that (re)appears in my dreams. Dreams full of the longing with which our memory tricks us. The idyllic memories of the desert of my childhood are shattered just as the plane touches the ground. Suddenly I can feel the past unveiling itself in front of me. All I can see now are the sandstorms, the suffocating heat, the smell of onions, and boys calling me *joto*.

What will they ask me, what will I say? After more than fifteen years we have become like strangers. When those moments of silence arrive, we try to fill them with something, anything.

—How is the weather in California?

It's always warm…

—Is the ocean pretty?

Yes, very much…

—Is it close to the border?

No, it's about…

—How long did your plane take?

Only one hour…

—What kind of work do you do?

I work in a library…

—What's the name of the town where you live?

When they finished asking me those questions, almost in the same order as the last time, I, too, try to fill the moments of silence with the same questions of a year ago so we can postpone the inevitable one.

—At what time are we going to church on Sunday?

We'll go to the ten-thirty Mass.

—Do you remember *Güero*, what happened to him?

He is married now and has two children.

—How is my *tía Ramona*?

She must be in her nineties by now.

—Is Don José still working in the onion fields, how old is he?

No, he does not work anymore. He is eighty-five and he keeps asking about you.

He still remembers me from that morning twenty years ago,

when I first showed up to work in the fields. Yes, I remember him too, and the smell of onions...

And we start again the same cycle. Then I sense they want to ask the question they have not asked for five years. The one I warned that if asked again, I would leave on Sunday instead of Monday night, even if I had come in on Friday at noon. I know they want to ask, to reassure themselves. I don't want to answer it and I don't want to leave either, as I had threatened. I really couldn't. How could I live with the guilt. I want to get up and ask for a cup of coffee, at eleven o'clock at night! Instead, I ask for an aspirin. "The plane ride made me a little dizzy," I say while getting up to go to the kitchen.

Monday has finally arrived. We had run out of things to ask each other by Saturday morning. On Saturday night, I wanted to go to sleep at nine. My father had gone to sleep at five. "Don't bother me now," he said, as he kicked the newspaper around. It's yesterday's. There was no Spanish-language paper today. It's Christmas Day. Don't they understand the need of this seventy-five-year-old man, with only a third-grade education? He has to read the newspaper. He's read it every day as long as I can remember. "If only I could learn the alphabet in English, then I would learn the language," said my father as he drank his third cup of coffee that morning, "then I could read the one you bought," as he picked up my copy of the *Los Angeles Times* and then threw it on the table.

"Don't go to sleep yet," I hear my sister threatening from the kitchen. She wants me to talk to her. "About what?" I want to say, but I don't. "What do you do on weekends?" she asks me. "I stay home and watch television or I go out with some friends to eat." She wants to know if any of those friends is someone special, but she does not know how to phrase the question. She wants to get to know me again, I am her brother. She has a right to know me again. But I don't let her into my world. It's ten-thirty already and we end up watching television. I ask her about a new musical group that appears on the screen that I don't recognize. She knows I have allowed her to enter a little bit into my life when I add, "They are very handsome." Then she asks me about my Cuban friend, the one who died this summer in Chicago, the one who was only thirty-three. And then she adds, "Are you being careful?"

It's time to go the airport. My father is not coming. "It's almost time for me to go to bed now," he says. I approach him to shake his hand and say good-bye. We embrace, briefly. I catch him looking at me. In those eyes, filled with tears, I see a quiet reassurance. The same one I felt when, as I child, I lulled myself to sleep on his lap. It's him, wanting to tell me, "I love you..." I know he wants to add, "no matter what." I also want to tell him, "I love you, too..." Neither one of us says it, but we both know it. It's our secret.

Smell of Coffee

It's seven-thirty and I have not heard the usual noise from the kitchen nor the *corridos* coming from the radio. Usually all of that starts to happen at about six in the morning. I get out of bed, getting dressed quickly. It's early May and it's a bit cool inside the house. I see that my father is still in bed under the blankets. I ask him if he would like some coffee. "Yes, that would be nice," he says.

It's been ten years since my mother's death and she still seems to be present in the kitchen. I open one of the cupboards and there they are, the flasks in which I got her to organize all of her herbs. There is *ruda, estafiate, poleo, manzanilla, tila, hierba-buena, zabila,* and…But we don't know what ache they will cure. My mother would have known it, just like she knew all the family history: "Your *tía* Romualda was not related to my mother… Your *tío* Felipe is younger than me, but he's also my *tío*… His mother is *la abuela* Ins…"

I see her in the kitchen, by the stove, preparing *papas con huevo* for me and my father. She is beaming, radiant with joy at seeing her boy come home, if only for a few days. I see her preparing the potatoes separately for me, without onions and chile. I see her hardly being able to move around the kitchen. "It's the weight, and the years and the pains and…" she would say. It is also the indelible mark of a car accident that ruined one of her arms and one of her legs. Several times I asked her if she remembered what happened. Her vivid recollection surprised me. "It was a Sunday morning, about six-thirty. Very few cars were around. We saw the truck zigzagging and Don Valerio hardly had any time to pull off the road when we were hit. My *comadre,* Soledad, died right away. And that *p—borracha.* She kept screaming because her knee was bleeding and I could not feel my arm or my leg and your brother's face was covered with blood. And you know what was her name? Esther, just like me."

The water is boiling now and I prepare two cups of coffee. My father has made his way to the kitchen. I know he sees my mother there, preparing coffee and breakfast for the two of us. He asks me if I want to go to the cemetery to visit her grave.

We don't say much along the way. We don't find that much to say these days anymore. Over the phone we always talk about the weather. When I ask him about the rest of the family he says, "They're all fine." Later, I find out from my sister that my *tío* Celso was in the hospital, another cousin, whom I have not seen in several years, got married and some other distant relative died. My father did not go to the funeral. He says, "Death is on the loose around that neighborhood." He will visit the relatives later. I did ask him about his "other sons." This time he did not pretend he did not know what I was talking about. "They are fine," he told me. One of them just got married and the other one is expecting a baby soon. I guess I should feel something for my half brothers and sisters but I have never met them. I also ask him about his younger brother, the one everyone made fun of because he "walked and talked" funny. "He's fine, he's a strong man," says my father. He had to be in order to survive all those years of solitude and humiliation.

The old part of the cemetery looks very much like the one where we visited my *abuela* Mariana's grave. She was the one who died the year I was born. The one I always felt I knew from all those visits to the *campo santo* to take flowers to her. The newest section of the cemetery looks very much like any other American cemetery, the lawns are nicely kept, always watered and so green. Almost all the graves look the same, very inconspicuous. There are not statues of angels and virgins and Christs. But here, only a mile away from the river, "the other side" is very palpable. The graves are always adorned with flowers, not just Kmart floral arrangements. Some have geraniums, carnations, and a few others have roses. I don't remember the way to my mother's grave, but my father seems to know the way quite well. She has a couple of flower bouquets. Mother's Day is this Sunday. I am about to ask my father about the flowers when he says he was here a couple of days ago. This would have been their fiftieth wedding anniversary. We both want to cry but we can't. *Los hombres no lloran* was what I heard all those years. My father walks toward his old truck and I say I have sand in my eyes as I rub them, at the same time trying to unlock the knot on my throat. We break the silence when he says now he owns a piece of land, right next to my mother. "She forgave me for all those years…" he says, sobbing, later that night after he's had a couple of beers. "Couldn't you find a job here in El Paso?" he asks as we are getting ready to go to bed. How can I tell him that I don't find anything here that I feel is my own. The Lent sandstorms seem to have blown away any remnants of me.

The next morning, over coffee, I ask him why he is not listening to *corridos* on the radio. "Because they have some new ones I don't like," he says. I also ask him about the two trees in front of the house, the ones I planted twenty years ago when we moved in. "They died," he said, "we tried to get them back…" I'm almost sure he then whispered, "…just like we tried to get you back."

Life Is Sweet

I see his hands, hardened by age, by the hot days in the fields: cotton, onion, chile, and sugar beet, "and also in construction," my father adds proudly as he lifts the blankets to cover himself up. He's had a mild stroke and has lost part of his hearing and eyesight. He cannot read the newspaper anymore as he has done everyday for the last fifty years. I offer to read him the front page but he's now ready to go to sleep. It's only 10 A.M. and he wants to take a nap before going to the doctor.

His daily routine has been interrupted overnight: up at 5 A.M., drive to the store to buy the Spanish newspaper by 6 A.M., 8 A.M. visit to the neighbor next door for a third cup of coffee and a quick breakfast, always with chile, the hotter the better. After a quick cigarette with his eighty-year-old friend Don Ezequiel, he comes back home to reread the paper and then a nap before lunch, when the social worker will come in to deliver a hot meal. The same one he will take to Doña Rafaela's in exchange for beans with chile because "that tasteless crap has no salt." He tells this to Doña Rafaela, after she's prepared some food for him.

I ask him for the paper and he gives me the front page, mixed in with the sports and society sections. Now he sleeps most of the time. He says he gets short of breath just by walking over to visit Don Ezequiel, less than 50 meters away. He's supposed to use the inhaler the doctor gave him. He says he can't find it and then adds, "Besides, it's all a conspiracy to get rid of old people." That's why he did not go to get a flu shot when the visiting social worker made an appointment for him. "I forgot about it," he told her when she asked him about it a few days later. At least the stroke, and the weight of seventy-eight years of age have not taken away his sense of humor. "All I need is a sleeping pill and some vitamins and I'll be fine," he told me when I called him from California.

The doctor's appointment is at three but he insists that we leave at one. It's useless telling him that it's only a thirty-minute drive. "But you have to go up to the mountain area," he says and he gets up to get ready. It's the same two hours ahead of time when I need to go to the airport or when we used to work in the fields.

He seems a bit nervous when we get to the doctor's at 1:45. The nurses already know him, "*¿Cómo está hoy, Don Mariano?*" We sit down and wait less than twenty minutes when they call his name. He turns to me and gives me an "I told you so" look before he asks me to join him in the doctor's office. "You can ask him what's wrong with me. Ask him to give me some sleeping pills." We both know he can ask the doctor himself. The doctor speaks Spanish. He's really afraid they are going to keep him here. "That's what they did to Doña Rafaela and all she had was a headache. They ended up operating on her and she never left the hospital." When he gave me the news over the phone, he reminded me of his theory, "I told you they just want to get rid of old people, but not before they get all the money they can from our Medicare." Maybe he was right.

When the doctor comes in, the first thing my father says is, "I can hear better and I can also see much better now." He just told me he wished he would regain his vision, "God Almighty will grant me that favor." It's odd to hear him invoke the name of God. He, who would go to church only for weddings and funerals, never staying for the whole ceremony.

After the doctor finishes checking the usual blood pressure and pulse, he asks my father a few questions about the medication he was given during the last visit. In spite of what my father says, the doctor knows my father has not been taking the medicine.

He turns to me and even if we don't say anything, we are probably sharing the same thoughts, "It's all a conspiracy, right?"

"I want to live until the year 2000, life is sweet," says my father when the doctor reminds him he's not to smoke anymore unless he wants to kill himself. "Are you smoking now," he asks him again. My father's response is not quite what the doctor expects, "I'm not buying cigarettes anymore." It's the same answer he gave me over the phone when I asked him about smoking. The doctor makes it very clear to my father and me, "No more cigarettes." More than seventy years of smoking has destroyed his lungs and it's obvious it was the main cause of the stroke, however mild, that affected his vision and hearing. "What about the spray I gave you last time?" asks the doctor. My father says he forgot it at home. "But are you using it like I told you?" My father says he is, but the doctor and I know it's not true. He looks at me again, and with that same "it's all a conspiracy" look from a few minutes ago.

It's already dark when we get home, although it's only 5 P.M. "It's time to go to bed," insists my father. He'll probably be able to sleep tonight, even if the doctor did not give him any sleeping pills. At least he knows he won't be in the hospital, all alone. Before long he's already sound asleep. I get close to him and I notice those same hands that caressed my face when he put me to sleep. I want to reach over to him and touch his hands, touch his face, but I can't.

It is exceedingly difficult for most of us to discard the assumptions of the society, in which we were born, in which we live, to which we owe our identities; very difficult to defeat the trap of circumstance, which is also the web of safety; ...virtually impossible to envision the future, except in those terms which we think we already know.

~James Baldwin

ROBERT VÁSQUEZ-PACHECO has been walking the fine line between community activism and art for a long time. Born in the fifties, he is a Nuyorican gay writer and longtime community activist. Growing up in the working-class South Bronx of the sixties, he discovered sex and drugs during the summer of love. A child of the seventies, his writings, primarily non-fiction and poetry, have been published in a whole mess of places, from the journals *Art and Understanding* and *The James White Review* to the anthologies *Sojourner: Black Gay Writers in the Age of AIDS* and *Asian American Sexualities: Dimensions of the Gay and Lesbian Experience*. Infected with HIV in the early eighties, he was a member of various progressive artist collectives, such as Gran Fury and Los Cuarto Gatos. Surviving into the nineties, he is working on his first book of novellas (*The Elements*) and a first book of poetry (*Calling Down the Spirits*).

BRUJO TIME

➤

Robert Vásquez-Pacheco

The old woman thought it was for a woman. She brought all he wanted with an excitement based on a simple error. She thought the object of his attention was a woman. Once again it was easier to leave her safely and comfortable in her mistake rather than bring her rudely into modern times. Charlie knew that her enthusiasm and her creativity might cool if she knew that she was helping a man bewitch another man. Politics are one thing, but this was real life. Consequently, she drew from ancient reservoirs of knowledge based on the perpetual battle for power and control between men and women. At the end, she stood behind the counter, regarding him with a neutral expression, the simple amalgam of too many complex emotions to be displayed on her ancient features at one time: conspiratorial excitement, remembered lust, magical confidence, and the sympathy of the rejected lover. As this was his first time here, they both decided to start simply. Besides, as a smart businesswoman, she knew that if it was too successful, he might not come back. It is always better to escalate slowly. He understood that. Even though he had been smitten with Brett the first time he met him, he knew better than to push too hard in the beginning. Let time work its magic. He paid for his purchases and she gave him specific instructions on how and what to do. He knew a little. After all, you couldn't grow up in a family of women without picking something up. But what he needed called for a degree of expertise that the women in his family refused to share with him. This classified information came under the title, "Things men shouldn't know." Even though the women in his family had conversations in front of him that they would never have in front of their men or any other straight man, this was an inherited wisdom that was entrusted only to the females of the tribe. So after exhausting the limits of his meager knowledge, he had decided to consult a professional.

He had grown up knowing very little about this stuff. His family had raised him to be a good boy, to be an American success so they didn't weigh him down with the burdens of their culture. He spoke Spanish badly. He knew little of his people's history, habits, or culture. They had decided that he didn't need them to be an American success. Charlie was better off free from his Puerto Rican identity, from the loudness, tackiness, and superstition that ruled the lives of his family members. He would not have embarrassing statues or mysterious substances around his apartment. His family would do that for him. He would simply do well, unencumbered by the past, becoming a modern-day Hispanic. He was the carefully constructed repository of his family's American dream. So he knew nothing about how to handle difficult bosses or how to still the wagging tongues of the envious or how to positively influence a case, legal and otherwise, or how to capture someone's heart. He was free of his family's powerlessness. His brother would always call him *el blanquito* with a combination of horror and admiration.

He had passed the *botánica* for months, ignoring it as yet another unnecessary element of the urban landscape. Like the *cuchifrito* place on the corner, it was a humiliating reminder of a culture slowly disappearing, a cultural dinosaur moving slowly toward extinction. But as the months passed and he found that his relationship with Brett wasn't going the way he wanted, the place had subtly developed a concreteness that commanded his attention and curiosity. He started to notice it walking home from work. It had emerged from its two dimensional surroundings, growing its own extrusive reality. Within weeks, its transformation from neighborhood eyesore to neighborhood landmark was complete. As the weeks passed and his frustration increased, long buried memories of various "magical recipes" began to float up from his unconscious, bobbing like so much psychic flotsam and jetsam. He began to remember little unnecessary things, like what to do to sleep better or how to chill out people who were paying too much attention to you. Actions long considered bewildering superstitions resurfaced and were just as quickly drowned once again. But for all his conscious delving into memory, Charlie could not remember what he needed now. He could not remember what to do about love.

Being a responsible man not given to impulsive acts, he decided, after much deliberation, to cease his speculation and consult a professional. Being an independent man used to doing things for himself, he would simply ask for advice and direction rather than involving a stranger in his predicament. Finally the cancellation of a much anticipated evening together (dinner, a movie, and spending the night together) drove him to the *botánica*. Although fueled by frustration and chagrin, he wandered into the *botánica* casually, as if he were a tourist. The old woman behind the counter was not surprised by his suit or his bad Spanish or even his timid request. Once he told her what he wanted, she was the soul of efficiency. She moved behind the counter in a flurry of graceful activity, tossing useful tidbits of information at him all the while. It was always either love or money. Like a true expert practitioner of her craft, she repeated her instructions to him as she placed everything in a plastic bag that said "Thanks for coming!" The second time she told him, Charlie took notes. Better to be safe than sorry. Fortunately, he saw none of his neighbors as he emerged into daylight again. He understood his actions to be a sign of how much he cared for Brett and it warmed his heart.

That night he performed the first ritual to make Brett Byron Chadwick his. Sure enough, about an hour after he was done, Brett called him to apologize for canceling their date. Brett asked if he could come over and spend the night. Although dumbfounded, Charlie immediately said yes. Hiding everything in a bookcase, he proceeded to spend a lovely evening with Brett. The next day, Brett spontaneously canceled his plans for the evening and gave Charlie the evening that he had originally promised him. This was even better than Charlie had anticipated. The old woman knew her business. Then Brett left town on business for ten days. He didn't call once, but then he never called when he was traveling. Floating on the high of two nights together, it didn't bother Charlie that Brett didn't call. What bothered him was seeing Brett a week later with another guy on the street. Charlie quickly ducked into a store to avoid an ugly scene with the common guy Brett was with. After an evening of anger, he decided to do nothing, at least not directly, to Brett. Maybe he had screwed the ritual up. He remembered watching *The Sorcerer's Apprentice* with Mickey Mouse where Mickey screwed up a magic spell and got into trouble. He had probably just screwed something up. He was unfamiliar with all this stuff. He simply repeated the ritual, slowly and methodically.

After two weeks, Brett still hadn't called. Charlie left numerous messages for him but none were returned. He bumped into Brett one evening at a bar they both liked. Brett was fine with him, as attentive and sweet as he always was. He apologized profusely for his behavior. He claimed to be very busy at work. Although he focused his attention on Charlie for the rest of the evening, they did not go home together. Brett claimed to be tired. He promised to call him soon so they could hook up. That night alone in his Ikea-furnished apartment, Charlie wondered what went wrong. He had meticulously followed the instructions. It should have worked. The spell had worked at least for a short while. It just hadn't stuck. It was time for something stronger, more serious. Three days later, Charlie returned to the *botánica*.

The old woman behind the counter seemed surprised to see him again. He explained the situation, how the "woman" he was interested in just wasn't giving him the type of attention he wanted. This time, the woman asked him specific questions. How long had they been going out? Were they sleeping together? What exactly did Charlie want? She asked him if he wanted to step into the back for a consultation, but he said that was unnecessary. He simply needed to "turn up the heat," so to speak. Everything else in his life was fine. The old woman stared wordlessly at him for a while. The store was quiet. It smelled of aromatic herbs and incense. He felt uncomfortable beneath her intense stare. She reminded him of his grandmother. His grandmother would stare at him silently for long moments and then sigh, shaking her head.

This second ritual was more complicated. It entailed various "offerings" and the recitation of a prayer in Spanish for seven days. He spent that week in a state of quiet anxiety. Except for Brett, everything else in his life was fine. Although his career seemed to be blossoming, it didn't seem as important as it had before. Even his supervisor had commented on how well he was doing. It was only a matter of time before he would achieve the type of success that he deserved, the success that his family had groomed him for. But Charlie would never understand his family's role in his American success story. Like a good American, Charlie believed his success to be the product of his individual effort. But despite that effort, Brett eluded him and Brett's mistake (which was to not love him) affected him more seriously than he had imagined. His confidence in himself, that quality of "whiteness" his brother commented on, had been diminished in some way. It hurt his heart and it hurt his pride. After all, he was quite a catch. Most of the kids he grew up with were in jail or working in places with no future like Burger King or the neighborhood cleaners. There were many guys who would be happy to date him. He didn't understand why he felt this particular rejection so strongly. It was almost as if Brett was rejecting everything

Charlie had done, rejecting the persona that Charlie had created, as if that man weren't enough. Intelligent, classically handsome, hard-working, upwardly mobile, cultured, Charlie knew he was a prize. Yet all of these things meant nothing to Brett. His behavior was beyond Charlie's understanding.

Two days later, Brett called him at work. He was going up to his family's vacation house in rural New Hampshire. He invited Charlie to come with him. A nice weekend alone, just the two of them. Charlie immediately accepted. This time the magic seemed to be working. He canceled his plans to see his parents that weekend. After all, he could see them any time. He made up some excuse. His mother was disappointed but she understood. Right after work, he did a little shopping for the weekend. As he was walking home, he saw the old woman from the *botánica*. Unfortunately she had seen him so he couldn't cross the street to avoid her. That would be too obvious. She looked different in the daylight, smaller, more fragile. He was a little ashamed of being seen talking to her in public. Now the neighborhood would know that he went to the *botánica*. She asked how things were going. He felt slightly put off by her nosiness. He told her that he and his "girlfriend" were going away for the weekend. She suggested he get an article of her clothing, just in case. Preferably something she had just worn, like a dirty pair of panties. It sounded vaguely sordid and desperate to him. Stealing a pair of Brett's Calvin Kleins seemed so ghetto to him. He ended their conversation quickly and went home.

The weekend went splendidly. The house was beautiful, like something out of Martha Stewart's magazine. Brett was wonderful, except for one little thing. They had rented some movies to watch in the big country house. They were entwined together on the sofa in front of a roaring fire. Charlie made some comment about the film they had just seen. Brett looked at him and said, "That's what I like about you, Charlie. You're so Portarican." Then Brett kissed him. Charlie was slightly offended by his comment but he decided not to bring it up until they were driving back to the city. Driving through Connecticut, he delicately broached the subject. Brett was nonchalant. "You just remind me of the Portarican guys I know. You all get so touchy about family stuff." Charlie decided to say nothing more. Brett dropped him off on his doorstep with a passionate kiss. At least this time, the magic was working.

He saw Brett once again that week. Then he didn't hear from him for almost three weeks. Shopping one Saturday with a friend, he saw him with another guy. His good friend Richie saw Brett too, archly pointing out to Charlie that Brett seemed very interested in the guy he was with. Then, in the spirit of friendly bitchiness, he asked what was up between him and Brett. After all, Charlie had told him they were dating. Richie commented on how ghetto the other boy looked. Charlie told him to ignore them. Richie hinted at having more information but Charlie refused to discuss it with him, feeling embarrassed and confused. Even though Brett professed to like him a lot, Brett's behavior told him something different. Richie said, "Girl, it's *brujo* time."

The third time he entered the *botánica*, his objective was clear. His frustration had increased along with his anger. Brett was playing hard to get. He was also playing the field. His rejection of him had shaken Charlie's confidence. Brett's being out in public with another man shamed him. His desire for Brett's love had now been tempered by an equally strong desire to control him. Those turbulent desires were tempered by another feeling, a new element in his emotional landscape: the desire for revenge. He would make Brett pay for his gamesmanship. This time the old woman said, "*Vente, mijo.*" She took him into the back of the *botánica*. It was a little office with two chairs and a little table. The table held various artifacts: a bowl of water, a lit candle, a vase filled with cheap flowers, a bottle of Florida water. She sat down across from him and lit a cigar. She closed her eyes and sat quietly, smoking her cigar. "*¿Quieres este blanquito?*" she asked him. Charlie was shocked at her question. How did she know that it was a man that he was pursuing and how did she know he was American? She opened her eyes and looked at him enigmatically. Her eyes looked shiny in the dim light of the room. The cigar smoke surrounded her, making her look like some ancient priestess. He was confused since he wasn't sure whether she was asking him whether he wanted Brett or whether he loved Brett. *Quieres* meant both. Charlie decided not to deny anything. "He's playing with me," Charlie said in English. "*Pues, se acabó el juego,*" she said. Then she told him what to do with the Calvins he had snatched. She also told him to prepare a special meal for Brett.

Three days later, Charlie invited Brett over for dinner. The setting was very romantic, complete with candles and a special incense the old woman had sold to Charlie. Brett was as charming as always. He brought flowers, a bottle of good wine, and a joint of wicked pot. The evening went perfectly. Brett ate everything Charlie fed him. The sex they had that night was the best ever. Lying in bed later, Brett confessed that he liked Charlie a lot and he wanted to see more of him. Charlie was elated. They started seeing each other regularly. After a couple of weeks, Brett started leaving clothes at Charlie's house, an old-school indicator of commitment. So it had happened. After all that hardship and struggle, it seemed that he and Brett were finally boyfriends. He had finally gotten what he wanted. The days and nights sped by in a flurry of togetherness. It was only after that initial blissful period had passed that Charlie became aware of something a little off, something not all there.

Despite Brett's time commitment and passionate sexual interest, despite all the wonderful times they shared, something was still lacking. It was something so important yet so simple he had almost ignored it. Brett hadn't used the L-word yet. Charlie was sure it would only be a matter of time before Brett professed his love. Charlie had already confessed his love three weeks into this new phase of the relationship during an incredibly passionate night of sex. He couldn't help it. Besides, Charlie thought that his profession might trigger a similar response from Brett. It hadn't happened. As the weeks passed, the relationship seemed to settle into something very steady. When they were together, Charlie had Brett's undivided attention. That was great, wonderful, and still Charlie felt that vague dissatisfaction. Hesitantly he admitted to himself that he wanted more from Brett. Yes, in very significant ways, Charlie had what he wanted, but Brett had never said, "I love you."

The weeks went by, moving inexorably toward the holidays, when Charlie remembered that he hadn't seen his folks in a while. He spoke to his mother regularly but he rarely made the trip uptown to see them. He decided one night to cancel Brett and travel uptown. Always glad to see him, his mother commented on his happiness but Charlie declined to elaborate on the source of his joy. He spoke about his success and work and his impending promotion. Later he sat with his aunt and his mother in the small kitchen while his father sat watching the game. They were drinking coffee as his mom washed the dishes. His *tía* Lola was the most modern of his mother's sisters, speaking in Spanglish most of the time. While Charlie's mother washed the dishes, she talked about her daughter Esmeralda, whom everybody called Pupu.

"*Esa nena está loca.* You know, she's really chasing after Rojelio."

"*¿Todavía?*" Charlie's mother asked. Pupu was notorious for losing her head over guys.

"*Mija,* she even started doing *brujería* on *el pobre.*"

Charlie's mother turned from the sink, soapy water dripping from her hands. "*Pero, mija,* doesn't she know?"

Charlie sat up and, in his most nonchalant voice, asked, "Know what, Titi Lola?"

Lola glanced at her sister. "Well, *mijo.* You shouldn't do love *brujos.*"

Charlie felt a twinge of apprehension as he tried to look relaxed. "But why?"

His mother turned back to her dishes. "Remember what happened with Estelle's sister," Lola said. "Uh-humm," his mom said, nodding. Charlie vaguely remembered some cousin's involvement with a married man that left her pregnant and alone. He had always thought that she was just stupid.

"I don't get it, Titi."

Titi Lola sat back calmly, taking a Newport out of her bag. "*Nene,* you can't create love. It has to happen naturally." She lit her cigarette, holding it like an old-time film star.

Again Charlie's mom murmured her assent. She said mysteriously, "If it's meant to be…"

Titi Lola put her hand on his arm. "*Nene. Los muertos* are very
fickle. What they give you—" she took a drag from her cigarette,
the curling smoke reminded him of the woman in the *botáncia*—
"eventually they'll take away."

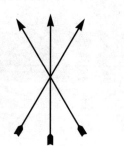

ROBERTO ECHAVARREN was born in Uruguay. He is a distinguished award-winning poet and critic who has translated an anthology of John Ashbery's poetry into Spanish. Sr. Echavarren was Professor of Comparative and Latin American Literature at New York University from 1976 to 1994. His first novel, *Ave Roc*, from which this story is adapted, was published in Buenos Aires to wide acclaim. He lives in Montevideo.

AVE ROC

———▶

Roberto Echavarren
Translated by Edith Grossman

It was clear you weren't going to get a job. You weren't interested. It was clear you weren't a prostitute. It was clear, too, that your family wouldn't send you any more money. You depended on friends and acquaintances, on a waitress in a snack bar along the beach. She worked the morning and early afternoon shift. Every day she gave you a lunch of rice and beans with pork or hard zebu imported from Brazil. At night you hardly ate anything, except when you had a joint and then you were hungry for desserts or sweets. Your great, your only escape was the rock band you formed with Raoul, our classmate from film school, and two of his friends from a meditation group he attended. It was your idea to call the band From the Other Side. I took photographs of you wrinkling up your nose to show a carnivore's fangs.

There was no external clue to pin you down, you had invented a new vehicle that would carry you over to a different shore. The three other members of the band provided a sounding shell, a gaping cave from which you were born over and over again. They gave birth, you were the unknown factor. You went in and out of the cave dressed in wolfskin, in black vinyl or leather pants.

Your clothes, like mine, were ancient rags sold for pennies by the blacks near the beach, fishnet T-shirts, torn tight trousers, and fisherman's pants, cut off sometimes or rolled up, and pointed-toe boots of cracked black leather or blue suede. You bought the vinyl pants at a women's boutique near the Sunset Strip. I had never seen a man wear them before. You didn't wear loud shirts like the other musicians did, or the batik prints that were all the rage then and there. Now when I look at the old photo-graphs from your first year of concerts, I can see that Raoul and Pete and Tom were perfect illustrations of those times, trademarks of everything transient, the liberal exponents of an incomplete, tentative spirit. Not you. Their long sideburns emphasized their machismo, even if they were bohemian; their collarless silky shirts said that their Eastern meditation group smoothed, or "spiritualized," their male aggression. Now I'm looking at a photo of Tom sheathed in an orange velvet suit. His moustache balances his "daring" longer hair; he looks like a pathetic clown. Your companions weren't dangerous. They responded to the call of the times with a clumsy, predictable compromise. They were secondary symptoms, the instruments of your consecration. They did not understand what you intended to do, but they followed you as they had followed their other gurus.

They were your apostles, only you weren't Christ. The New Testament didn't move you at all. It seemed embarrassing, awkward, a problem of Jews tired of their own law. It had been contaminated, in your memory, by the unctuous sound and the saliva of your elementary and high school teachers. The Old Testament, or "sacred history" as the priests who taught you called it, was another matter. Cain and Abel, or Saul and David, or David and Absalom: stories of wicked crimes. The legend of Cain and Abel represented the superstition of completely evil and completely good characters. Abel seduced, Cain terrified. Both you and I were Abel, an Apollo with tame, almost limp hair the color of honey, although more and more we were Cain, a turbulent Dionysus, more iconoclastic than jealous. But Saul's jealousy of David led straight to despair: David was a musical Dionysus; Saul, unlike Cain, only a lovestruck spectator who tried and failed to kill the object of his impotent love. With Absalom the perspective changes, since he, a rebellious version of Abel, hangs by his entangled golden hair in the twilight, while David, grown old, is doomed to run him through the back with a spear. Absalom, hanging from the tree like a sacrifice, receives a ritual blow of the lance. The blood of Absalom is the most disturbing of all, it splatters in all directions, it is the other side of Saul's impotent rage. David "laments" his annihilation. The blood, in any case, splatters victim and victimizer, the offering and the offering arms.

The Black Haze, the first bar that hired you to play, every night for a month, was a third-rate hole, even if it was on the Sunset Strip. I'd never been with drunken old women and stupefied sailors before. The audience seemed like extras in a 1940s spy movie, the place could have been called Tavern at the End of the World. Sometimes lost tourists wandered in. Occasionally a few teenage girls, cheap and undecided as to whether or not they were prostitutes, stood together at the door. At first it seemed that your band didn't belong there at all, but after a couple of weeks some friends of Tom and Raoul started to come by, and later on a bunch of students I didn't know, their eyes lined with kohl.

You lined your eyes, too, and kept them open, fixed on the top of the back wall. The wall was dark, relieved only by a glimmer of light that filtered through the velvet curtain at the entrance. This helped you to concentrate, to pretend that you were part of the show, although at first Raoul sang most of the songs, your lyrics, and now and then you blew into the harmonica Charles had given you years before. But Raoul became more and more involved with his instruments, a synthesizer and an electric accordion, so you began to sing, first in a whisper with your back to the audience, then facing the sides of the stage, and finally you closed your eyes, swayed your hips slowly, then frantically, until you collapsed on the stage or fell onto a table.

While Raoul or Pete smiled at the slightest provocation, you never, or almost never, laughed, except for a dramatic outburst from time to time if you wanted to win over some agent or club owner, or suggest to your friends that an orgy was about to begin. In every photograph you looked alert, detached from the other musicians, with a burning turned-inward glance of alienated indifference or disdain. You knew that this strategy allowed you to give the only gift worth having, a mask the others could not produce. They, we, recognized it. The guru's disciples could not tolerate the implicit cruelty of your gaze, but they accepted your gaze all the same, shaking with fear as eunuch priests of Isis. You were the musical equivalent of Monica Vitti. You sang for yourself, with the gyrations and disconnectedness of an impromptu monologue.

Raoul echoed your moods. He took on that job. He was a

shrewd improviser of special effects, different accompaniments for each of your repetitions: "Go into the night." Tom, the drummer, exiled himself in the rhythm, oblivious to what you were saying or doing. Pete played a versatile guitar, rock riffs or flamenco taps. The bus honks its horn. "Driver, where are you taking us? To where my sister lives, I know, and to that other door farther down the hall. Hi Dad, you're dead, and Mom, who's in charge? The laughing's over. Nobody's here." The rhythm accelerated and you spun around embracing the microphone. "Fall down with me."

At this point I stop. Why fall? Why with you? Why are you falling? I stop and wonder about this, the fury of your climax, the blast of the trumpet added on at the end. "Yoga," you used to say in Tampa, "helps me control my orgasm." But then what was your sense of an ending, an end by exhaustion? You wanted the gig to end, because you were into something else, theater that does not end, your diaries, iambic lines that everybody remembers, that anybody can remember, unlike a novel or a film (although nobody remembers anything, not even poems). Actor or poet, actor and poet, troubadour. Dancer. A huge black girl with a shaved black head taught you, she danced at Garazzi, the second club on the Sunset Strip where the band played.

"You have to please me all night long, I'm waiting." On the other side of the wall you were lying face down on a mattress with your elbows raised and your hands at the back of your neck. The camera slid along your skin inch by inch, glided under your armpit, over a chain it doesn't touch and a microscopic medal glued to your back by sweat, your briefs, first from behind. The air turns to glass, nobody's here, just a chain of clear glass beads. The silence is wild, nothing exists except for the glass atmosphere. Fine! A pup, a natural child, our son, shouts. Except for this, and in its place, every night's performance was in the clubs. When you weren't singing with From the Other Side, you went to any of the bars in the area and sang with any band that was playing, it didn't matter which one, real and forgotten, night after night. Nobody remembers those groups today, but you were the pimp of the bandstands: stamping your boots you squeezed on to any stage that made music on the Sunset Strip. Suddenly you had become the god of the city, there was no other, you cleared the boards like Bagoas, Alexander's eunuch, you outdid him, in fact, in any theater of the empire, a paradoxical reversal. "Where can I hide? Nobody forgets me," you said, "they want to hear me and ogle me all of the time. I'm splitting," you said, but nobody gets out of here alive. "I know that," you said, but for the rest of the night we'll go from one podium to another, you here and there, in the catacombs, in the nick of time, babes thrown into the rivers, avenues, novelties or novellas sold with metal studs, boots, and the din and blare where I find your voice. "I'm here to stay. Everything has to be as it is." I translated, read as if they were rosary beads each of your callused, velvet knuckles. "Follow me." Fall, free, I fall, free, follow me. Truth rings only in fiction. "Follow me as I fall." Now when I think of you, now when I take the time to think of you, the others grow small. They don't disappear, they become the size my life requires so that I can think of you. Sometimes you defied comprehension. Sometimes you explained yourself too well.

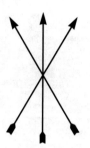

Photo: Star Black

JAIME MANRIQUE is a novelist, poet, essayist, and translator. Born in Colombia, he has been published extensively both in English and Spanish. In English he has written the volume of poems *My Night with Federico García Lorca* (The Groundwater Press, 1995; new edition Painted Leaf Press, 1997); and the novels *Colombian Gold* (Clarkson N. Potter, 1983; new edition, Painted Leaf Press, 1998), *Latin Moon in Manhattan* (St. Martin's Press, 1992), and *Twilight at the Equator* (Faber and Faber, 1997). In 1999, his autobiography, *Eminent Maricones: Arenas, Lorca, Puig, and Me*, will be published by the University of Wisconsin Press. Mr. Manrique has taught in the MFA program at Columbia University, Mount Holyoke College, and New York University. He lives in New York City. This piece is excerpted from a novel-in-progress, *Señoritas in Love*.

SEÑORITAS IN LOVE

→

Jaime Manrique

Manolo was very excited, which, if you know Manolo, can be cause for alarm—he has the energy of a hurricane. We were going to N.Y.U. to hear Ramón Ariza give a talk. He was a famous Cuban author who had escaped from the island a couple of years ago and was now making his first public appearance in New York. Because Ramón was one of the few openly gay Latin American writers, and because he had suffered persecution and incarceration for his beliefs, he was one of our heroes.

The weather had suddenly turned chilly, reminding us that we were in late November, that winter was around the corner. Ramón Ariza was lecturing in a small auditorium in the Spanish Department. Though he was well known in Latin America, and two of his novels had been translated into English while he was still jailed on the island, he was not exactly a household name in New York. We were such ardent fans that we had left early so we could get front-row seats. Manolo had brought his camera and tape recorder to document the event, which he considered of historical importance.

By seven o'clock the auditorium was packed with an audience of mostly older, academic-looking women and a dozen men, though few seemed openly gay. Ramón arrived accompanied by the department chairman. Up until this point, I just knew the crush-inducing photo of him on the editions of his books published in Spanish. He was older now, in his mid-forties, but he was still handsome, though thin, borderline thin, so thin that it was hard to say if he had the virus. He had prominent cheekbones, sunken cheeks, and big, black intense eyes, and a mane of brown hair. Though he had a stocky, strong peasant build, there was something coquettish and queenie about his manner as he stood there while being introduced.

While Manolo took photos like any vulgar paparazzo, I found myself completely unable to take my eyes off Ramón. I loved his two novels about life in rural Cuba just before and right after the revolution. I also thought he was one of the greatest poets in the Spanish language. Even if he hadn't been jailed, tortured, his manuscripts destroyed, I would have been a big fan of his work. But of course the story of his incarcerations and his confrontations with Fidel added a whole other mystique to his persona. In Latin American artistic circles, which were traditionally left-wing and pro Castro, Ramón was considered a pariah. I, too, was divided in my admiration of Ramón—I considered myself a socialist and yet I couldn't forgive Fidel Castro for his treatment of homosexuals. As far as I was concerned, I was tired of putting the needs of the people above my own. Either I was considered one of the people—homosexuality and all—or I wanted no part of a system that wanted justice for all, except the homosexuals. Castro's track record spoke for itself, indicting him as someone who had perpetrated great crimes against gay people. So I often had found myself arguing with my Latino friends who were pro gay rights but also pro Fidel and who therefore dismissed and ridiculed Ramón.

Ramón was a magnetic speaker. As soon as he began to talk, he turned on some kind of inner light that made him shine like a true star. He was charming, deadly serious, irreverent, subversive as he talked about his life and the evolution of his work under communism. He had as many bad things to say about the Cuban communists on the island as about the Cuban exiles in Miami whom he called materialistic, racist, homophobic. I was astonished by his courage and his determination not to simplify his talk into black and white issues. Ramón was telling us about how one of his novels had been confiscated by Fidel's police and all the existing manuscripts destroyed and how he had had to rewrite it from memory, when suddenly a male voice in the audience cried, "Liar! It's all lies!"

All the heads in the auditorium turned in the direction the voice had come from. Four younger men stood in the back, against the wall, looking defiantly at Ramón and at the rest of us. "You are a liar paid by the CIA," one of the men said. "Tell us how much they pay you to lie about the revolution."

Intense whispering was heard in the auditorium. "Faggot," one of the men called. "Faggot. You should all be dead."

"¡Malparido hijo de puta!" Ramón screamed, losing all control, blanching, shaking. "If you were a man you wouldn't scream from up there. You'd say it to my face."

Like a stampede of hungry beasts, the men raced down the stairs in Ramón's direction. Pandemonium broke out in the auditorium. The ladies in the audience started screaming, Manolo began to snap pictures and before I knew it, the four men started beating Ramón, who fought all of them with incredible fury. Two of the men had pinned Ramón against the wall and were hitting him. Seeing this, I couldn't let the four goons beat one person so I decided to help Ramón and started throwing blows. When Manolo saw me enter the scuffle he joined in. Suddenly I realized some of the screaming ladies had entered the tussle and were hitting the attackers with their umbrellas and pocketbooks. One of the men ran out of the room, and as soon as they saw him flee, his companions followed him.

Ramón was on the floor bleeding, so I knelt to assist him. "Careful," he said. "Don't touch the blood. I have AIDS."

I froze. It was the first time our eyes met. He seemed surprised, hardly believing that a total stranger had come to his help. We were surrounded by a chorus of women. "Ramón, ¿estás bien? Ay, Dios mío. Somebody call an ambulance. ¡Ay, pobrecito!" was heard all at once.

Ramón had bunched a hand against his nose to stop the profuse bleeding.

"He has to go to the hospital," one of the ladies said.

"My car is parked right outside," another one offered.

Ramón placed a hand on my shoulder to help himself up. "Who are you?" he asked suddenly and I saw paranoia in his eyes. Perhaps he thought I was a Cuban agent. Later I would learn that he behaved in the States as if he were still in Cuba—he was suspicious of everyone and saw conspiracies everywhere. He had escaped the island but had brought the police state mentality with him.

"I'm a fan," I said. "I love your books. I'm a writer from

Colombia. And this is my friend Manolo, another fan," I said, nodding in Manolo's direction.

Ramón winced and decided I was telling the truth. We helped him get up and into the elevator. When he was inside the car, it occurred to me that I should go with him. I told Manolo I'd call him later and, accompanied by the driver and another woman, we headed for Saint Vincent's Hospital in the Village. The women were academics who knew Ramón and had written papers about his work. I was the only stranger in the car. They talked among themselves with great animation without paying attention to me.

The waiting room was a madhouse, and when Ramón's turn came I helped him fill out the forms because he was still bleeding. It turned out he had no health insurance. One of the women with us, whose name was Sara, pulled out her American Express card, gave it to the attendant, and said, "Here's my card. You can charge everything to me."

Finally, a nurse came out pushing a wheelchair and whisked Ramón away. The women and I chatted for a while about Ramón, whom they worshipped, about themselves, the places where they taught, and about me. They were Cuban refugees who had been in the States for decades, though they still talked about Cuba as if they had left it yesterday. Both were in their fifties. Sara was plump, matronly, and very proper; Sonia was her junior, thin, full of nervous energy. Sara spoke slowly, measuring her words with precision. Sonia had a spitfire delivery. Sara was seductive in a motherly way; whereas Sonia was edgy, almost sharp. When they spoke about Castro and Cuba and how Ramón had been treated, I saw another side of them. I saw that they were strong, determined women and that they could be formidable adversaries.

Finally, I suggested that they should leave; that I would wait for Ramón and take him home. I convinced them that they could leave the situation in my hands. The women talked to the nurses, and when they were satisfied that Ramón's cuts were minor, that he would be discharged that night, we exchanged kisses and they left.

A couple of hours later a dazed Ramón appeared, accompanied by a nurse. I walked up to him. He looked surprised to see me there. "I told Sara and Sonia they could leave. That I would make sure you'd get home all right."

Instead of thanking me, he said, "Why are you doing this? You don't know me."

"I told you earlier, I'm a fan. That's why." I became apprehensive that I sounded like a groupie. I added, "I'm also a poet. I'm writing my first novel."

"Who's your favorite poet?" he asked aggressively. The way he put the question it sounded as though if I said the wrong name all communication between us would be over. The people pleaser in me wanted to guess who his favorite poet was. I did not want to alienate him, but I did not want to lie. Martí sounded like a safe bet, since all Cubans are nuts about Martí, but I did not care for his poetry, though I certainly liked "Guantanamera." "You mean, of all the poets in the world?" I asked, trying to gain time.

"Who comes to mind right now?" he asked, point-blank.

"Cernuda," I blurted. "Luis Cernuda."

"I love Cernuda too," he said and tried to smile. Ramón looked awful: his face swollen, his nose wrapped in a bulky, wet bandage. His shirt was liberally covered with dry blood. He had a black eye, so inflamed that it was shut. There was also blood splotched on his hair. He took a step in my direction and wobbled, as if he were dizzy. I offered him my arm.

When Ramón gave his address to the taxi driver, I felt déjà vu. The address he gave, 690 Eighth Avenue, was just next door to O'Donnell's Bar, which I had lived over for more than a decade. When I told him about this, Ramón said, "This is a good omen, don't you think?"

Was he flirting with me? I wondered. We were silent riding the taxi uptown. Ramón seemed morose, and he was drowsy from the sedatives and painkillers they had given him. The taxi stopped one door past my former abode. When I saw how weak he was, I offered to help him to his apartment. He accepted my offer without protesting. We climbed and climbed, all the way to the sixth floor. Several times we had to stop so that Ramón could catch his breath.

"Now that you're here," he said when we reached his door, "you must come in for a cup of coffee."

After we entered the apartment, which had half a dozen locks, Ramón secured it from the inside, sliding all kinds of chains and bolts across the door. For a moment, I was alarmed. Then I relaxed, as I realized this was just routine for him. Later, when I knew him better, I understood that he still felt as if any minute the Cuban Secret Police would break down the door of his apartment without any notice. We walked into the living room, which had a window looking in the direction of the Hudson. Because it was night, all I saw were the lighted silhouettes of some tall buildings.

Despite the fact that a couple of Ramón's books had been translated into English and into many foreign languages and that he had received some important cash awards, the apartment was shabby. A primitive oil landscape depicting the Cuban countryside hung in the living room. It was the only decoration. Ramón indicated that I sit in a sunken couch. He said he could offer me a Cuba Libre or a cup of coffee.

"Whatever you're having, it's fine," I said.

"Oh, you're so accommodating," he said coquettishly. "Coffee it will be. I'm going to write after you leave. I need a shot of caffeine to keep me awake. I feel so groggy from the damn sedatives."

I wanted to say, Forget about writing tonight. What you need is to rest. What was it in him that awoke my need to want to play Florence Nightingale? Was it that he had AIDS? Or was this part of my Al-Anon disease? I could hear Dallas screaming in my ear, "Keep the focus on yourself!"

Ramón served two mugs of strong black coffee and sat on the couch, at the opposite end. There was no light on in the living room but, because of the light on the buildings and billboards outside, no other illumination was needed. We sat there bathed in a muted neon glow that was a hodgepodge of colors, so that the place seemed unreal, like a stage. It looked like neither night nor day, as though time had ceased to exist at that moment and we were in a room in another galaxy where neither the sun nor the moon were the main sources of light.

It turned out that Ramón was also a client of Tim Colby's, and that he had moved into this apartment shortly before I moved away to Bank Street.

"I wonder if I ever cruised you," he said.

"Are you flirting with me?" I asked.

His face changed colors but he looked at me even more intently. "It's cultural, you know."

"I was hoping it would be more specific than that."

His face got even redder and mine got very warm. "Tell me the story of your life. I want to know everything," he said.

"My life's really boring." I wanted to talk about the people who had attacked him, but Ramón dismissed them as "Castroite scumbags" not worth talking about.

I was full of questions: I wanted to ask him about Cuba, about growing up in the countryside, about the early days of the revolution, about the persecution he had endured, jail, torture, and finally his escape. By comparison, my life had been dull and lackluster. Later, it occurred to me that, as a successful writer who traveled and spoke to audiences, he was probably sick and tired of having to repeat his story wherever he went. So much of it was public record, anyway. The truth is that I had never had many gay Latino friends. When Bobby Castro died of AIDS, he had left a large void in my life.

Right away, a spark was created between Ramón and me. Though we were strangers, I gabbed away about my childhood, my adolescence, about coming out as an adult in the States, about my writing. At every turn, he found some point of identification with my story. Like me, he had grown up with his mother's family. Like me, both his maternal grandparents were country people. We both had developed a love of books in early adolescence and had started to write when we were barely out of puberty. I had arrived in the States in my late teens. At that point, his experience and mine diverged. But everything that had to do with Latin America, with growing up in a culture of machismo, united us in a potent bond.

We had been talking for a couple of hours when he asked, "What was the worst time for you when you were an adolescent?"

I didn't have to think about that one. "Sunday afternoons," I said.

"Exactly right," he said. "It was the same for me."

I talked about the terror of those sweltering afternoons in Barranquilla when the world seemed to come to a standstill. Many of the people in the city went to the soccer stadium and, if I didn't have a plan—for example, to go to the movies with Wilbrajan—the afternoon seemed endless and I felt a loneliness that was unbearably painful because I thought it would never end. As much as I hated school, where the boys tormented me for being an intellectual sissy, I preferred it to being at home when my mother and sister had gone out to visit friends and I sat by the window reading a novel. Next I talked about Tarzan, the only known homosexual in Barranquilla, an outcast who was supposed to prey on the boys. How I was both drawn to him and repelled by him. How I sat by my window reading and studied him when he went by the house, strutting like a peacock in his tight jeans and close-fitting T-shirts over his muscular torso. Here Ramón interjected that in Holguín, where he grew up, the only known homosexual was also an outcast, and that he dreaded he'd become one. I talked about discovering Oscar Wilde through the movie *The Trials of Oscar Wilde* and reading all his works. And the devastation I felt when I thought that, like Wilde, I would also be put in jail for my homosexuality. I talked about my first experiences with a neighbor, and about experimenting with animals, which was very common in Colombia, especially in the countryside. From reading his novels I knew that he, too, had done his share of that.

SEÑORITAS IN LOVE • 133

It was dawn when we stopped exchanging anecdotes. The lights on the buildings and billboards were out and the sky was a satiny ivory tent above Manhattan. I was so tired I was barely able to get up from the sofa. Ramón suggested that I stay and sleep on the couch. "I promise not to molest you," he teased me. There was no chance of that, I thought. Bandaged in bloody rags, he looked most unappealing. However, as we faced each other in front of his door, a momentary awkwardness ensued. We hugged, the way old friends do, but as we pulled away, our faces brushed and we kissed lightly on the lips. At that moment, it surprised me to find out that I was romantically attracted to him.

"Let's talk later today," he said. "Maybe we can catch a movie."

"Okay," I said, feeling myself blush.

When I stepped on the deserted sidewalk of Eighth Avenue at dawn, I felt light-headed, younger. Suddenly it hit me that another, entirely different life—risky but thrilling—had begun.

The ringing phone woke me up. "*Buenas tardes,*" said Ramón's voice.

"What time is it?" I asked.

"It's noon, Sleeping Beauty."

Though we had just met, he was talking to me as an old intimate friend, and I liked the familiarity. I sat up on my bed and yawned.

"Should I call you back later?"

"No, it's nice to hear your voice. How are you feeling this morning?"

"My face is even more swollen than yesterday. But I'm not in pain." Ramón paused. "Hey, want to go see a movie later this evening?"

"Sure," I said. We had already established that we were both movie nuts and that we liked many of the same directors. "Do you have anything in mind?"

That night we met across from Lincoln Center to see Jean Vigo's *L'Atalante* which had recently been restored and which we hadn't seen before. There were few people in the audience and sitting so close to Ramón, being so aware of his breathing, once in awhile touching as we shifted positions on our chairs, heightened the trancelike mood created by Jean Vigo's masterpiece. Afterward, we walked out of the theatre discussing the film. It was a cold night, but we were both feeling so exhilarated and energized by the movie and our discussion that we walked down Broadway, to 43rd Street. Before I knew it, we arrived in front of the door to his building. It was like déjà vu: instant replay of the night before. It also felt as if a whole year of knowing each other (not a measly twenty-four hours) had gone by. It was like being with an old friend.

"Want to come up for a drink?" Ramón asked.

I hesitated; I didn't want Ramón to take over my life; I needed to get back to my old routine.

"I promise not to keep you up very late. Just a quick cup of coffee."

I didn't want to go home, yet I demurred. I wasn't sure whether he was just being polite. But I said yes because I didn't want the night to end. Inside his apartment, after we took off our jackets, we sat down in the same exact spots where we had sat the night before. Our eyes met. Ramón leaned over and took my hand. "Look," he said. "I like you. I am attracted to you, Santiago."

I squeezed his hand. With his red bruised face and bandages he looked quite monstrous. I closed my eyes so that I could see him the way he had appeared before the men attacked him in the auditorium.

"But I understand if you don't want to get involved with someone with AIDS."

With my eyes still closed, I put a finger to his lips. "Hush," I murmured. "I like you too," I added, to my own surprise. Until that moment I hadn't thought the potential was there for a romance. I opened my eyes. Now he looked handsome to me. "I don't care about the HIV."

"I don't just have HIV," he insisted. "I have full-blown AIDS. Last year I almost died of pneumonia. It's a miracle I've recovered this much. One thing I can tell you is that I never want to be that sick again. Once was enough. I know what's down the road so I don't want to lie to you."

I reached over, took his face gently in my hands, and kissed his lips. "I don't care," I said, not sure if I really meant it.

He took my face in his hands. "Then let's be lovers. I'm not into games and I don't have the time for a long courtship."

What can I say? I didn't want to reject Ramón because he was sick. I'd be a hypocrite if I didn't admit that I was terrified of what had happened. Was getting involved with a man with AIDS the ultimate Al-Anon caretaker dream? *Involvement* sounded like too light a word for the demands such a relationship would make.

All this was too much for me to deal with on my own. I called my free therapist—my Al-Anon sponsor. I was apprehensive about how Dallas might react. Would he approve of the affair? After all, how wise was it to get involved with a sick man? What kind of future was there in starting a relationship with someone who had no future? Ramón wasn't just positive—he was sick, the next time he got sick it might be fatal. We hadn't discussed the T-cell count or the various hospitalizations, etc., but I had already known enough sick people to realize that in Ramón's case the illness was quite advanced.

I voiced my hesitations to Dallas, whose advice was, "Santiago, it's not the length of a relationship that matters, but the quality of the time you have together." After I hung up, I thought about what he had said. I was thirty-five years old: I knew that the chances were slim that anyone of Ramón's exceptional qualities would ever appear again.

My fears hadn't been completely quelled by Dallas's words. I wanted to talk with at least one other person before I saw Ramón again—before we had sex. We had kissed passionately and I knew that kissing was all right, that the chances of getting HIV that way were almost nonexistent. I also knew that the best way to stay HIV-negative was not to share needles or have sex with an HIV-positive man. Lots of guys were having sex with positive men and were staying negative, but I couldn't just reject the idea of having sex with Ramón (whom I passionately desired) just because I wasn't quite sure about all the dos and don'ts.

I called Manolo but got his machine. Though I didn't feel comfortable discussing the nitty-gritty of sex with Laurette, I called her to get her take on the situation. Laurette heard me patiently, and then remarked, "When you're an old man, Santiago, you're not going to regret the affairs you had, but the ones you didn't have." More than anything else I would hear in the next few weeks, this made up my mind. I would not reject Ramón just because he carried the virus.

Right away I understood that I was getting involved in a threesome: that HIV was the third party in the equation—a noisy, insistent monster who would always come between us.

Born, raised, and educated in Texas, **JOEL ANTONIO
VILLALÓN** currently lives in San Francisco. His work has
appeared in literary reviews, anthologies, and newspapers.
He is still trying to finish a collection of linked short stories,
Caliche, which he now hopes to complete before the year
2025.

Awakened from Their Dreams

➤

Joel Villalón

Remember, we were young then, the day Rudy whispered, "Mooooooonrise." The wind sifted through the cornfield. A beam of light shone on my face.

"Mooooonrise," Rudy said.

Alex reached to the sky, flashlight in each hand, waving to the stars, "Mooooooonset!" Alex cried.

"Mooooooonrise!" They continued shaking.

Sweat slid down my face, and I couldn't breathe. I lay in a circle drawn on black dirt in a clearing in the field behind our house. Corn stalks swayed in the wind, and blackness beyond the beams surrounded me.

Remember, we were young then, and my world at that time ran east and west for the most part, the two miles of Jefferson Avenue, the street we lived on. Wood house by tiny wood house sat side by side, east and west, until you hit a road perpendicular at either end. For two miles you passed ditches, blue, pink, yellow houses, mesquites, live oaks, palm trees, toys everywhere, broken-down cars, brand-new pickups, and at least thirty-one types of rosebushes I'd counted so far.

Rudy Castillo lived next door, in the house to my east. His yard was neat to the point that you were scared to walk barefoot on the grass for fear you might slice the bottom of your toes, the blades were so cut. Their wooden fence stretched low, and bird-houses perched high above the clotheslines on tall railroad ties at each corner of their yard. Yellow and red and orange bougainvillea sprouted from a cylinder of tires piled high.

Alex Martínez lived in the peeling house to our west and didn't have grass on most of his yard. He said his yard, like his father, was fast going bald with age. So, on the days when Mrs. Castillo watered her bougainvillea and lawn, Mrs. Martínez swept the dirt with great speed, so the ground of her yard lay smooth and free of stones. And days when Mr. Castillo pushed the mower with a handkerchief sticking out his shirt pocket, Mr. Martínez changed the oil in his car, lying on the road with a red bandanna tied around his head.

"Moooooooonrise," Rudy whispered through the screen.

"Yes, Sunset," I said through my window, and I listened to his reply.

"Sunrise," I called at the other end of my house.

"Yes, Moonset," Alex said. The message was passed.

Now remember, our world was a road running one mile each way. Cotton fields to our north. Cornfields to the south. Our world held two stores, one church and a billboard of flowers twenty-five feet high. This world of mine, our town, we called Nopalitos.

And in Nopalitos, summers are dusty and windy and hot, and the games we played consumed sweaty nights. Tribes of Indians with flashlights and plastic hatchets met on empty lots planning attacks on *los* Cowboys with *pistolas.* Sunrise led raids from the fields, and Sunset guided his assaults from the street. At the dinner table, my brothers, the Cowboys, yelled, "You play with Susie and stay out the fields!"

"No! I'm older, and I'll do what I want."

"Out!" they shouted. "You stay out!"

And Momma asked, "But why?"

"No, Momma. Didn't no one listen? We said, 'No!'"

"I'll do what I want."

"You wanna bet?"

"You bet I wanna bet!"

"Daddddddddyyyyyyyyy!"

Daddy tapped his fork on his glass of water, "Mari: no."

"But, but Momma, tell me, what do you say?"

And Daddy said no.

So later that night, Alex and Rudy led me out back to the fields to that clearing in the corn. They told me to lie in a circle they'd drawn in dirt. I lay on the ground, and they danced with their lights calling sounds to the sky.

"Mooooooonrise," the flashlights twirled.

"Mooooooonset," called the other.

I burrowed in the dirt watching their faces from below. Their eyes rolled from side to side as their shoulders bounced up and up and up. Corn stalks wavered above them. Stars flickered beyond. And for years thereafter, I passed details in secret from one house to the other, not in betrayal of my brothers, but so as not to betray who I was. Cowboys and Indians was only a game. And I knew I should be permitted to play.

I sat with my mother in our backyard during those Indian raid nights. From where I sat, I could see down the yards to where the last porchlight shone. A line of tall corn separated our yards from the rest of the world. Beyond the first row only darkness approached. Even at night, I could feel the ground's heat. My hair stuck to my neck. "Momma," I'd say and tell her what was going to happen across all our yards. From the fields and streets. On the lots, from the trees. The flashlights. Yells. Commands and the cries.

She looked at me, crocheting yarn that came from the basket to her side. "How come you know all this?"

I sat, leaning, listening toward the field, "I know, 'cause I have ears."

"'Cause you have big ears," Momma said, "and sometimes big ears hear too much. Now, I'm not telling you not to listen, but I tell you to be careful to choose what you hear."

"I don't have big ears. My ears are small," I sized them with my fingers.

"Well, you have bad eyes, so of course you can't see that your ears are much bigger than they are, can you? *Cabezonas* always have bad eyes, don't you see? And bad eyes, I don't have to say, run on your daddy's side of the family."

"My eyes see fine," I said much louder. "I'll count the stars tonight for you."

And Momma said, "But what is the use of counting, my girl.

You will count only stars that you only see. And that doesn't tell me how small your ears are."

Time passes, of course, and those games at night, the tiny spotlights whirling through the sky from yards and the fields, moved down the street in both directions as our brothers passed this game, their inheritance, to the young. My brothers wanted to drive cars, and Alex and Rudy stopped calling through windows.

"Sunrise," I whispered. He appeared at his window.

"Talk to you later. I'm late, and I've gotta go."

"Sunset," I whispered at the other end of the house. I waited. "Sunset," I called again. I waited. "Ruddddddyyyyyy!" I yelled aloud.

My father tapped his fork at the edge of his plate. We watched him as he looked at my mother and whispered, "*Los indios y los vaqueros* now want to wear ties." He looked at my brothers. "They've jumped off of horses and slid into pickups without even a thought of saying good-bye. Without even a thought of burying the dead. They fought and killed, and just like that," he snapped his fingers high in the air, "they've rolled over in their bed and awakened from their dreams."

I remember Nopalitos those days stopping at Cantu's for *raspas* in May. I slept in one room. My brothers in the other. I washed the dishes. My brothers worked the yard. So when the boys stopped playing and decided to become men, I simply couldn't run down the road and ask others to play.

"*Los vaqueros* now want money," my father'd say, "the pleasure they find is the pleasure they pay for. No more running through fields with *pistolas* in their hands. They now drive through our streets with guns mounted in their trucks. The pleasure they seek is the pleasure they take. No more running in *pestosos*, sweating like pigs. They now have 'blow dryers.' They call themselves 'boys.' The pleasure they want is the pleasure to be man."

For weeks after they stopped, I sat with my mother in the yard drinking juice. The chants and flashlights were faint, far away. The cries sounded different. The wind made them small.

"So tell me, big ears," Momma said, "what'll happen tonight? What manure have the boys planned?"

"Maneuver, Momma." I stretched my legs out front. "Maneuver. Not manure. Nothing happens tonight, because the boys've chosen not to play."

"And tell me, big ears, what does the girl choose to do?"

"The girl, the girl chooses to play alone. Like always."

"And what'll the girl play when she plays alone?"

"The girl will play at sitting with her mother like she's done every night since she was little. The girl will sit with her mother and learn how to sew. The girl will sit with her mother and choose what to hear."

"Can't the girl tell her mother how many stars light the sky?"

"What's the use, for the girl will count only those stars which she sees."

And Momma stopped her sewing and looked at my face for a moment. "Since when have you ever listened to anything I've ever said." She shook her head. "Marisa, when the night's clear and dark, the stars are many, and the task of counting is long. When the night's very young, you may count only one. And when the night's cloudy like tonight, you can't see stars at all. But on those nights like every night, you can count, in your mind, all those stars you don't see." And Momma stood and walked five steps to the patio and pulled from the toolbox a flashlight and pushed its glow to my face. Without saying a word, she walked to the gate at the back of the yard. She shone rays through the corn. The light was direct and moved soundlessly over the long leaves as my mother jerked her wrist from side to side. She turned and waved for me to follow and stepped forward, fading into the field. I rose and walked through the gate into the tall corn. My heart again hitting my chest, my arms feeling the itch from the leaves scratching my skin as I trailed the heavy silhouette before me, following my mother's moving beacon.

EMANUEL XAVIER author of the poetry collection *Pier Queen*, survived hustling on the streets of New York City and dealing drugs at the clubs to become a two-time Nuyorican Poets Cafe Grand Slam winner. His work has been published in *Best Gay Erotica '97*, *Urban: The Latino Magazine*, *Mia Magazine*, *Men on Men 7*, and many other fierce publications. Emanuel's frank and shameless writing has offended many critics and delighted fans. Father of the House of Xavier, "Banjee Hustlers" is his latest half-paradoxical, half-appropriate contribution, and is taken from the forthcoming debut novel, *Christ-like* (Painted Leaf Press).

Banjee Hustlers

→

Emanuel Xavier

Mikey felt the presence of undercover cops lurking inside The Sanctuary as he casually guarded his drug spot underneath the statue of St. Therese, who was watching over him. Mikey had a wicked smile engraved on his youthful face, fully aware that they could never touch him. The paid-off security guards knew he was the life of the party and would never allow "Maggie" to lay a hand on the club's designated dealer. Mikey and the House of X were as much a part of The Sanctuary as the discoball hanging from the ceiling of the condemned church where New York City's most famous nightclub was located. Besides, unless you knew the secret password of the day, Mikey would deny knowledge of any drugs, curse you out and send you on your merry way.

However, for forty bucks, Mikey would touch your hand, the cold vial of coke or K contrasting against the feverish warmth of his Latin machismo. A wink from one of his pearl-black eyes, the one below his scarred eyebrow in particular, would be your signal to take the merchandise and disappear into the sweaty madness dancing around what would otherwise be early Sunday Mass. The music pounded like his mother's fists when Mikey was too young to fight back but old enough to develop an insatiable dark side.

A hundred bucks and Mikey would drop to his knees and feast on your supremacy with starving lips which, at the age of three, already knew hunger and submission, thanks to older cousin Chino. Two hundred and the gates of banjee heaven would spread wide open while you ripped through his soul like the needle on the record high above the altar from Dominick X's deejay booth.

They both still belonged to the House of X, a godless gang of vicious gays whose wrists were only limp because of heavy knives used to slash their enemies. They were the kind to travel in packs, terrorizing the West Side Highway piers with loud exaggerated laughter, shady comments, and unapologetic homosexuality; the ones who would go to jail for "mopping" clothes or cutting up ex-boyfriends and were looked after by heartless criminals named Bubba. When your own family puts you out on the streets of New York as a child for wanting the same sex, you create your own family, or "house," and deviance becomes a way of life, self-destruction giving you the only fleeting glimpses of survival.

The House of X and The Sanctuary had a lot in common: they were both christened in chaos, blessed in blasphemy. Neon lights, pin-lights, spotlights cast hues of red, blue, and green over bitter souls and crumbling Catholic statues, glaring down with decadent beauty. Within these realms, the outside world meant very little if nothing at all.

From the deejay booth, Dominick served as God himself over the dance floor blasting commands with every rhythm and beat, featuring an immaculate record collection of house and techno to entertain the children. Voguing pier queens, possessed with the Holy Ghost, battled each other underneath Dominick's booth for the glory of his flashlight to shine upon them. Walking, screaming, twirling, they threw shade all over in preparation for the next ball where Dominick would canonize them with trophies.

The highest of all angels was legendary Damian X, the dark prince of voguing arm control and posing, who was battling Flaca from the House of Pendavis, not far from Mikey's spot. They created a fortress of spectators curiously involved with the intensity of the arrogance between the two of them. The battle was over who was the best but had more to do with a guy named Cesar, whom Flaca was supposedly dating.

"Get huh! Get that skinny ass bitch!" Mikey cheered his sista on. "Serve huh Damian!"

Damian danced more ferociously as Dominick spotlighted his every machinelike move. Dominick mixed in Damian's favorite house classic, "Love Is the Message," as Damian served the floor with pops, dips, and spins, driving the crowd into uproarious frenzy with his incredible energy.

"Work Ms. Damian! Bring it, bitch! Bring it to the ballroom!" Jorge X appeared from out of the darkness, taking over where Mikey left off.

"Walk for me! Feel the love break!" Jorge continued.

Damian, mean-spiritedly exaggerating Flaca Pendavis's

trademark moves, mocked him in public. The crowd around them screamed support for Damian by chanting, *"Pendavis! Pendeja! Pendavis! Pendeja!"* Flaca struggled desperately to keep up to the music, eager to show any signs of success in the face of oppression, but Damian had far too many skills. Damian moved to the music, or was it the music that moved to him? He held his hands together and spun his sinewy arms around his back full circle, dislocating them and clicking them back into place. Damian flung his long muscular arms into the air and his silky wet black chest glistened naked under the blinding lights. His fierce eyes pierced through the smoky air, shooting Flaca down with a million daggers. The audience roared and Jorge jumped in, kissing him excitedly, while Damian's face succumbing to an undeniably enchanted smile. Dominick mixed in Junior Vásquez's "X," Flaca's ultimate humiliation. The battle was over and the category was closed. Damian X was once again a force to be reckoned with as Flaca and the angels from stained-glass windows looked down at him with jealousy and contempt.

Mikey, now in his mid-twenties but still looking nineteen, was thirsty but unable to leave his spot because potential buyers would get confused about his designated location. Mikey simply caught Damian's attention with a penetrating stare, smirking in his sexy way before some shirtless muscle queen interrupted him with, "Yo, Mikey! Wassup, kid? Got any vitamin C for my cold symptoms?"

Mikey sized him up from balding head to construction boots, contemplating either a price or an excuse.

"Pookie says hello!" the wrinkling gym bunny insisted nervously while sweat raced down his bulging hairless pecs.

Arresting his pale blue eyes by raising an eyebrow, Mikey wondered if he recognized him from a previous encounter.

"Fifty bucks, papi!" Mikey half smiled, upping the price an extra ten bucks.

"FIFTY?" The daddy freaked out, digging deep into his tight-assed daisy dukes for extra cash and working up enough nerve to ask, "Is it any good?"

Mikey's smile grew mysterious with anticipation. "About as good as those steroids you're on!" Mikey snapped, watching the guy's face crumble to once holy ground.

"All right, I'll take it!" He hurried, handing Mikey the money quickly before Mikey changed his mind and called security.

Mikey pulled out a yellow pen, marking the fifty dollar bill to make sure it wasn't counterfeit before putting it away in the left front pocket of his baggy jeans. He pulled out a half gram of cocaine from his right pocket and reached over to surprise him with an unexpected hug while slipping the vial into his hand.

"By the way, I fucked your boyfriend the other night while you were in L.A.!" Mikey revealed into his ear. "Wouldn't you like to know if he was any good?"

With that, Mikey pulled away, giving him his signature wink. Wounded, the Chelsea Queen turned from Mikey and walked away humiliated, losing himself somewhere on the dancefloor.

Mikey was approached with yet another opportunity for revenge.

"Hey, Mikey, can I get half a gram?" asked Hector, a tacky cha-cha queen Mikey vividly remembered from his days living in the South Bronx.

"Shouldn't you be off smoking crack somewhere with my ex-boyfriend!"

"Mikey, that was years ago!" Hector begged. "Besides, Juan Carlos is dead!"

"Yeah, but you ain't! So, you betta get out of my face 'fore I beat you like the bitch you are and you could join him!"

Hector held himself back, gagging at Mikey's cold words.

"*Pero* Mikey, I've got money!"

"I don't need your welfare checks! Now fleece!" Mikey yelled loud enough for those around them to hear. Out of nowhere, three security guards were produced.

"Wha? Wha's da problem hea?" the one named Steve asked in a rugged deep voice.

Mikey said something to Steve in his ear and, without a chance to defend himself, Hector was grabbed by six brawny arms and carried out of the club screaming.

"*¡ME LAS VAS A PAGAR! ¡MALDITA, ME LAS VAS A PAGAR!*"

Mikey's face glowed like a crowned prom queen as he watched Hector being thrown out of the club.

Meanwhile, up in the deejay booth, Dominick watched his sistas prancing back and forth, longing to be out on the dance floor with the rest of them, dancing to his own mixes.

"WORK, MAMA, IT'S OVAH FOR YOU!" Jorge materialized from behind, racing toward Dominick with excitement. "The children, they live!"

"I didn't know you were here! Had I known you were coming, I would've baked a cake!" Dominick joked, mixing in the sample of a song he wouldn't play for hours to come just to fuck with people's heads.

"That's too wicked!" Jorge shook his index finger back and

forth, signaling a "no."

"Have you noticed all the pieces out there on the dance floor tonight?" Dominick continued, his pale white skin lighting up.

"Um-hmmm!"

Using his flashlight, he pointed them out to Jorge. Shirtless bodies, flooded with his glory, threw their arms in the air and screamed for Dominick's attention. Dominick ignored them and searched for Damian, who was standing by the speaker closest to Mikey, surrounded by an entourage of worshipping followers. Damian stared back with two shining arrogant eyes fixed on his ex-boyfriend and best friend.

"Did you scc him serve Flaca Pendavis?" Jorge asked.

Dominick grinned, still staring at Damian.

"You still love him, don't you?" Jorge snatched the flashlight away from Dominick and searched for Mikey.

"Yeah and you still love Mikey!" Dominick came back without missing a beat, exchanging a knowing stare with Jorge.

"WHATEVER!" they both shouted. Rolling their eyes in unison, they fell into a fit of laughter.

"Excuse me, Miss Thing, but you're blocking my spot!" Mikey barked at some queeny little Puerto Rican from the House of Revlon, standing in front of him. "You're gonna have to move!"

"Eh-Q me?" he asked, no, *demanded*, turning to raise a perfectly plucked eyebrow to enhance what was meant to be a threatening stare.

"No, there is no excuse for you!" Mikey said, unimpressed. The Revlon's eyes widened with disbelief.

"WHY can't I stand here?"

"Because I said so!"

"And WHO are you?"

"SOMEONE YOU'RE NOT!" Mikey tucked it quickly into his sentence, "Now, would you PUHLEASE move!"

"Miss Thing, you are too fierce!"

"Thanks, I wish I could say the same for you! NOW MOVE!"

"Bitch, don't try it!"

"SECURITY! SECURITY!" Mikey yelled out nonchalantly, checking his nails.

From the deejay booth, Jorge and Dominick stopped laughing to watch the commotion along with everyone else looking into the spotlight. Steve the security guard and his henchmen emerged once again to haul the offending party out onto the streets. The Revlon crashed violently against the ground on the other side of the velvet rope, excommunicated forever.

"You know, I lose more customers that way!" Dominick sneered to Jorge while Mikey laughed sadistically up to them from down below.

"Do you s'pose that's why people don't like us?"

"You think?"

Laughter once again prevailed in the deejay booth.

Damian pushed and shoved his way toward Mikey's spot while Dominick conveniently mixed in a record, repeating the words "Bitch Get Out." The crowd got louder and unsettled.

"WORK MS. DOMINICK!" someone yelled out as Damian swam through the crowd like an eel, feeling up a few half-naked bodies along the way.

"Damian! Damian, thank God you're here! Did you see that beast try it with me?" Mikey asked.

"Did you see me turn Flaca inside out?" Damian ignored his question and asked his own.

"Enough about you, let's talk about me! I'm parched! If I give you two drink tickets, would you get me a Corona?" Mikey begged.

"Bitch, I don't need your lousy drink tickets!"

"Oh, that's right, you slept with the bartender!" Mikey snapped his fingers in Damian's face.

"Fine, have it your way, but I expect a bump of K for the pageant winner when I return!"

"Wait!" Mikey stopped him, changing his mind. "Better yet, why don't you stay here first! I've gotta spring a mad leak before I'm stuck here for another hour!"

"Well, you would WANT to hurry it up or I'll just split and your customers will come together!" Damian said, annoyed.

"I'll be just a second! When I get back I'll let you go flirt with your favorite bartender, ah-ight?"

Damian returned Mikey's wink with an evil stare before nodding his head up and down halfheartedly.

"Ah-ight! I be out!"

Gliding like he owned the club, Mikey made his way to the bathroom, where he discovered a notoriously long line waiting for the private stalls to do everything but pee. There, the love of Mikey's life, a twenty-two-year-old banjee boy named Eric Santiago stood in front of the line.

"Hey, where ya goin'?" someone yelled out to Mikey who paid him dust and walked straight up to Eric, smiling back at him with a glow on his smooth ivory skin.

"Hey, papi!" Mikey smiled, lowering his blushing face to disguise his unexpected shyness.

"Hey!" Eric returned with a rugged yet tender voice.

"How ya been?" Mikey continued coquettishly, zeroing in on Eric's recently shaved head.

"Ah-ight!" Eric blushed.

"His dark puppy eyes were fixed on Mikey, who was biting his lower lip. Both stood there smiling moronically, the cheerleader flirting with the quarterback, before one of the stall doors flung open and three drugged-up rave kids stumbled out onto the puddles of dirty water on the bathroom floor. Mikey casually stepped over them. Eric, right behind him, locked the door.

Without any forewarning, Mikey pulled his zipper down and whipped out his Latin pride, taking a mad piss in front of Eric. Eric noticed the color of Mikey's cock was darker than the rest of him.

Mikey sprinkled any remaining fluids before tucking it away inside his Marvin-the-Martian boxer shorts. Zippering up, he announced, "Well, what are you waiting for, a personal invitation?"

"I can't pee in front of other people!" Eric admitted nervously.

"That's ah-ight, I won't look!" Mikey lied. "I promise!"

"Yeah, right!" Eric giggled before shifting over to the toilet, blocking Mikey's view with his broad shoulders.

Mikey, however, reached over Eric's shoulder to catch a glimpse of his uncut beauty.

"Ooh! It's a masterpiece!"

"You little bitch, you lied to me!" Eric burst out with laughter, hurriedly zippering up.

"I couldn't help it! It's like going to Paris and not going to see the Eiffel Tower! Y'know? It's probably just as big!"

"I can't believe you spooked my tray!"

"Ay, papi, you got nothing to be ashamed of! Trust!"

Confused about whether to kiss him or not, Mikey instead pulled out a half-empty vial of K.

"You like?" He raised his scarred eyebrow devilishly.

Eric's smile stretched across his rugged face. "Only if you feed it to me!"

"Papito, I'd feed you lots of things!" Mikey pulled out a Snuffly, scooping up a full bump from the vial before offering it to Eric ominously.

"How do you use this?" Eric asked.

"Ay, *loca* please! *¡No te hagas!* Just put it up your nose and take a deep breath!"

Following Mikey's instructions, Eric felt the powdery substance race through his nostrils, leaving behind an aspirin-like taste down his throat, a cottony feeling quickly taking over him as Mikey did the same.

Eric, in a K-hole, stood there staring at Mikey in bewilderment, traveling to distant waterfalls before Mikey broke the ice, asking that all important question that every coke and K queen needs to ask after taking a bump, "Is my nose clean?"

To his own surprise, Eric reached over and passionately licked Mikey's freckled nose with his warm tongue. Hovering over Mikey with his breath caressing him, Eric tickled Mikey before grabbing him by the waist. Pulling up to meet lips, Mikey and Eric's tongues danced to their own sweet music. Mikey's heart beat out of control, in spite of bitterness and multitudes of bad experiences, like the very first time. It didn't matter that someone was banging on the door for them to get out or that they could be seen through the cracks on the door. At that moment, Mikey and Eric were the only ones in the whole wide world, removed to their own private island. Eric's mustache softly brushed Mikey's thick goatee, holding on to one another's dreams while the words "Mikey X is a slut!" "No he isn't" "Yes, I am!" bounced off the wall of the bathroom door.

Tired of waiting for Mikey and desperate to see César before Flaca got to him, Damian impatiently paved his way to the bar. Ignoring the customers vying for his attention, he slithered up toward the bartender who watched with lustful eyes.

"Can I get a Corona and a Sex on the Beach?" Damian flirtatiously leaned over the counter, practically sitting on César's tongue.

Struggling for an intelligent response while his oiled skin glistened underneath the bar lights, César fell short with, "We've had sex in more interesting places."

Within earshot, Flaca watched them ferociously, the hair in his nostrils quivering with anger.

"Too bad you had to get involved with that *pendeja*...I mean Pendavis!" Damian snickered.

"THAT'S IT! IT'S CURTAINS FOR YOU!" Flaca hollered above the music before furiously pulling out his pocket knife and lunging insanely through the crowds toward Damian. Club kids screamed and got out of the way as the glistening metal made its way into Damian's left arm, stabbing him underneath flashing strobe lights. Damian hollered as the blood quickly gushed out all over himself and Flaca. Flaca, pulled away by the crowd, dropped the knife to the ground as César jumped over the counter and grabbed Damian who was still in shock from the attack. Through the madness, Damian's quickly infuriating eyes met with Flaca's frightened tearful ones. Breaking loose from César's tight grip, Damian jumped on top of Flaca and knocked him to the ground.

"BITCH! BITCH! LOOK WHAT YOU'VE DONE! I'M GONNA KILL YOU!" Damian bashed Flaca's face repeatedly with his right fist, a nameplate ring cutting deep into Flaca's skin. Flaca's eyes blurred as they bloated with blood.

César pulled Damian off and the crowd engulfed Flaca like a flock of pigeons devouring bread. Underneath the disco lights, Flaca lay on the dance floor with his face quickly swelling. Choking in a pool of blood, he was unable to let out more than a whimper. His legs were spread and his arms were stretched in a pose he would have never deemed possible.

"Dominick! Dominick! Damian just got stabbed! Maggie will be here any minute!" Steve yelled hysterically into his walkie-talkie as the doormen announced the police's arrival at the front door into his headphones. Dominick and Jorge scrambled around each other with the flashlight, watching in awe as César helped a bloodied Damian out onto the streets. Flaca was on the dance-floor, almost unrecognizable. Grabbing Jorge's hand, Dominick anxiously shifted the flashlight over to Mikey's spot, where he once held court.

"Shit! He's gone!" Jorge yelled. "He's gone!"

"Fuck!" Dominick lowered the music—Mikey's signal to leave the club immediately.

"Steve, find Mikey and get him out of the club NOW!" Dominick screamed into the walkie-talkie as the church doors burst open.

The dance floor flooded with God's wrathful light as an ocean of blue and cold air spilled into The Sanctuary.

"LIGHTS! LIGHTS!" Police officers infiltrated the club and Dominick's deejay booth, ordering him to turn on the lights and turn off the music. One of the officers, reaching for the microphone, made the dreadful announcement, "ATTENTION EVERYBODY! THIS CLUB IS CLOSED!" The words echoed, bouncing off sacred walls and raising loud angry curses from pissed-off club kids while others raced to the nearest exit.

Still making out, Mikey faintly heard the music lowered. He loosened his lip lock and pulled away from Eric.

"Wow, that shit was good! I think I've lost my hearing!" Mikey referred both to the kiss and the drugs.

Eric laughed his genuinely intoxicating laugh until the room stopped spinning and Mikey became dimly aware that the music had stopped altogether. Catching on to Mikey's inquisitive look, Eric opened the door to discover they were the only ones left in the bathroom.

"Did we take that long?" Confused, Mikey grabbed Eric's sweaty hand and led him out of their private paradise.

"Something must've happened!" Eric said, disoriented. Whatever K was left in his system made him feel nauseous.

Suddenly, the entire bathroom was washed with light. Mikey struggled to look beyond his blinded eyes, vaguely recognizing Steve's husky figure.

"MIKEY! MIKEY! OH MY GOD! YOU'VE GOT TO GET OUT OF HERE! THE CLUB'S BEEN RAIDED! MAGGIE'S EVERYWHERE!"

"¡*MIERDA LOCO!*" Mikey screamed, looking back at Eric with all the fear of the world in his eyes. Steve grabbed Mikey with a wrestler's grip and pulled him away, violently waking him from this dream.

"NOOO!" Mikey freed himself from Steve, racing back into Eric's arms. "Eric! Eric! I'm sorry but I've gotta run!"

"I'll come with you!"

"No!" Mikey insisted, "I mean, you can't!"

"MIKEY, WE HAVE NO TIME FOR THIS! SAVE THE ROMANTIC SHIT FOR LATER!" Steve yelled.

"Eric," Mikey pleaded, "if I get caught and you're with me they'll take you too!"

"I don't care!" Eric begged.

"Yeah, but I do!" Mikey grabbed the back of Eric's head tightly with both hands, resting his forehead sweetly against Eric's. "I'm sorry but I can't do this to you!"

"MIKEY! YA! LET'S GO! LET'S GO!" Steve said, furiously annoyed.

They stared briefly into each other's eyes before Mikey kissed Eric with words he could never express and raced out the door forever.

Mikey was near tears as Steve directed him through a series of back doors and long tunnels until they were out on the streets, somewhere far from the main entrance. Mikey froze when he noticed the number of police cars, sirens, and screaming queens going off by the church. The words of cousin Chino—"If your mami finds out, she'll leave you like your daddy did!"—flashed across his face.

"Eh-Q me, offisah? Can you puhlease tell me wha is goin' on hea?"

A tall husky police officer looked down to notice a skinny black man wrapped in white fur addressing him from behind huge Jackie O sunglasses and surrounded by an entourage of faithful fans staring up at him. The officer held back his smile.

"Ees these club goin' tah reopen?" Princess demanded to know, one hand on his leathered hips, the other pointing a long bony finger toward The Sanctuary.

"Not tonight, it won't!" The cop, unsure, was still trying to figure him out.

"But offisah, I pay twenty DAHLAHS to get in!"

"Princess! Princess, don't! You'll get yourself arrested-ed-ed!" one of the house children begged. The others giggled among themselves, fully aware that Princess was always on the guestlist. "I'm sorry..." The police officer did not know whether to say ma'am or sir. "I don't know if it's ever going to reopen!"

Princess dropped his jaw, twisting his neck haughtily with exaggerated concern. The officer walked away, confused.

From the back seat of Steve's car, Mikey lit up a cigarette and watched the chaos outside with hopes of finding Eric or one of his sistas. As Steve drove by, avoiding the congested traffic, the cross on top of the church reflected on the windshield. Mikey watched Princess chasing after some cop, arguing about the closing of the club while others were escorted out in handcuffs. Farther up, he noticed an ambulance swarming with a multitude of drugged-up party people, revolving lights reminiscent of the red ones Dominick used on the dance floor.

"That's either Flaca or Damian in there!" Steve said, automatically locking the doors.

"WHAT?" Mikey's eyes bulged out of his head, struggling with the door to jump out of the car.

"*Cógelo con* take it easy, okay! Flaca stabbed him in the arm! It's Flaca you should be worried about!"

"When the fuck did all this happen?" Mikey was unable to see who was inside.

"While you were in the bathroom with that kid!" Steve revealed a hint of bitterness. "Why do you think Maggie showed up?"

"Fuck, man!"

"Damian beat the shit out of her with whatever arm he had left! Flaca's lucky if she's still alive!"

"What's wrong with that bitch?"

"I don't know, but you guys are always fuckin' wit' somebody! How many times do I have to tell you? You had me throw out two guys today! I knew this would happen sooner or later!" Steve was yelling like the father Mikey never knew. Mikey rolled his eyes and pouted in the backseat, "Oh, daddy, just shut the fuck up and drive, will you?"

"I'm telling you, *uno de estos días te van a matar!*"

Mikey's beeper suddenly went off with Dominick's home number and secret code—666.

"*Ya cállate* and give me your cell phone, it's Dominick!"

"*¿Qué tú te crees? ¿Que yo soy* AT&T? I don't have a cell phone wit' me!"

"*Pues*, pull ovah to the nearest phone!"

"AT ALL! I'm taking you straight to my house on Long Island…" Steve mumbled on and on incomprehensibly.

"I DON'T THINK SO!" Mikey snapped his fingers on the air, forming a semicircle.

Steve continued, ignoring him.

"Ay c'mon Steve, it could be an emergency!"

"Mikey, I'm responsible for you! If anything happens to you, they would kill me!"

"Steve, the police don't know who the fuck I am! I could be standing right in their face, they'd ask me to get out of the way! Besides, I gotta find out if Damian's okay!"

Steve, still driving, tried to avoid Mikey's pleading eyes until Mikey put his arms around him, flirtatiously begging him, "Please!"

Always a sucker for Mikey's come-ons, Steve pulled the car over to a pay phone, only a few blocks away from Sanctuary, pressing the button to unlock the doors.

Mikey kissed him on the cheek before jumping out of the car. Janet X raced toward him with bloodshot eyes, still tripping on a hit of acid.

"*¡Me cago en Dios!* Just don't take your sweet time like you did in the bathroom!" Steve groaned.

"*Ay bendito,* Mikey! Did chu hear 'bout Ms. Damian?" Janet was taking a deep drag from his Virginia Slim while his long curly hair waved in the wind to reveal his blemished face, tainted with acne and tons of makeup.

"I think he's okay but I gotta call Dominick back!" Mikey studied Janet's tight Chicle jeans and implants, which bulged out of a bright red bustier underneath a motorcycle jacket.

"I don't think he's gonna vogue f'awhile!" Janet's breath formed thick misty clouds in the cold January air, "*¡Es un escándalo!* The *locas* ah screamin'! They got all pretty up to get thrown out onto the streets thanks to *la Flaca pendeja, ésa!*"

Janet took another long drag before noticing Steve inside the car.

"Stevie? Stevie? Ay, Stevie! *Papi chulo,* I didn't know that was chu inside da cah! *¡Espérate que tengo que contarte algo!*"

Jumping inside the car, Janet harassed Steve while Mikey took the opportunity to slip a quarter in, dialing the number on his beeper.

"Hello!"

"Hello? Mikey?"

"Yeah! Dominick? What the hell is going on?"

"I'm at my house with Jorge."

"No duh!"

"Where are you?"

"A few blocks from Sanctuary, by some bodega."

"Is Steve with you?"

"You mean daddy?"

"Yeah."

"He's in the car with Janet who's chewing his ear off as we speak."

"Janet?"

"Si! La Janet! I ran into huh on the way to call you back, but you still haven't answered my question!"

"Flaca stabbed Damian in the arm and Damian fucked her up fierce!"

"Is he gonna be okay?"

"Who? Damian? Not if Maggie finds him! Listen, Finnigan, come over to my house!"

"Bitch! Are you for real?"

"Just bring your tired half Puerto Rican ass over, ah-ight?"

"Dominick?"

"What?"

"I think I'm in love!"

"Good-bye!" Click, dial tone.

Mikey hung up the phone while Marsha, a black homeless thirty-something drag queen, approached him, a thin ratty shawl wrapped around his torn-up pink dress, still wearing the bonnet Dominick gave him last Easter.

"Hey Mikey! How ya doin' baby? Oooh chile, I is stahvin'! I do anythin' fah a dahlah! You got a dahlah? Baby, please tell me ya got a dahlah!" Marsha shivered violently to show how cold he was.

"Mama, I ain't got no small bills but I'll give you a ten if I could find one!" Mikey went through his pockets until he pulled out a ten. Marsha smiled with joy to expose his rotting teeth while the lampposts cast a sickly glow on his coal-black skin.

It was three weeks later and they were all together again, having coffee at Café Rafaella. Dim candles enhanced their hungover faces. Damian featured a bandaged arm while Dominick tried to conceal the bags underneath his frustrated eyes by hiding behind his trademark drooping sunglasses. He was miserably depressed about the closing of The Sanctuary. Jorge argued about waiting forever for a "damned tiramisu!" while Mikey stared out the window, hoping to catch a glimpse of Eric walking by.

They had already discussed everything there was to discuss about the other night. The subject was about as worn out as they were as they waited for the mother of the House of X to arrive so they could plan their inevitable attack on the House of Pendavis. Damian suggested killing Flaca altogether while Jorge, the hopeless theater queen in the gang, preferred the old *West Side Story*-like battle at the piers.

"Are you goin' out tonight?" asked Mikey, changing the subject, the question directed to no one in particular.

"Where is there to go?" Jorge logged on.

"I dunno…maybe The Attic?" Mikey suggested, hoping to God maybe that's where Eric could be.

"The Attic? That place sucks!" Dominick interjected bitterly.

"Well, if I go I'm going with Chris!" Jorge revealed, almost whispered.

"Chris? Chris Infiniti? Chris? My ex-boyfriend Chris?" Mikey silenced Jorge with a stare.

"Oh, you'll get over it!" Damian jumped in defense of Jorge, the tiramisu finally making its way to their table.

"I thought Chris was going out with Jason Aviance?" Dominick wondered out loud, Jorge holding back his comment by stuffing his mouth with dessert.

"Wait a minute! Back up! Didn't you go out with Jason Aviance too?" Damian asked, looking at Mikey as if the word "whore" was stamped on his forehead.

"They weren't 'going out'! They were just fucking!" Dominick clarified, Mikey nodding his head in agreement.

"Yeah, besides, Jason is cheating on Chris with Mark Magnifique!" Jorge took time out from his expedition to defend his date for the evening.

"That's because Jason found out Chris slept with Damian!" said Dominick, casually dropping the bomb to make Jorge choke. "But I ain't one to gossip so you didn't hear that from me!"

"Bitch! I only slept wit' him 'cause I got locked outta my apartment!" Damian yelled.

"Did he ask you to pull his nipples while fucking him?" asked Mikey, happily turning the conversation over to Damian, mocking him by pinching his own nipples and comically feigning orgasm.

"I wouldn't talk if I were you, 'Ms. Fifty Dollars Grandpa, Seventy-five the Lover Can Watch!' Besides, weren't you the one who got fucked up the ass by Mark?"

"Mark? Mark Magnifique? HA! Mark THINKS he fucked me but he was so high he can't remember it was actually Jorge he fucked!" Mikey belted out. Jorge pushed his dessert aside, defeated.

"That's right! He turned you out on his leather couch!" Damian said, excitedly turning on Jorge.

"How did you know he had a leather couch?" Dominick caught him, the whole table silently waiting while Damian gasped for a quick answer.

"Because…I fucked him…on that leather couch!" he let out a second too late.

"Yeah right! YOU fucked Mark Magnifique! With what, Miss Thing? Your nail filer?" Dominick and the others burst into hysterical laughter and Damian's face crumbled like ashes.

"FUCK YOU ALL!"

The laughter eventually quieted, leaving them back where they started, waiting humorlessly for their house mother, late as usual.

Still dwelling on the previous revelations, Mikey turned to Damian, asking, "When did YOU munch on Chris?"

"When you was going out with that Chelsea queen, whatever his name was!"

"Cliff?" Mikey asked, raising his scarred eyebrow, contempt in his eye.

"Yeah! Cliff!"

"I'm surprised you never slept with Cliff, considering how much you wanted him!" Mikey quickly blinked his eyes at Damian as if hoping to find a chicken in Damian's place when he opened them.

"Who? Cliff? Bitch, please! It was cute for him but I don't do steroid-enhanced bodies!" Damian said defensively.

"*Ay loca*, pleeease!" Dominick snapped, raising his hand up to Damian's face like white trailer trash on the *Jerry Springer Show*. "What the fuck was Troy, Fernando and all those other gym bunnies you slept with?"

"Yeah 'Ms. Big Cup'! I mean, 'Ms. Big Cunt'!" Mikey said, injecting imaginary steroids into his own ass, his face contorting in pretend pain.

Damian, who wanted to jump Mikey over the table, couldn't resist laughing.

"I didn't know you slept with Troy?" Jorge asked, aiming the question at Mikey. He had finished with his tiramisu. "Didn't YOU sleep with Troy?"

The conversation was once again on Mikey's lap, who quickly scanned the café with hopes of finding Sista Mama heading toward the ill-fated table.

"Yeah! I remember you were going out with Geo at the time! Oh! I'm sorry!" Damian gleamed. "You weren't going out with Geo! You were just getting fucked by him on a regular basis!"

Mikey returned on cue with, "Yeah, but haven't you heard the latest! Geo is now FUCKING your ex-lover Hector!"

Jorge and Dominick, joining forces, let out an astounded "Oooooooooh!"

Speechless, Damian contemplated a comeback, the wrath of

heaven and hell in his crunched eyes. "Yeah! Well, I heard Geo was messing around with your little boy-toy Eric!" Damian lied.

Mikey rolled his eyes, unimpressed. "Bullshit! Eric doesn't SEE Geo! If anything he feels threatened by him! Besides, it's all about Eric!"

Managing to shut up everyone at the table once and for all with his bittersweet revelation, the entire café was invaded with tangible silence when the tall black woman they referred to as Sista Mama X finally arrived in all her wicked glory. Chanel sunglasses decorated her shaved head as Sista Mama sailed toward their table like an African goddess.

When they left, Marsha was outside begging for money with her Easter bonnet.

"Hey Mama! Whas goin' on, girrrl?" He waved ashy hands at Sista Mama and the rest of them, his smile revealing a slew of missing teeth.

"Wassup Marsha girl? I dig your lubly ensemble!" Sista Mama extended hand to allow Marsha the honor of paying her homage.

Marsha dutifully kissed her callused hands with dry lips.

"Ms. Damian, ah heard 'bout what Flaca did to you at da Sanctuary! You okay, honey?"

"Yeah! I'm ah-ight!" said Damian, half-convincingly, shaking his bandaged arm.

"Back in da days, I got cut by Spiffy LaBeija at the Legends Ball right hea!" Marsha pulled up his dress to point a gray finger at a scar on his upper left thigh.

"The Legends Ball?" Jorge turned to ask Dominick.

"Prehistoric is more like it!" Dominick laughed.

"Anyways!" said Marsha, brushing him off, "Did I not set that bitch's hair on fiah da next day? Das right! I lit huh up!" Marsha accentuated the 'I lit huh up!' part with finger-snaps.

"I remember that baby! She jumped into the Hudson screamin'!" Mama laughed while reminiscing. "She wore wigs and hats till they found her floating dead in that same river three years ago. Her hair never did grow back."

"She had it comin', attackin' po' lil' me!" said Marsha, hands on his bony hips.

"Are you taking notes? This is you in ten years!" Dominick said, teasing Damian.

"Oooh, honey chile! I is stahvin'! I'd do anythin' fo' a dahlah!" Mikey said, mouthing off Marsha's trademark lines simultaneously with him.

"Really? Would you vogue for us Mah…?" Mama silenced Dominick with a stare that was too late.

"Shuah, baby!" Marsha convulsed without a second to spare to some imaginary song in his head, arms flopping in the cold air, legs twitching to unheard rhythms. His audience was appalled, desperately waiting for Marsha to stop. Passersby were beginning to stare.

"Uhhh, okay baby!" Mama pulled out a few singles from her baggy slacks. "That will be all for today! The category is now closed! Here's your trophy. Now, walk for me!"

Marsha happily took the money, the others pulled out more.

"Go buy yourself sumthin' good to eat so you won't be *stahvin'!*" Dominick handed him a five, then handed him another. "While you're at it, go buy yourself a new hat, 'cause that one is ready to pick up and walk its own category!"

Marsha was excited as they waved good-bye, heading toward

the piers, leaving behind a homeless transsexual with a wad of money in his wrinkled hands and a lonesome tear racing down his charcoal face.

At the Christopher Street piers, Mikey rolled a blunt to keep warm while Damian and Dominick fought over some leftover K Mama had left behind for them, before heading off to her girl-friend's house. Staring out into the empty darkness of the Hudson River with "Master Blaster" playing from somebody's car in the distance, Mikey remembered the first time he ever stepped foot on the piers. Choking on a mad puff, Dominick slapped Mikey on the back really hard.

"Yo, chill out bitch!" Mikey managed to say between coughs, the air windy and cold.

Except for a few desperate hustlers, the piers were empty. New Jersey lit on the other side, Mikey imagined himself getting an apartment close to the PATH train with Eric. Damian and Dominick were still arguing over the last few bumps of K. Mikey, in his own hole, recalled the days when the piers belonged to voguing faggots and house music blasted from parked cars. All that was left was the carcass of a soul, the piers once so full of life were now so full of death. Graffitied walls, once boasting "The House of Ninja Rules" now featured "Rest in Peace Supreme. We Love You!" The lampposts, which once served as spotlights for battling houses, were lifeless. The nightfall served the twelve-year-old who sucked some old man's dick behind the bushes— "Yeah! Suck it baby! Suck that dick!"

In his drug-enhanced daze, Mikey turned to watch the cars drive by with locked doors. The West Side Highway was haunted by the ghosts of men who once walked in the arms of other men, women who once kissed the lips of other women, men who dressed as women, women who dressed as men and children who dressed as adults. However, in spite of death and AIDS, the houses still prevailed, lingering in the hearts of a new generation living out the legends of the past.

A speeding cab suddenly stopped not far from where they stood. Janet X dashed out of the passenger seat with one high heel stiletto on, struggling to run in a pair of ultra tight cut-off shorts and a red lace bra, his bread and butter.

"HELP! HELP!" Janet screamed at the top of his lungs. Mikey and the others made out his bloodied face through the darkness.

"HE'S GONNA KILL ME!"

A big black cabbie jumped out of the car, caught up to Janet, pulled his weave to yank him to the concrete floor, ripping open his shorts to expose Janet's tucked cock, punching him repeatedly in the face.

"YOU FAGGOT! YOU FAGGOT!" he screamed. Janet's fresh blood warmed his clenched fist, using his long nails to scratch his face.

Before he could swing another near fatal blow, the cabbie was pulled away by six arms, one of which went on to punch him in the face, snapping the bone in his nose. Someone else kicked him in the stomach, making him cringe to the ground before getting bashed in the mouth. Unable to scream, belting out a groan, his mouth quickly filled with blood. Trying to cover his face with both hands, someone else kicked him between the legs, followed by another kick to the ribs, cracking them as the blood in his mouth mixed with vomit. Through swollen eyes, he could only make out three shadows hovering above him before getting kicked in his right ear, knocking his face into a pool of blood and vomit.

Janet watched in awe before they raced off, disappearing into the night, police sirens blaring somewhere in the distance. Holstering himself up against the floor, Janet stared through tearful eyes at the deformed figure before him, blood streaming through the hand that held an ardent face. Slowly pulling himself off the cold cement, Janet limped toward him, eyes fixed on his disfigured face while holding his hair back with one hand, the other reaching to touch a swollen cheek. The driver, still alive but closer to death, caught an angry glimmer in Janet's eyes.

"See wha happin' when chu mess wit' faggots! Now chu could tell all ya friends that chu got beat by faggots!" Janet screamed, gathering enough energy to give the sprawled body one last kick.

That night while sleeping on Dominick's couch, Mikey dreamt he was in a desert, the sun beaming down harshly, burning the skin right off him. Mikey, alone in the emptiness, sat underneath an ominous tree with the sand beneath hot as coal. Blinded by the brightness of the sun, Mikey could make out the shadow of a huge black bird sailing down toward the tree, thin legs clutching on a limb.

"Why are you still here?" the crow asked.

"I dunno!" Mikey said, sweat dripping down his tanned face.

"You've been here all your life!" the crow continued. "Hiding in the desert from your reality. Imagining yourself persecuted like myself, wanting only to survive, to feed the hunger. Driven away. Driven away in flocks. But you're not like me, always perched somewhere up in a tree, waiting, waiting for a chance to feed on the corn which gives life. The only one who persecutes you is yourself!"

Mikey forced a smile on his dried out face.

"Now tell me! Why are you still here?" the crow asked once again, his feathers ruffled.

Mikey contemplated the question for a moment before responding.

"Because this is all I know!" Mikey's smile became wry. "Suffering and pain. At least here no one can hurt me! No one can make me suffer. I can sit here for eternity in solitude. Waiting. Waiting for someone to come along to take away this loneliness."

With this, the crow turned, spread itself in benediction and flew away, vanishing over Mikey, leaving him behind still smiling wryly, alone in the desert.

MIGUEL FALQUEZ-CERTAIN was born in Barranquilla, Colombia. His most recent volumes of poetry are *Palimpsestos* (Silver Medal, Ibero-American Poets and Writers Guild in 1996), *Usurpaciones y deicidios* (finalist at the second Latin American Writers Institute poetry contest in 1990), and *Doble corona*, all published in 1997. Other books: *Habitación en la palabra* (1995), *Proemas en cámara ardiente* (1989), and *Reflejos de una máscara* (1986). He was co-screenwriter and co-director of *Emma Zunz* (1978), starring Virginia Rambal and Elizabeth Peña. He is currently the associate editor of *Ollantay Theater Magazine*, and is a contributing editor of *Realidad Aparte*. His translation into English of Gabriel García Márquez's monologue *Diatriba de amor contra un hombre sentado* had a run in April of 1996 at Teatro Repertorio Español in New York. The story included was originally published as "¿Y cómo es parada, Padre Infante?" (Medellín: Editorial Transempaques, 1994) and was runner-up in the "Carlos Castro Saavedra" International Short Story Contest. It was translated into English by the author.

WHAT'S UP, FATHER INFANTE?

Miguel Falquez-Certain

So, Father Infante, what's your story? For a long time now I've been hearing a lot about what's been happening to you. The truth is I never saw you again after the day I graduated from high school and today, when least expected, I see you coming into the Rex Cinema. The lights are already out and I could see only your silhouette between the big curtains and the lobby. My stomach turns and my eyes follow you in the dark: with your flashlight on, you are walking briskly down the aisles looking for a place to sit. I hesitate for a second and decide to follow you, filled with that morbid curiosity caused by so many years of piled-up hate and resentment. Little by little I realize that you're not looking for just any seat but rather for something in particular, since I see you have ignored some empty spots. I finally see you already sitting next to a kid whose apparent beauty is revealed by the flashing lights coming from the screen where *The Four Hundred Blows* is being shown today.

Do you remember the day you showed up in Barranquilla? We were all hanging out in the basketball court drinking sodas when you suddenly came out of the church. The high-noon sun was hitting straight down on you, the hoop and the pavement which was simmering in the 104-degree heat.

Curiosity got the best of us and we immediately surrounded you because we wanted to know everything about the new priest who had arrived as a hero from that faraway Cuba we now hated so much. Kennedy was our new hero. Can you imagine, the first Catholic president of the United States. Even though we were only twelve at the time, you looked pretty young to us. You were that sort of man who has a slight blue hairy growth even after having a close shave. And you almost had no lips, just a line that hardly suggested them, and they reminded me of my father's. Your white cassock was spotless. All was peachy, full of laughs and pleasantries. You were quite a character who had succeeded in fleeing from the evil that had taken hold of the island.

But something threw us off, though. You didn't like Jack Kennedy, and for starters you told us that he was a third-rate president. We didn't appreciate that but accepted it: we really hoped that some day you'd come around. We didn't think it was that hard since Kennedy had started the embargo against Cuba and was already planning the "Freedom Flights."

We used to get the heebie-jeebies listening to your stories about that island of faithless people who had bartered God for bearded Fidel. We started telling you at the top of our lungs that we understood you quite well, that in the Alliance for Progress comics, which were distributed to us by the Jesuits at the end of Mass on Sundays, your stories were explained very well: parents who had been betrayed by their own children, reporting them to the militia, and who ended up dead at the firing squad just for not sharing their views. Can you believe it? A bunch of atheists who didn't honor the Fourth Commandment.

Or that one about the brainwashing they'd do on school-children: the schoolteacher would ask her pupils whether they wanted any ice cream and when they'd say yes she'd tell them to ask Baby Jesus for it. After the children would do as she'd asked, the schoolmistress would wait a while and then would order them to ask Fidel for ice cream. The children would gather in front of Castro's huge portrait and beg him for ice cream. No sooner said than done. A few seconds later, a line of militiamen would barge in carrying cones to distribute among the over-joyed children who were now yelling jubilantly, squealing with pleasure. You had to be a monster to do that to children who hadn't even reached the age when they could make sense of things.

We told you that it'd be a different story with us. We were Eucharistic Crusaders, we had been consecrated to the service of the Holy Virgin, and for Her and Her Son we were upholding the Christian Faith even if we had to die for it. Now that the Second Vatican Council had allowed us to study the Bible in depth, we had it down pat, and every Saturday we'd go to Carrizal to catechize and bring food for the poor who live there. The Scripture classes were a thing of the past; we now felt like Baby Jesus at the Temple and, holding a Bible, we used to get into heated theological arguments, especially with Martha, my parents' washwoman, who was a Jehovah's Witness.

Of course, that was nothing compared to you. You were a true hero who had suffered in your own flesh Castro's persecu-tion for just being a priest and because, as it was your duty, you had taken the Sacraments to millions of Cuban Catholics, because Cuba was a Catholic country and it had always been, and just for that they put you in jail and fed you bread and water, but you didn't lose heart because you were really tough and a man of God to top it all off, and you didn't care either when they shot you on your foot and you offered everything to God on behalf of Cuba, the Cubans and even for Castro's soul, such an infidel.

Right away you showed us your special shoe with a black rubber platform so you could walk normally after the operation they had performed on your foot to take the bullet out. Of course we couldn't notice the platform because it was black like the shoes which, by the way, were so shiny that they looked as if they had been polished by one of the shoeshine boys who hang out at Bolívar Square.

And then you started to tell us about the precarious conditions your beloved Cuba was in, about the persecutions of Catholics similar to the stories we had heard about in religion classes that mentioned the Roman catacombs and the first Christians, and about Fidel and the Castroites who were a bunch of bums, who had never heard of showers and who stunk like skunks, as you used to say, and we'd crack up. But you really killed us when you told us the nickname they had for Fidel on account of how filthy he was—"Slime Bucket" you said they used to call him, and we really burst out laughing because we thought you were just great.

It was a pity that you didn't like Jack Kennedy, the first Catholic president of the United States of America and who, as Brother Beto used to say, could convert all the American heretics to Catholicism when they'd finally realize how good he was, that the Catholic Church was the real one, that it was the only one that could save their souls from Hell's fire.

How sorry we felt when we heard the bell ringing. We were so happy and we said good-bye to you, screaming that we'd see you again, no two ways about it, that you definitely were a cool priest.

To tell you the truth, the real truth, Father Infante, I was always a very religious kid. My mom used to tell me that when I was three years old my nanny used to take me by the hand to Lourdes School just across the street from home where my sister Betty, the oldest, was a boarder. The nun of the Order of the Presentation of the Virgin Mary and their pupils made me their pet; they started inviting me to all the school's festivities. My aunt Lydia had given me a tiny missal that I always carried with me, and nanny Angela would take me in my baby carriage through all the school halls while I was "reading" from my missal, like a real grown-up, as my aunt Lydia used to say. Marie Pousepin's nuns found all this very cute, so much so that their beautiful faces would blush with joy and their extremely white headdresses would shake like jelly in a quake. It was there that I went to elementary school and had my First Communion.

When I graduated to the Jesuits' school, Father Infante, the change took me by surprise: it was a closed religious world that had inner recesses and violent punishments—flogged hands and cruel humiliations. We had left behind the one hundred lines we had to write as punishment, the harsh scolding that started with tears and ended up with hugs and smiles. Instead, we had to attend mass daily at seven o'clock in the morning and conform to new, stricter rules: punctuality, attendance, conduct, study progress, personal appearance, gala uniform on Sundays bearing the school's coat-of-arms. The Eucharistic Crusade came later: the field trips to spread the Gospel, the imposing parades, all the paraphernalia needed to battle against the heretics.

Perhaps getting myself ready for what would be your Marian Congregation, Father Infante, one day I joined the recently founded Loyola's Legion. Ignatius, the general who had given up everything to create the Society of Jesus, Loyola, the invincible Loyola, who could only be compared to the Pope. And me, surrounded by my cassocks, my surplices, all sorts of incense, and my makeshift altars. It was a challenge to memorize the names of the 533 different objects that make up the liturgical world. I had to prepare myself to become a priest.

So it happened that I was very religious even though puberty was knocking at my door: pent-up desires that were making me very anxious—the world shattering my thus far placid, innocent way of life.

Yes, Father Infante, you had to be aware of my deep-rooted religious faith, especially when you became our teacher of World and Church History in eighth grade. I was really interested in those subjects and by then you already were the head of the Marian Congregation. Father Molina had been removed from that post and you were going places. So young and qualified. Your image as a religious hero from Fidel's Cuba surely helped you quite a bit.

At the beginning, your relationship with the class was quite cordial. You didn't discriminate against anyone until the day, with no warning whatsoever, you started to have it in for me. This was so sudden that I was puzzled because so far you seemed to be fair. But little by little you showed your true colors and I stopped deceiving myself once and for all.

I was a good student and devoted a lot of time to reading those stories about popes and pirates. And without warning you started to taunt those you considered "weak." It wasn't easy for me to understand how you could be on the side of those who could make our lives impossible. Some of us were the kind of helpless creatures who had been too spoiled by their parents: the youngest sibling, or the only begotten son, or perhaps the only male among females. We were that sort of child who would ask for the sun, the moon, and the stars and everything would be granted to us with no problem at all. Maybe we'd cry a little so that our parents would take pity on us and we'd get away with murder. We didn't know how to fistfight for any reason at all like the rest of our schoolmates and we didn't practice any sports either. Too fat or too skinny, too pretty or too ugly. The general line was being broken in front of the majority's fuming eyes that was used to impose its purported normality. And then we were left out in the cold and pushed around; the best spots on the school bus, in lines and in the classrooms were taken away from us. And our moods became darker with time, forcing us to lead isolated lives or join esoteric cliques closed to everybody else but the initiated. Books, poems, plays, movies, schoolwork—those became our haven: the only way we could conquer our conquerors.

For many years I tried to figure out why you didn't become our leader, our friend, but rather our most rabid persecutor. As we distanced ourselves from you and my admiration became a deep-rooted hate, I started to suspect that deep down you were a lot like me, as if you had seen your reflection in my face.

Many years later, after my hatred eased into indifference, I began to find out things about you that proved me right.

I remember that you used to mimic any kind of slight affectation you could find in any member of our little group and this would be met with approval by the toughies in our class. For you, it was a big joke; for us, the worst humiliation. It was easier for us to deal with our classmates' wickedness but what we resented the most was your acquiescence and participation. After all, they were our age, but you were a "grown-up" and, most importantly, our teacher, the one who was supposed to keep them under control. But instead, Father Infante, you proved to be a true collaborationist, like a joker in a poker game, enjoying the gibes and jeers performed by the clown of the moment and we were the target of your ridicule.

Yes, Father Infante. Do you remember the day when you decided that I was a homosexual? I, on the other hand, will never forget it. We were attending your World History class. The Society of Jesus' schools were very particular, like no other school in Barranquilla. At St. Joseph's there were divisions and classes. Each school grade had its own division with several sections, so the First Division was composed of twelfth grade with Sections A and B. I was in eighth grade and belonged to Section A (the taller kids) of the Fifth Division. But what really differentiated divisions from classes was that in the former each student had his own fixed desk where he always sat. And in those old desks we kept our school supplies as well as a rag and wax we used to polish the desks. Classes, on the other hand, met in individual groups at smaller classrooms and, there, anyone could sit wherever he pleased. At least in theory, because in practice there were certain unwritten rules of the game that were respected by all the classmates in their sections. Instead of individual desks with drawers, these classrooms had long, flat tables with individual folding metal chairs. Each table had room for two and either you chose your mate or he chose you.

Caraballo had chosen me. Abimelech Caraballo—nick-named, I never knew why (although years later, when I was familiar with Puerto Rican slang in which "ducks" are "fags," the irony became obvious), the "Puerto Rican duck," since in Barranquilla we called "ducks" the people who crashed parties—was a real character. Almost without realizing it, he had become a member of our inner circle: five classmates who got together at recesses, after class, weekends and at the desks. I say "without realizing it" because I couldn't stand the Duck. Perhaps it was his colossal tackiness. He must've been my age: thirteen years old. But he also had something that attracted me at the same time: his alleged sexual knowledge and his much boasted-about exploits. Indeed, Duck Caraballo spoke freely about his night out at the whorehouse or about the way he'd fucked a she-donkey in the farm Sunday night or about the faggot he'd screwed for thirty bucks. Of course, all this piqued my interest due to my repressed sexuality and my absolute virginity. Duck Caraballo was a big talker and to tell you the truth I didn't believe everything he said in my clique, although when he was alone with me he definitely put an emphasis on homosexuality. He insisted that you could have great pleasure fucking a fag because the anus was tighter than the vagina.

"Shit, fag, I know what I'm telling you," he stressed, using the epithet as a tag; in Barranquilla, he-men called each other either faggot or nutjob.

"Why is that?"

"'Cause it's smaller and it's better when you come 'cause you have it tight," he would conclude triumphantly and burst out laughing. "You should try it."

"I don't know if I could."

"But of course," he would caution, "you have to be very careful. The only snag is that a fag could have clap in the ass and you could catch it. So, if you're going to fuck 'im, you'd better squeeze lime juice in his ass and, if it hurts, then you'll know he's got it big time."

In a way Duck Caraballo was in love with me. Or rather, he was attracted to me and he was always ready to grab my butt and start the game of I-grab-your-butt-so-you-can-also-grab-mine. That's why he always wanted to sit next to me because he liked me and in that way he could take advantage of any situation to grab my ass.

The classroom was rectangular with big windows and two long halls on each side. At the back of the room, stuck in a corner, there was a platform and, on top of it, the teacher's old desk, so he could be higher than the rest of the class and be able to observe not only his pupils but also anyone who might venture into the halls. There were three rows of ten desks that sat two students each, although it was very rare to have a section with more than forty pupils. That day, Father Infante, Duck Caraballo and I were sitting at the third desk in the middle row. And you started your lesson.

Aware that you had it in for me, I had studied hard the assigned two chapters of the textbook the previous night: Queen Elizabeth I, Francis Drake, and the buccaneers in the Americas. And as I expected, you asked me to stand up and recite. And I rattled off names, dates, and circumstances with complete accuracy. I was so good that I expected you to congratulate me and give me an A+. But you didn't.

To answer the teacher's question we had to stand up and wait for the sadistic attack from the Grand Inquisitor. When I was about to give the finishing touches to my brilliant speech, Duck Caraballo grabbed my ass. He left me speechless for a split second that seemed to me like an eternity, and then I reacted compulsively and irrationally, throwing my English leather briefcase to the floor in a tantrum.

You couldn't figure out why I had cut short a splendid disquisition or what was going on among my classmates right behind me who were having a field day, laughing and making all sorts of disgusting noises.

Anselmo Echeverri, who was one of my most hated enemies, said on the sly that my reaction was exactly what a fag would do, but you managed to hear him and joined the mocking gang. I felt I was going to die and let myself drop on the metal chair while you were saying that I should act like a man. Right away you gave me a B and I didn't have the guts to argue with you. I accepted it without complaints and when I thought the ridicule would never end, the bell rang, sending us to the 9 A.M. recess.

From then on you became my most rabid persecutor. You started to spread unsubstantiated stories about me that made their way to my classmates. I, who at thirteen, hadn't yet tasted the joy of sex.

My turn finally came to request admission to your Marian Congregation. Before a group of older students presided over by you, the Spanish Inquisition opened its doors: your cunning questions were filled with contempt to blackball me, Father Infante, blackballing was your game and you got the upper hand. I tried again and again with the same results. Until one day I just gave up, joined the Boy Scouts and graduated from high school with honors.

I heard the buzz about you after graduation but didn't care

anymore. Your wicked image melted away and disappeared with time, recurring only in my darkest nightmares.

Until today when I see you again when least expected. I've stationed myself at the back wall next to the exit curtains so I can spy on you with joy. You're not wearing a cassock—not even the collar you're nowadays allowed to wear. Not at all. You're dressed like a civilian, like anyone else. Right there, thirty feet away.

The flashing lights on the screen show a thirteen-year-old Jean-Pierre Léaud, playing Antoine Doinel, Truffaut's alter ego, running in the countryside looking for the sea that will shape his destiny.

And I start to slowly face mine, my heart running wild, discreetly walking in the dark aisle until reaching the spot where you're sitting and shockingly discover that the beautiful young man next to you has his fly open and his hard penis, shining in its pristine whiteness against the Cinema Rex's intermittent shadows, is being held by your priestly hands.

You're taken by surprise. You hesitate for a second and raise your frightened face and recognize me at once. Hatred, terror, and shame successively travel in a frenzy through your tearing eyes, and I falter but keep on going.

Antoine has finally reached the sea and bathed his radiant body with its silvery waves. Freedom, at last!

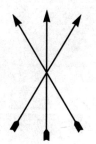

DIONISIO CAÑAS was born in Spain. He is one of the most important poets and critics of contemporary Spanish letters. The author of many books of poetry and criticism, he is also a historian. Sr. Cañas is a professor at the City College of New York. He has lived in Manhattan since 1972.

Lord Cornbury's Ear

→

Dionisio Cañas
Translated by Doris R. Schnable

I was fascinated by the portrait of Lord Cornbury dressed as a woman; I didn't care whether it was authentic or not. A poor example of American Colonial art, painted by an unknown artist, that simple and taunting portrait hypnotized me from the first day I saw it.

Every time I entered the New York Historical Society, I stood, paralyzed, in front of this painting of the New York governor who had dared, at the beginning of the eighteenth century, to dress as a woman (or at least that's what I believed), so that an artist could paint the only official portrait of his "reign"; since Lord Cornbury, more than a governor, was really a full-fledged Queen with a hairy chest.

But it was his ear, his enormous ear, that slowly but surely sucked me in. I introduced myself into its gelatinous edges, I cavorted in that forest of hair and spongy flesh, I sailed through the humid canals of that shell of flesh, I gyrated and drew to myself urban noises, the silence of History. And without knowing how, I found myself there, firm, scared, looking at a sunrise in 1702, far removed from the twentieth century.

"I would like this one to be my personal bodyguard," said Lord Cornbury as he pointed his gaunt finger at me. I was thunderstruck by that command, and shame and fear went like lightning through my body. I was a British soldier and, as you know, British soldiers should not show in their demeanor the slightest bit of emotion.

The other soldiers also never flinched when, in the morning, Lord Cornbury would inspect the troops dressed in a woman's gown and hat. The day he chose me for his personal service, when I returned to the barracks, the soldiers were laughing and talking behind my back. I lowered my head, did not speak to any of them, but I kept asking myself: "Why did this faggot choose me?" When silently I would talk to myself, I heard strange noises of a brutal city in my head. I heard the steps of thousands, the screeching of rubber tires in the streets, the voices of multitudes that moved rapidly from one place to the other.

When I appeared in Lord Cornbury's quarters, he was already wearing his governor's attire. As soon as he saw me he said: "Come here. Take your cap off. Let's see, let's see..." And with his exquisitely thin fingers he took my ear, he pawed it, he caressed it, he looked at it, he looked at it again. Like a good British soldier, I remained silent, unmoved. At the beginning that game disgusted me, later I began to enjoy it and, slowly, the silky flesh that caressed my ear every morning became familiar to me.

True or not, the rumors of Lord Cornbury's wedding in England, to Katherine, Baroness Clifton of Leighton, were making the rounds. It was said that he had chosen his future wife, among a group of even more beautiful noblewomen, because he had liked her ears. On his wedding day Lord Cornbury did not kiss her mouth; he kissed her ears. And during the welcoming banquet by the members of the British colony, the newly appointed governor devoted his speech to the praise of his wife's ears. During the panegyric, Lord Cornbury went to such extremes that he asked all the men present to come and feel Lady Cornbury's ears, so that they could see that he was not exaggerating.

Lord Cornbury had arrived in New York with incredible credentials: a cousin of Queen Anne of England, he had been a Member of Parliament for sixteen years, and he was a veteran of King William II's army. He had seven children with Katherine and, in spite of his extravagant behavior, no one ever doubted his masculinity. It was, however, a well-known fact that he loved ears.

The biggest scandal surrounding him was the attempt by an ignorant sentinel to arrest him. At sunset, Lord Cornbury used to take walks along Broadway, or to amble along the parapets of the fort, alone, dressed in one of his wife's frocks. One night, a newly arrived soldier, unaware of the governor's habits, saw, in the evening, a prostitute that seemed to look for men as she walked close to the fortress walls. The soldier stopped her and the prostitute, Lord Cornbury, began to slap him, insult him, pull his ears. The poor soldier insisted in his duty to arrest her, even though the prostitute claimed to be the governor. Rudely he took her to the barracks and when he got there he saw the pale faces of his superiors, and they began to hit him while apologizing to Lord Cornbury. The governor, without skipping a beat, rearranged his dress, looked at the soldier forgivingly, pulled his ears and left.

After that incident Lord Cornbury asked me to accompany him during his nocturnal strolls. I would follow him without saying a word. I saw him withdraw into himself, as if he were enclosed in thoughts that transported him to another place, another time. During one of those walks, without looking at me or stopping his stride, he said: "Do you believe that one could have lived other lives?" I asked him: "Excuse me, Sir, I know not what you mean by that." And then he told me: "Well, whether you believe that we human beings can live various lives, in different times, in other ages." "I know not, Sir," I answered, "I do not know a thing about that." Lord Cornbury went on walking, as if he were thinking about what he had said to me.

I was fond of Lord Cornbury and I believe he also was fond of me, but his wife I hated. Lady Cornbury was famous because she would borrow clothes—that both she and her husband could wear—from New York aristocratic women, and later she would fail to return them. Every time she visited someone she took something away: some candelabra, dishes, a small painting. People had to tolerate such abuse because she was the First Lady, the governor's wife. When they saw her carriage, the only one in New York at the time, they began to hide all valuable objects. It was useless, because when they least expected it, one of Lady Cornbury's servants would arrive, and, ordered by his mistress, would ask for money, cups, knives, or other things that were never returned. When the governor's wife died in 1706, the wealthy families of the City were free from her abuses. Because of this, they happily paid for her funeral and her grave at the Trinity Church cemetery.

From the moment his wife died, Lord Cornbury was irremediably saddened. During our strolls along the parapets, he would dress in black, like a widow, speaking to himself and some-times, without looking at me, he would address me. One evening he said: "Eustachi"— he used to call me that way in order not to pronounce my name—"do you believe that people truthfully love one another or do we only need one another? Or to love is to need?" "Well, Sir, I do not know a thing about that," I answered. "But Eustachi, you do not love someone?" he told me. "Yes, Sir, I love my mother." And Lord Cornbury, for the first time during those walks, turned toward me, looked at me and smiled. In that moment I heard strange noises of an immense city in my head, I heard the steps of thousands, the screeching of rubber tires in the streets, the voices of multitudes that moved rapidly from one place to the other.

The two years that followed his wife's death were terrible. Lord Cornbury borrowed money from everyone, he kept the colony's income taxes, he forced upon the community the morals of the Anglican Church, and engaged in all kinds of abuse toward the inhabitants of New York. His injustices were such that his cousin, Queen Anne, decided to remove him from office and ordered him to return to England.

But when, in 1708, Lord Cornbury was going to sail (his children had left already), his creditors arrested him, turned him over to the city's sheriff, and put him in jail. His imprisonment was a blessing for me since for a whole year I went to see him daily. In some way his disgrace allowed us to get to know each other and, in spite of the gossip, I spent two or three hours with him every afternoon. He would caress my ears, he spoke to himself, with-out looking at me. Whenever he began those long monologues, he would say: "Eustachi, tell me…" even though, of course, he never expected an answer. He would speak of palm trees, oceans, coral reefs, of men of color, fruits and exotic birds. Frequently, he repeated two phrases: "Oh, Lord, why have you made me this way?" And, "*Putana, putana...*"

During that year of imprisonment I told him: "Sir, I would like to have a portrait of you." He answered: "Well, but who is going to pay for it?" I told him not to worry. Thus with some money I had saved, I looked for a mediocre Dutch painter who lived in the lower part of the City. I asked a friend of mine, a prostitute, to pose for the artist. I told him to paint only the body of a prostitute but to dress her in a noble woman's gown, with a grande-dame posture, with a fan in her hand, on a dark background and with a folded panel of red drape on the right section of the painting. When the painter finished that faceless portrait, we went with the painting to the jail where Lord Cornbury was imprisoned. There the artist painted, on the canvas, above the body of the prostitute, Lord Cornbury's face, lightly turned sideways, showing his enormous fleshy ear. The Dutchman said he would not sign the painting and that he did not want anyone to find out about it.

Some months after the painting was finished, Lord Cornbury's father, the Count of Clarendon, died in England. The ex-governor paid some of his debts with the paternal inheritance and could thus return to London, where again he occupied his seat in the House of Lords.

Frequently I looked at the portrait of Lord Cornbury I had in my house. I do not know if I was endearing to him or not, whether I was only a diversion, my ears a fixation. What I do know is that one day in 1723 they came to tell me that I had received a package from England. I went to collect it, I took it home, I opened it. Wrapped in a piece of paper was Lord

Cornbury's embalmed ear.

With the ear there was a letter signed by one of his children. The letter read: "Sir, my father, who died some months ago, and who has been the bane of our family and of all of England, entrusted us to sever his right ear, to embalm it and to send it to you. I do hope it has arrived intact. The other, the left ear, we also severed, but that one we gave to the dogs."

I placed the ear on a small table in front of the portrait of Lord Cornbury. Every now and then I put flowers there. But his face made me as nervous as it did the first day I met him. In my head, his words still echoed: "Eustachi, tell me…" and the strange noises of an immense city, the steps of thousands of hurried people, the friction of wheels that were not iron nor wood, trumpets that blared discordantly.

I do not know whether he loved me a little or not. Now among his papers in the archives of the New York Historical Society, I look for a letter, a sign, a reference to that soldier who inherited Lord Cornbury's ear.

Photo: MA

ERASMO GUERRA's stories have appeared in *The James White Review* and the anthologies *New World: Young Latino Writers* (Delta, 1997), *Gay Literary Travels* (Whereabout, 1998), and *Men Seeking Men* (Painted Leaf, 1998). He is a writing fellow at the Vermont Studio Center, and the editor of the forthcoming anthology, *Latin Lovers* (Painted Leaf Press).

BETWEEN DANCES

→

Erasmo Guerra

Marco didn't want to dance. He didn't want to get back onstage and do his last number for the night. The hour had dragged its naked ass to three in the morning and everything hurt and ached. The scrap between his legs felt raw from pulling on it too many times and from having too many strange men suck it in his hotel room between dances. It hurt to even touch it.

He stood behind the back curtain, listening to his song and its forced cheer collapsing like soap bubbles. What was he doing here, he wondered. The question inevitably asked itself at some point during the night, the interrogative words loud and demanding as the songs that blared over the speakers. He lanced those suspended moments with whatever thin excuse he found or let them fall and shatter from their own weight. They always did. If he ignored them long enough. Tonight, with exhaustion weighing him down, he thought it better to be done with it, to part the curtains and go out before the DJ decided to start the record again. He pushed himself onto the stage and stripped to his white briefs without choreographing any of his moves to the music. He then slipped behind the curtain again, to the narrow corridor backstage. The gay dancers, the ones who admitted it, stroked off here. The straight ones jerked off on the other side, in the main room with the lockers. In whatever part of the theater he stood, however, the same dingy smell of sweaty crotches and damp bills penetrated his senses.

He had little more than a minute now. A minute to get himself hard and back out for his second song. This was the *spectacular* part of the live show to which the ads in the papers referred: an uncompromising view of his body. The audience expected him hard, but already he could hear its hiss of disappointment once he went back out there again. He didn't care, though. He only wanted to get back to his room to sleep.

Marco moved to the end of the corridor and pulled off his underwear. He made sure his money was still in his sock and then laced up his boots slowly, steadying his breath, searching for a fragmentary thought or image that could get him off. He sat on his clothes spread over the radiator and stroked himself to the guy in the pool, the one in the porn magazine he had bought last week. Marco called him out from memory. He didn't have enough time to get the magazine from his locker and didn't want to deal with the guys in the other room. He heard their voices, pinched and shallow, as if tightly holding their breath. They were arguing about the female strippers they had picked up after last night's show, and more than likely were passing around a joint. His concentration splintered and broke so that in his mind there floated the disembodied parts of the tanned guy, the aquamarine water, the long white pool chair. The john

Marco had been with earlier that night suddenly swam into his head. That guy had been as worn as a seat in the theater, stained and banged up and suspiciously mute. Looking at him, even by the warm lights of the bed-side lamps, had made Marco want to leave the business and the city altogether. Thinking about the guy in the pool had helped then. He wasn't much help now.

Marco tried to call in the other guys from the magazine, the way he sometimes did when he had the magazine with him, turning the pages quickly, holding each picture for a moment, all of them building to an eventual rush of blood to his dick. When that didn't work, he simply prayed, making a *promesa* to San Juditas, the way his mother taught him. San Juditas was the patron saint of lost causes, but this particular night, even he was of no use. Marco pulled at himself, slapping the dead skin against his hips, forcing blood to it, but it remained limp. Patrick appeared at the other end of the corridor, by the edge of the steps. He stood there naked, pulling on his own soft dick.

"Sorry," he said. "Didn't know you were here."

"That's all right," Marco offered. "This thing ain't getting up anyway. I think I killed it."

"Forget it. It's the last dance. There ain't nobody out there."

Patrick came down and stood off to the side, stroking himself without apology. His eyebrows butted into a single thick line. The rest of his face, though handsome, looked hammered by a stony seriousness. All the dancers had that aggravated look when they needed to get hard.

"Here," Patrick said, spitting into his hands and grabbing Marco's dick.

Marco watched the stairs, afraid one of the other guys would find them. Patrick didn't seem worried though. He massaged

Marco's bruised flesh, taking it in the palm of his hands and finally his mouth. The second song came up then, Boy George singing a remixed version of "Do You Really Want To Hurt Me." The lyrics were a bit pathetic, but Marco preferred them over the melodramatic love songs that most of the other guys danced to. Those songs never felt honest to him. The red lights came on full and bled under the back curtain. His cue. He was hard, but he couldn't feel it. His dick seemed to belong to someone else. He kissed Patrick, and feeling nothing at all, his entire body numb, rushed out onto the stage.

No one clapped. The few men that remained for the last show didn't care about Marco's hard-on. They didn't seem to care about anything. They were either too drunk to notice him or had fallen asleep, heads back against the seats, mouths open. Marco danced anyway, as if enjoying himself, though he knew he didn't have to. This was the last dance and he could do more dancing and less showing. He could enjoy himself moving around the stage instead of pretending so the men could get off or think he might be fun to be with in a private show. He swung his arms overhead and rocked his pelvis, his soft thrusts leading him across the stage and up the ramp that plunged into the field of empty seats. He always tried to make a show of it, giving the men their money's worth, since the muscle guys did nothing more than strike poses as if in a bodybuilding competition and the others strutted around, winking and pointing at the men in the audience as if they were in some defunct lounge act.

Marco could dance, and had been dancing since before he was even able to dress himself. His mother would button and zip him into his clothes, sometimes forcing him into wearing a cheap clip-on tie. His father would have already eaten his dinner and left the house for whatever place the dance was going to be. He was one of the musicians for the band Los Chamacos del Río. They played all of the Valley, even once played El Show de Tony Perales. The whole family went to his gigs. Marco and his little brother enjoyed the late nights, running among the dancing bodies, playing tag or hide-and-seek, licking the beer caps they collected. The adults were either too drunk or set on getting laid or into a fight to care about whatever they did. Even their mother got swept up, dancing with her brothers, one after another, exhausting them and crippling their already bad feet, lamed by their pointy boots. If his mother ever sat out a song though, she usually caught Marco and his brother sliding on their knees, across the polished floors of the dance hall, as they liked to do. She'd clatter over in her spiked heels and yank them to their feet, cursing them as *hijos de la mañana* and pull them back to their table where she'd make them sit there with *las cuatas*, their twin sisters with lip-glossed mouths tight as the ironed curls in their hair, their only words a whine or moan about how they would rather be at home watching television or talking on the phone. His mother would ignore their complaints, biting her painted fingernails, or pouring herself another vodka grapefruit. She'd slug back her obvious disappointment that she couldn't dance with the musicians, not even her husband. Then she'd look over at Marco and wink, as if he'd suddenly become her little prince again, her king, as she liked to say, and she'd pull him out to the dance floor when the next *ranchera* or *corrido* shot out with its shattering *grito*.

Tonight, at the theater, the song didn't go to the end. The DJ stopped it before the second chorus. *Let's hear it for Marco*, he monotoned into the microphone. A weary clap struggled up from the back, but it was too dark for Marco to notice who it was. He hoped it was Chris. He hadn't seen Chris in months.

As the last dancer did his number, Marco went to his locker for his magazine. He needed it for the finale. He didn't think he would have Patrick's help again since he found him in the main room, sitting on one of the benches, listening to the other guys talk about how they were going back to the strip joint. Dallas, one of the muscle guys, leaned up against the lockers and worked his oiled dick with one hand. With the other he held a porn magazine.

"I know you ain't going," he told Marco, then turned to everyone else. "Kid gets his rocks off watching us. We should start charging him."

A thin laughter broke out like the distant rumble of a subway train. Everyone seemed too battered to offer any more. The other dancers were preoccupied with getting themselves ready for the finale or ignored it altogether and lazily picked at the blackheads on their chins or laid out on the benches with their arms over their eyes. Even Dallas gave up and flung his magazine into his locker. He posed for himself in the mirror. With his distended muscles and burnt-orange skin, the results of too many hours in a gym and tanning booth, Dallas looked like a sideshow freak on the Coney Island boardwalk. All the muscle guys did. Not every john liked them though. Marco worked the post-adolescent look. Under the colored stage lights, he looked younger than his age. One night, when the female strippers came to the theater to wait for Dallas and the other guys, the women flocked around him in their gaudy dresses. They tousled his hair and wondered if he was legal enough to dance.

He went to the other side of the backstage, but even with his magazine and the other naked guys standing by him, he couldn't get hard for the finale. He looked for Patrick, but Patrick must have stayed by the lockers because he wasn't around. Marco thought it might be for the best. He didn't want Patrick to think he was interested in him.

Onstage, Marco stood with a limp dick like everybody else and he thought about those women again, figured they had it easy. They could fake their excitement.

The muscle guys huddled together, slapping one another on the ass and bending over to fart into what remained of the audience. Marco looked out into the shadowy seats. The stage lights were on full, but he still couldn't tell if anyone in the rear seats was Chris.

Backstage, Marco dressed quickly and then went out to the lounge where a few crumpled old men waited for the final exit parade of dancers. He didn't bother. The stragglers usually didn't have any money, or the money they did have was never enough to buy off his fatigue and need for sleep. He checked the theater, the box office, and then the DJ booth, but those places were empty and Chris was nowhere. His only surprise came from the sudden need to see him.

He slipped into the bathroom to splash water on his face. He avoided his reflection in the mirror. He'd wasted too many years looking at himself in mirrors and in the reflections of glass store-fronts and car windshields. He knew what he looked like, and at the end of a dance marathon, he could feel it to his teeth. His eyes would be lined in heavy red strokes, weary from watching too many men watch him. His face would be greasy, slick pores opened wide or clogged with the beginnings of pimples from staying up late. His father had told him that he wouldn't get any more pimples once he started dating girls. Marco figured he meant he wouldn't get them once he started having sex, but here he was in his early twenties, having more sex than he wanted, and his face still broke out with regularity. He hoped the blemishes made him look young, like a hormonal adolescent, like some of the johns said. He wanted to believe them, pushing out the dream he'd been having lately, a dream in which he went to a bar and waited for the men to come to him, but none do, until finally another hustler comes up and talks to him as if to make a proposition. Marco tells him he's selling too and the guy combusts into a fireball of laughter. It isn't until he goes to the bathroom that Marco sees how old he is, wrinkled and spotted with an age no dim room could mask.

Standing there, in the bathroom with its unsettling blue light, Marco had the vague sense that the particular night of his dreams wasn't too far off. His twenty-fourth birthday was only a few months away and then what? He didn't know. He only started thinking about what he might do or where he might go that night, after the last guy left him feeling as if he'd really earned every dollar. The money was far from easy now, and he knew he soon wouldn't be able to make any. And he had nothing saved. All the money he made was spent on bills or rent or food. The money disappeared faster than a yellow cab hurtling down Broadway.

"Thought you'd already left," Patrick said, out of breath and smelling of smoke. "You going out tonight? The Factory should be hot around now."

"I couldn't dance another song." Marco reached for the paper towels to dry his face. He couldn't remember the last time he'd gone out to a club after a night at the theater. It must have been about the time Chris stopped working, or soon after. He looked at Patrick who said nothing, leaning against the sink, a faint expression of concern darkening his forehead.

"You going back to your room?" Patrick asked.

"No," Marco said and then lied, "I'm meeting a friend downtown."

He said it only to discourage Patrick from making any proposals. He didn't want to go dancing with him, back to the hotel room, or to Patrick's apartment as they had the last time. More than anything though, Marco wanted to believe that Chris waited for him.

He dried his hands and thought this would have been the end of it, he would throw the paper towel into the wastebasket and leave the theater altogether, the damp paper putting out whatever embers of interest smoldered in Patrick's crotch. But no, the rejection only seemed to fuel Patrick. He asked Marco if he wanted to share a cab. He was headed downtown too. Marco could have said no, but he accepted the offer. He thought he may as well go see Chris.

The ride was quiet except for the incessant hollow sound of the vents. They spewed an air so hot it was as if the car was coughing up all the heated air it had swallowed during the summer months. Marco tried not to think back to that time, hoping the heat would burn away each thorn of memory.

"You're not going out to Flashdancers with the other guys?" Marco asked.

"What for?"

"I thought you were into that."

"I'm not. I don't like going there at all. It's pretty sleazy going there to buy those whores. I don't do that. I have a girlfriend."

"Jennifer, right?"

"Jane."

Patrick said her name with a dull smile like he had the night she walked in on them at Patrick's apartment. Marco couldn't remember what she looked like, the anger and surprise that had percolated into his eyes that night had washed out her face.

"I hate cheating on her," Patrick said, his voice serious and apologetic. "She's too much of a good friend, you know. Sometimes I think we're better friends than lovers, but I like her. It's like she knows what I'm thinking and I know what she's thinking. Like soulmates or something."

"Does she know you dance?"

"Yeah. She's even come by a couple of times with her friends."

"Nothing about the theater shocks me either, I guess." Marco looked out at the dim impressions of the city. "I don't think I could ever get involved with anyone who does this for a living." The words came out flat and measured. Marco had said them so many times. "It's too much to worry about. Like what if he falls in love with somebody, you know?"

"Well, my girlfriend doesn't have to worry about that. I don't really like men all that much." Patrick squeezed Marco's leg as if in consolation.

Marco moved his leg away. "What's all that much?"

"Well, money makes the difference."

"Is this where you tell me how much I owe you for your help back there?"

"Nah. I wanted to do that. It's on the house."

The cab made a sharp turn onto Second Avenue, sliding them closer together. Patrick had a sweet stink to him, like the incense some drivers burned in their cabs. Marco imagined the heated smell unfurling and spiraling around him, dizzying him, making him doubt what he thought he wanted. He'd made up his mind that he would never go home with Patrick again or with any straight guy. He didn't want that. The experience always left him feeling used like no john could, because at least the johns paid money. The straight guys never gave him much of anything other than a momentary thrill, the fleeting thought that he might be their first. He didn't believe that anymore. Chris had convinced him that when a guy at the theater said he was straight, it only meant straight to bed and straight up the ass.

"Where are you going anyway?" Patrick whispered. "To see a boyfriend?"

"No, just a friend."

"You don't want to go back to my place? We don't have to do anything, you know, just hang out or whatever."

"What about Jennifer?"

"She's gone to Toronto to visit her folks."

"Wasn't that where she was supposed to be the last time?"

Patrick smiled at him slightly and then opened his mouth to say something, but his lips hung there, his teeth a faint glow from the passing headlights of other cabs rushing through the black streets. He said, "You're not like the other guys, Marco."

His name wasn't Marco, but he used it at the theater and hardly answered to his real name anymore. Patrick wasn't Patrick's real name either. His girlfriend had cried out some other name that Marco didn't remember now.

"Let's go back to my place," Patrick said, his voice low.

"My friend is waiting for me."

"He's really waiting for you?"

Before he could insist that he was, the cab stopped on East

17th by the gothic wrought-iron fence of Stuyvesant Park. Marco got out. Patrick slipped him a piece of paper on which he had scrawled a phone number and what Marco assumed to be his real name. Marco pulled out a few bills for the cab, but Patrick wouldn't take it.

"Call me and it'll be even," he said. "Besides, I scored more money than you tonight."

"Go ahead and think that," Marco said and shut the door.

Patrick put a loose fist to his ear in the shape of a phone. Marco nodded. The cab sped off and Marco walked down to the hotel where Chris lived.

Hotel Seventeen could have been any other roach-trap in the city were it not for the fashion photographers who used it as a location for their bohemian-inspired shoots and the small-time celebrity club kids who lived there. The residents were roomed according to the degree of their fame with the drag queens and trannies taking much of the top floor. Chris lived on one of the bottom floors, in a narrow room with peeling wallpaper and a bankrupt bed. He lived little better than the homeless who pitched their cardboard shelters in the park and in the doorframe of the nearby church. Chris endured it because he wanted to make a short film about the hotel and its tenants, but Marco guessed it was because Chris thought he was among the fabulous.

The guy at the desk was new. He wasn't the fat-faced blond boy who worked during the day or the weathered thirty-year-old manager. The new guy seemed to suffer from anemia or anorexia, had long knotted hair and silvery half-circles punched under his eyes, and he was about as useful as the moon. He wouldn't buzz

Chris because it was past four in the morning and official visiting hours had ended at midnight.

"He's expecting me," Marco lied, more to himself than the desk guy.

The guy buzzed the room. Once. Then again. No answer.

Out on the stoop, Marco tried to think of where he should go next, if anywhere. He knew he didn't have the energy for an after-hours club or Patrick. If he wanted sex, he only had to walk back to Stuyvesant Park, wander the maze of benches and desiccated hedges, and wait under the pools of the sodium lamps. He didn't want that, though. He was afraid he might run into Chris there. All too suddenly, he didn't want Chris to find him, not just in the park, but at the hotel, searching him out as if coming back on night's bruised knees. He flagged a cab and rode back to Midtown, to the hotel he had rented for the weekend. It was easier than going home at that thin hour.

He bought a cup of tea and a bagel at the deli across the street from his hotel and went back up to his room. The woman at the front desk usually gave him a crummy room with a burnt-out television and a dead radiator. He didn't care most times. The worse the room looked, the colder it felt, the easier it seemed to get the men out of there so he could make the next dance. This time, his room was warm, and he sat on the bed, cross-legged, eating and listening to the clanging radiator and the orders being shouted across the street on the loading docks of the *New York Times*. He fell asleep to those snarling voices coming over the speakers, voices spitting out directions to the trucks that would deliver the morning paper.

JAIME CORTEZ is a San-Francisco based visual artist, writer and performer. He was raised in Mexicali, Baja California, and Watsonville and San Juan Bautista in Alta California. He was the editor of the zine *A La Brava* and the co-founder of the comedy group Latin Hustle. His work appears in *Queer PAPI Porn* (Cleis Press) and *2sexE* (North Atlantic Press). Cortez is currently working with Cleis Press, editing an anthology of queer Latino writings.

THE NASTY BOOK WARS

→

Jaime Cortez

I

When you leave a grapefruit on a countertop for several weeks, the membranes and fruity ligaments that hold together the pleasantly rounded shape slowly weaken. Gravity insinuates itself, and the citrus's hapless bottom begins a relentless downward migration. Eventually, the underside spreads and takes on the flatness of the counter, while the top grows ever thinner. This defeated grapefruit shape was precisely the shape of Ralph Duarte's head. On top of that, Ralph had no goddamned neck. His purple, liquor-swollen face sat squarely on his collarbones.

My father, possessed of a cruel genius for transforming physical defects into nicknames, watched Ralph at the wedding of Ligo and noticeably pregnant Chelo. Poor drunken Ralph was feeling particularly dapper in his rented tuxedo, his bow tie securely strapped somewhere in the vicinity of his double chin. Everyone got tremendous comic mileage out of Ralph's neckwear, but he went on dancing and drinking, obliviously shaking his beer gut and gyrating the sad bit of protoplasm he alleged was his ass. At some point that night, Daddy christened him "Head and Shoulders." The name stuck.

The women in the labor camp remained respectful, calling him Rafa as always, but the men were relentless, batting his new nickname back and forth across the blistering August garlic fields. He was a good guy about the name thing, though. When I called him Head and Shoulders, he actually laughed, releasing a great cloud of beer breath into my face. I decided I liked him despite his barfy smell.

Head and Shoulders' last day at the Wyrick Labor Camp came within a week of the wedding. Three INS vans descended upon the garlic field just before the midmorning break. He had already sucked down three very tall cans of Coors. He tried to dash across the field and hide in the cattails on the banks of the irrigation ditch, but he was too far gone on his breakfast beers. Tripping over a clod, he sprawled on the ground, arms and legs spread out like the Carl's Jr. star. His beer shot forth a geyser of foam but, amazingly, he *never* let that can go. The INS agents surrounded him and lifted him off the ground. With his free hand, he sheepishly dusted himself off. He winked at me, and raised his beer can to his lips, tilted his head back, opened his throat, and poured in the pissy remains. Conspicuously pregnant Chelo cried silently as Head and Shoulders bent his back and entered the paddy wagon. Ligo tilted his head, sucked his teeth, and intoned, "Oh well, at least he got to finish his Coors."

That evening, the foreman's wife cleared out Head and Shoulders' tiny rental room in the big house. She packed his clothes into grocery bags in case he should return, looking sadly at his undershirts, stiff and a murky gray from bad washings with colored clothes, insufficient detergent, and a Downy deficiency. The lone men who rented rooms in the big house always seemed so unable to care for themselves. She Ajaxed his one-burner hot plate for the next tenant to use. From behind the crook of a willow tree, my sister Erma, cousin Lola, cousin Chucho, and I watched her cleaning with particular interest. As soon as she left, we pried the window open, climbed into the room, and began rooting around, hoping to find a spare nickel under the bed, or matches or maybe even cigarettes. From inside the wardrobe, Erma and Chucho gasped simultaneously.

"Oh my gawd! Oh my gawd! Oh my gawd!" said Erma.

"What is it?" I shouted.

"Oh my god," added Chucho. Together they dragged out a grocery bag filled to the top with nasty girl magazines.

We swooped upon the bag, tearing it to pieces as we reached in to pull out nasty books. Each of us grabbed a handful and retreated from the others like wolves with a deer's legs.

"Ooooooh," I chanted, from behind my copy of *Cheri* magazine, "you can see her guts." I turned the centerfold around so everyone could see the tragically eviscerated blonde.

"Thass not her guts, stupid," snarled Chucho, "Thass her pussy." At twelve, Chucho was the oldest, and our resident sexpert. Little Lola was as confused as I was.

"How come isss all hairy?"

Chucho had had enough. "Stupid, you're a bonehead, Lola. Get out of here, this isn't for little kids." Lola became teary-eyed at the rejection and pleaded her case.

"I was just asking howcum iss all hairy, you don't have to throw me out."

"GET OUT!"

"I'm gonna tell Mom," she threatened, her voice quavering.

"All right, then," Chucho agreed, "shut up and don't ask any more stupid questions."

"I'm just asking howcum it's all hairy, that's all," she repeated.

"Look, little baby," said Erma, "when women grow up they get hair. Your mom has hair down there and when you grow up, you will too."

"No sir," said Lola in a tone that was half denial, half question.

"Yes you will," insisted Erma, "all kinds of hair, down to your knees probably. Like it or don't." This bushy prospect was too much for Lola. She began to wail.

"All right," said Chucho. "You girls get outta here. We've gotta take these books and put 'em someplace safe."

"They're not your books, you know," countered Erma. "We found them at the same time, so they're everybody's." Chucho was nearing the end of his patience.

"Stupid, these books are for MEN, not GIRLS! What do you want 'em for?"

"You're not MEN," shrieked Erma, "You're just BOYS! And the girls wanna look at the pictures." Teary-eyed Lola nodded her head in agreement.

"These books belong to the boys," Chucho proclaimed. "And we're taking them."

"Yeah, the boys," I added. I could not have been less interested in the magazines, but I was a dutiful foot soldier in the gender wars.

Suddenly Erma plunged her hands into the stack of magazines and made for the door with a bunch of them. Chucho grabbed her by the pigtail and pulled her back into the room and they began to fight, the both of them sliding on the glossy paper. Lola and I entered the fray and there ensued a tremendous ripping of paper, yanking of hair and centerfolds, and opportunistic biting. The girls were scrappy, but they were no match for Chucho's brutal rabbit punches and my size. In short order, we expelled them from the room and locked the door behind them. Erma, with a bit of crumpled centerfold still in her clenched fist, beat the door.

"Open the door, Jaime."

Red in the face and panting, I shouted back at her: "These are for BOYS, Erma. Go find your own books."

"THERE AREN'T ANY, SO THE BOYS HAVE TO SHARE, IDIOT!!!" Chucho brayed his evil laugh, right against the door, and Erma gave the door one last wallop with her bony fist.

"We'll be back, fuckers! And we'll bring help!"

Chucho and I collapsed on the floor, rolling around in the porno and kissing the centerfolds. It was sweet to have won the first skirmish of the nasty book wars.

II

In Head and Shoulders' darkened room, Chucho and I crouched by the window. "Do you see 'em anywhere out there, Jaime?"

"Nope. I think they're gone."

"You know the plan, right?"

"Yes. You only told me it a hundred times."

"I'm jus' checking. If you know it, tell me it."

"We hide the books under the bed, and fill the bag with Head and Shoulders' clothes. I run out with the bag, and pretend it's the books, and I hide them under the porch, and they'll see me, and think they know our secret hiding place, but really they don't 'cause you'll for really have the books and you'll hide them in the tractor barn, and tomorrow we can look at them all day."

"Perfect. They'll never figure it out. It's perfect."

I slipped out of Ralph's window, and Chucho handed me the bag. I made a big show of pretending it was heavy with books. I lurched to the front porch, opening the little iron-grill door that led to the space under the porch. As soon as I had disappeared beneath the stairs, I heard footsteps. Through a crack in the stairs, I saw Lola and Manuela. Shit, the girls had reinforcements.

"Ooh, Lola. I think there's something under the stairs. I think it's an animal."

"No it wasn't it was Jai—"

"Shut up idiot! It was an animal, I think it was a pig. We'd better lock it in before it eats Daddy's cucumber plants." Before I could scramble out from under the stairs, Manuela closed the latch on the iron grill.

"Look Lola. It's one of those wild pigs. See how wild he is."

"You better let me out, fucker!" I hissed.

"Ooh, the pig is mad, but he better not get too mad, 'cause his mami is right in the kitchen and she'll come out if he makes too much noise, and she'll wanna know what you were doing down there, and we'll have to tell her all about the nasty books." I glared at her through the grill. She smiled serenely. "You guys think we're stupid but we're not. Right now Erma and big Cookie are kicking Chucho's ass and getting those books back. That's what you get for not sharing with the girls, fuckers!"

"Open the gate!" I hissed between clenched teeth.

"Sorry. Retarded pigs have to stay in their cages till we say. Bye-bye!" Manuela turned heel and ran off toward the barn. I crouched beneath the porch for what seemed like a long time, and finally Manuela returned and opened the latch. I immediately bolted for the tractor barn. There I found Chucho pinned stomach-down underneath Big Cookie, who was counting out loud, her fleshy lips slowly intoning each number.

"One hundred five. One hundred six. One hundred..."

Manolo's ambush had been a rough one. Torn scraps of nasty books were strewn about them in a circle. Chucho and Cookie were filthy from rolling around in the oily dirt of the tractor barn.

"Those magazines are for men, you fuckers."

"Not anymore, Chucho. Now they're ours, and we're taking them."

"You guys are stupid, what do you wanna see naked girls for?"

"That's for me to know and you to find out. Now shut your hole and let me count to two hundred so I can let you go."

"Fuckers," spit out Chucho.

"You guys are the fuckers. If you had just shared, we would all have our magazines instead of kicking your ass all over the barn. Now stop squirming, you idiot, or we'll never get to two hundred."

III

Girls are, of course, far more advanced than boys in the realm of psychological torture and manipulation. For the next few days, Chucho and I were led on a raging game of follow the leader. We'd spy on the four of them as they'd gather and move on purposefully to some unlikely place like the garbage heap or the inside of an abandoned Chevy that rusted away on the edge of the fields. There they would huddle tightly, their eyes turned inward, backs obscuring their actions. Chucho and I would descend upon them with an "AHA!" only to find them empty-handed.

"Looking for something?"

"No."

"Then why did you say 'Aha,' idiot?"

"Just because."

"You'll never guess where we put 'em, Chucho. You know why? Because you're an M.R. and because we're smart. We might wait fifty-seven-hundred-millions of days before we even look at 'em. We're very patient. But if you're nice for once, we might let you look"—Chucho brightened—"at a staple from the pages." Mocking laughter lashed us as we retreated. Entire days passed, and we saw no signs of activity. I was rapidly losing morale and interest, but it had become a personal thing with Chucho.

"Jaime, I have a plan."

"What's the plan?"

"Secret. But you gotta be in the plan or it doesn't work."

"What am I gonna do?"

"It's a secret, stupid. Just do what I tell you. First we gotta find Lola."

"I think she's over by the trailer."

"Good. C'mon."

As we approached, we heard Lola holding court at an al fresco tea party in the garden behind the trailer. Kneeling in the dust, she contentedly served up mud pies and tin cans of water to her assembled collection of ravaged, special needs dolls, all of whom resembled nothing so much as extras from *Les Misérables.* The stellar hostess always, she even serenaded them with one of her patented fuck-up songs.

"Conjunction Junction, what's your fuck shuh? Lookin' at worse, and raisins and closets."

"Get her," whispered Chucho. I pounced from behind the trailer and grabbed her from behind. Chucho assumed the role of grand inquisitor.

"Lola, where are the nasty books?"

"I don' know."

"Don't be stupid, Lola, or we'll make you suffer."

Less convincingly now, she repeated. "I don't know."

"Gimme your hand, bonehead."

"Nooo." He took it anyway. He produced a little cereal box magnifying glass from his pocket. Holding her hand steady, he focused the sunlight to a tight white point. Lola was confused for a moment, but then howled.

"Oooow. Don't do that. You're cutting me."

"I'm not cutting you, stupid. I'm burning you."

"You're burning me." He pulled the glass away.

"Lola, if I use the glass longer, your whole hand will burn and you'll die and go to Hell with the Devil because you lied to me right before I killed you. Do you know what it's like in Hell?" Lola nodded through tears. Aside from Disneyland, Hell was the most-discussed and theorized destination among the labor camp children. Chucho refocused the beam of light on the back of her wrist.

"Have fun in Hell, Lola. Say hello to Frankystein and the other monsters." Lola opened her mouth wide, she was one of those delayed howl kids who held their mouths open for days before unleashing a cry. I clamped my grubby hand on her mouth just as the early rumblings made their way up her throat. The three of us watched the incineration process intently. Chucho was sweaty with concentration, and Lola's face turned a rich red. In the cruel beam of sunlight, her downy arm hairs curled slightly as they began to singe.

"OKAY!" she shouted, breaking free of my hand. "Okay, I'll tell you. It's in the frigilater. By the big house."

"Let her go. Next time, you don't take our stuff, Lola."

"Yes we will," she countered, flinging mud pies at our backs as we retreated. We were impressed by Lola's spunk but laughed anyway. The Gods of War were with us again.

IV

The nasty books were stuffed into the meat bin of the abandoned refrigerator. They smelled weird now, and many of the pages had oily dirt and footprints from Chucho's ambush in the tractor barn. Still, our joy was expansive as we repacked the well-traveled magazines into a burlap sack. We had only a few minutes to act before Lola and the girls found us. We grabbed shovels and a hoe from the toolshed en route to the garlic field. There, we hid behind the mammoth wheel of a tractor and began digging.

"This is perfect, Jaime, they'll never find our books now," grunted Chucho as he shoveled.

"Yeah, perfect." We buried the nasty books and headed back to the toolshed. On our way, the girls intercepted us but said nothing. We retreated, checking behind us all the way for some unexpected maneuver. Anything was possible.

That night I tossed in bed. In the bunk above mine, my sister lay silently. Silence was all we had shared through dinner, *Sanford and Son,* and the preparations for sleep. Our war had escalated, taken on its own momentum. No one seemed to care about the books anymore. It was now a war for the honor of the boys or the girls. This was a situation utterly untenable to a sissy like me. I wanted to tell her where they were, but that would show Chucho I wasn't a real boy. He would then sever my tenuous connections to boyness and force me to be with the girls or all alone. That was more than I could tolerate. Something was terribly wrong with me and my problem was greater than my language. I counted sheep, and then horses. Deep into my chicken count, I finally fell asleep.

For three days, we let the books lay in the soil like fleshy seeds. We were waiting, waiting, for things to cool down. On the fourth morning, at 6 A.M., I did not hear the rumbling of the tiller tractor. The smell of the blades slicing through soil did not waft through my closed window. The sight of the nasty books being cut into ever smaller bits with each pass of the tiller went unseen by any of us.

We headed out to play after breakfast. A late summer breeze kicked up dust and nasty book remnants. Grandma emerged from her kitchen to examine these strange pink scraps that littered the camp.

"*Ave María por encima!*" The Devil was hard at work, but she knew just what to do. She and her neighbor Doña María quarantined us in the house, and ran about like manic chickens, chasing down every scrap they could find and tossing it in a paper sack.

The burning of our war treasure was perfunctory and largely unmourned. For weeks afterward, scraps missed by *abuela* would appear in corners; bits of tit, snatches of snatch, hanks of hair, and bouquets of tightly clenched toes that skipped along the dusty camp. But the boys and girls saved every nasty scrap and placed it in a cigar box. Together, we thought, we would gather enough pieces to assemble this puzzle of adultness.

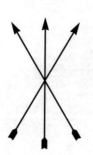

AL LUJÁN is a bastard!! He is a San Francisco-based writer, visual artist, performer, and filmmaker. He was raised in East Los Angeles and now makes San Francisco his home.

His artwork has been shown at Yerba Buena Center for the Arts, Galería De La Raza, Folsom Street Interchange, Four Walls Gallery, Artist's Television Access. His debut 8mm film was shown at Yerba Buena Center for the Arts, Cine Festival, and was picked up by Frameline for distribution.

His writing has appeared in *Beyond Definition, New Queer Writers of San Francisco, Best American Erotica 1995, Best Gay Erotica 1997,* and *SEX SPOKEN HERE,* writings from the Good Vibrations reading circle. He has also been published in *Drummer* magazine, *A La Brava* and *Manteca* zines, and an upcoming anthology from North Atlantic Books.

Al has performed throughout California. He is currently appearing with his new comedy troupe Latin Hustle, which debuted in January 1998 at Theatre Rhinoceros in San Francisco. He is a recipient of San Francisco Art Commission's Cultural Equity Grant.

RUBY DÍAZ

→

Al Luján

"Manny, damnit, cut it out! You're acting like such a little faggot!"
Ruby shouted at me one afternoon while we sat around on my
front porch, when I wouldn't stop ragging on her about the way
she dressed and put on her make-up. She was really pissed that
I would suggest that she cut her waist-long hair into the Dorothy
Hamill style that was so right-on that winter. I was only trying to
give her a little advice. After all, I did have two older sisters in
high school, who practically had to keep the boys back with cigarette lighters they weren't supposed to have and flaming cans of
Aqua-Net.

"For your goddamned information, Ruby," I snapped back
without thinking, "I am not acting, okay? And you know what?
A blue blouse with brown shorts will never, never, ever match
with pink eyeshadow, okay?"

That was it. I was out to my best friend, one of my only friends, Ruby Díaz. My only male friend was my cousin Freddy, who was sixteen, stocky, out of control, and didn't have any friends himself 'cause he'd beaten them all up. So he came around to shoot off my firecrackers at me or leave muddy blossoms in my mom's garden and blame me. Once he dangled himself off the railroad bridge, over the concrete banks of the L.A. riverbed, screaming as if he was losing his grip and begging me not to grab his hands or we'd both fall. Then he pulled himself up as effortlessly as though he were emerging from a swimming pool and told me, "See, that's how I can tell you love me, you started crying, you scared little baby." Ruby hated him as much as I did and would grant me asylum to her bedroom whenever I heard that his family was coming to visit.

My premature declaration caught us both off guard. We just stood there. Silent. Ruby and I were only fourteen. She was like my sister and my sisters were like glamorous and mean strangers living in the rooms down the hall. I didn't really want her to cut her hair. I was just acting the way my sisters did when they talked about other girls. We became friends the same day her family moved into the house next to mine, about ten years earlier. We grew up together. I watched her hair grow, from shoulder length to all the way down, just above the small of her back. Our mothers always joked about which one of them would make the tamales for our wedding reception—never compromising to work together. We would make vomit faces at the suggestion that we liked each other like that.

I always knew that I liked guys but I had never felt I could tell anyone. I never really wanted to and couldn't figure out why anyone would. I never rehearsed telling anyone 'cause I knew I would never have the nerve. Not Ruby, not my sisters, not even Joey, this really cute guy who worked at the corner grocery store. I'd had a crush on him since I was a boy. My mother always knew where to find me if I wasn't with Ruby or in the backyard. I was loitering at the store, comparison shopping and asking questions about the ingredients on cans of ravioli. He was young, but he had two kids already. I wanted to be one of them.

By then I'd already kissed two guys; one guy named Lardo who hung around the library and thought he had to wrestle me into a headlock to savagely french me behind the non-fiction section. The other was an older man at the record store who offered to buy me the tapes I wanted with his credit card, which looked like it was hammered out of solid gold, if I would only take a little "ride" with him. When my mom confronted me about all my new cassettes, I solemnly confessed that I stole them, took my punishment, and thanked God she didn't make me take them back to the store and apologize.

"What?" Ruby hissed. Her mouth and eyes were wide open.

"You heard me, Ruby, I am one. I like guys, okay? Are you happy now? See, you called me a sissy so many times you finally convinced me of it and now I've turned into one." (Actually, she wasn't the only one. My sisters, cousin Freddy, and even my father would occasionally refer to me as "sissy.") "See, you shouldn't have teased me so much about acting and talking the way I do. I can't help it. It really hurts, even when you're joking around, and you know what, it sinks in. Now I'll probably be a homo for a really long time, like Mr. Nash." Mr. Nash was this old, lanky, chain-smoking school crossing guard who swished from corner to corner, fanning himself with the STOP sign, even when there were no children crossing.

I bowed my head and shuffled my shoes around in that hopelessly marked-for-life manner. She just sat there speechless, pulled her long, brown hair forward, obscuring her face. She did that whenever she was embarrassed, angry, or just flirting with boys. She stood up, looked at me, and moved her lips but nothing came out. She turned away, snapping her head in the direction of her house. Her loose hair fanned out like a brown cape. It was beautiful and thick. I would sometimes help her brush out the tangles or braid it down to her butt when we had enough time before school. I wasn't really serious about her cutting it. I guess I was trying to model her after my sisters who mostly ignored me. I even stole their lip glosses to give to her (only after trying it on myself in front of the bathroom mirror).

I stood, turned away, climbed the five steps, crossed the porch, and went into my house without another word, letting the screen door hit me on the ass. I pulled the door, looking back once more. There she stood, motionless on the walkway facing her house. I shut the door and leaned back against it, exhaling what felt like lungs full of anxiety. I bolted the door as if I could keep out all those ugly feelings I had just conjured outside. I prayed: "Bad feelings, stay back, go away, be quiet."

Ruby lived two houses down on the same side of the street. Only the Puentes', an elderly couple's, blue stuccoed house separated her house from mine.

I remained there with my back on the door till I heard her hard, black shoes make deliberate stomping sounds down my walkway. All the way home I could hear her heels hit the floor, even across her lawn, it seemed. I heard her front door slam, then another slam. Her bedroom or bathroom door, I figured.

That afternoon, those sounds that are normally drowned out by the noises of cars, planes, televisions, and hysterical children seemed amplified. My thumping heart and voices I didn't want to hear. Ruby's mother pleading repeatedly: "*¿Qué te pasa? Contesta.*" Then louder. "*Dime, qué pasó.*"

"Don't tell, Ruby, please don't say it," I whispered.

"Ruby, what's wrong, *mija*, tell me, *¿qué paso?*" Her mother begged and pounded on the door.

"Don't," I prayed. It seemed as though Ruby gathered all her strength in her fourteen-year-old body to shout something back at her mom. I couldn't understand what, but I still jumped back and almost collapsed from fear. I'd never heard her roar like that. It gave me the chills. I went to my room and clicked on the TV to relieve my anguish with sitcom reruns.

My new life as an "out" fourteen-year-old was only twenty minutes old and I was in a constant state of panic. It was only Monday afternoon, which gave Ruby four more school days to repeat what I had told her to the entire student body before I killed myself under the bleachers on Friday. We guarded each other's secrets. We were no snitches. Didn't I, in fact, keep it to myself that it was she who marched down Whitter Boulevard in the East L.A. Cinco de Mayo parade with a crude papier maché Porky Pig head on and the front of her costume wide open so that everyone could see her pink training bra? She got the most applause and waved back enthusiastically, not knowing that she was exposing herself to the flashing cameras. Wasn't it me who let her know? And did I tell anyone? No.

But admittedly, this was different. I knew very well it was most definitely different. I hadn't sworn her to secrecy on her grandmother's grave. I figured that at least it was my last year in junior high. Perhaps I could volunteer to be bused to a school where nobody knew me. But that was still months away. I'd be beat up, teased, and pretty much insane by then. I still had the following day to deal with. I plotted. Of course I would deny it. Say things like "spurned lover," or "That lez-bean should talk." Perhaps I could turn this all around so that Ruby appeared like the fool I felt like. All I needed to do was rehearse for the inevitable.

That evening I stayed quiet through dinner. I gazed out the dining room window in the direction of Ruby's house, instead of talking as usual with my mouth crammed with food. My mom and dad welcomed the silence. My sisters, Morelia and Jacqueline (or as our father referred to them, Mo and Jack, completing his vision of having children named Manny, Mo, and Jack—much to our mother's surprise and mortification; you have to understand that he was a mechanic at Casa de Tune Up on Soto Street, and it was his passion), suspected nothing and just tittered among themselves about whoever knows what. No one noticed my craning neck and shifting eyes that looked out across the lawn to the side of the house that Ruby lived in with her mom and her obese Aunt Sarah.

Ruby's dad had left home about three years earlier. Her mom tried to explain it away, saying he had been deported back to Mexico and couldn't get back, despite the fact that we all knew he was Native American and from Wyoming. He used to talk about it all the time when he was drinking.

One afternoon as we rode the bus back from Hollywood after seeing a movie, we saw someone who looked just like him sitting in front of a check cashing place on Vermont Avenue with some other guy asleep on the sidewalk. Ruby veiled her face with her hair, looked at her hands, and played with her rings. I fought the urge to ask: "Hey, isn't that your dad?"

I rarely saw Ruby's Aunt Sarah because when she wasn't at the hospital getting her dialysis treatments, she was shut away in her dark room. I'd only catch glimpses of her as the ambulance drivers pulled her on a gurney up the driveway to the back door where Ruby's dad had built a ramp before he was "deported." One afternoon we were hanging out on her porch when Aunt Sarah was being returned. She looked uncomfortable on her back with a white sheet barely big enough to cover her. All that was exposed was her head with long, thin hair hanging over the edge of the gurney, and her stockinged feet that looked pink and swollen. She smiled at me and said: "Hi, Manny." She had sad eyes above her rounded cheeks. She looked nothing like Ruby's mom, her sister. All I could think to say back was: "Hi." I saw the painfully flushed look on Ruby's face as she fidgeted with her hair.

From time to time Ruby would tell me that she secretly wished her aunt would stay at the hospital or get deported, which I understood to mean she wished her aunt was dead. Mostly so that her mom could have more time to spend with her after work instead of taking care of Sarah. Ruby had no brothers or sisters but hardly felt like an only child. Money was scarce for her family too, which only made the resentment stronger.

After dinner I remained there at the table, watching the house as if I expected a banner to unfurl from a window that told me, "Everything is gonna be all right. Don't sweat it. Your secret's safe." Instead, an ambulance backed up into the driveway,

popped the back door, and unloaded Aunt Sarah. The sounds
of the outside world had resurfaced. One sister on the phone,
the other playing records, my dad in the garage banging on
something with his beloved tools, my mother's semi-beautiful
voice singing along with Juan Gabriel on the radio in the kitchen
as she washed the dishes, the sounds of cars, crying babies, and
planes.

I went off to my room to pick out something very masculine
to wear to school the next day. An ugly, never-worn-before Kansas
City Royals jersey given to me by somebody some Christmas ago
would do the trick, I thought. I practiced looks of horror and disgust in the mirror. "Ugh, me a fag?" I asked my reflection. "Nah,
never, impossible." I responded. I flexed, grimaced, and posed
tough for nearly an hour before going to bed thoroughly
exhausted, but not before beating up and pinning down my pillow,
growling: "Take it back, who's a faggot, punk?" I could swear I
heard it whisper back: "You."

Just after I fell asleep I awoke to the soundtrack of my bad
dreams still playing. Howling or crying, I got up and roamed
the dark house nervously. Lights peeked out from under the
doors to my sisters' rooms, but no noise. My parents' room was
dark. I looked out through the living room window. All of a sudden
an ambulance in Ruby's driveway switched on its lights and a
siren broke the quiet night. I jumped back about three feet and
clutched my throat to keep my heart from exiting that route.
My blood was electric and only slowed down as the wail of the
siren faded off down Soto Street. Poor Aunt Sarah, I thought,
and went back to bed, where I lay sleepless for most of the night.

I got out of bed and out of the house the next day fifteen
minutes earlier than usual. I didn't want to run into Ruby. We

usually walked to and from school together. We ate lunch together on the steps leading to the quad. I wasn't in any of her classes. Luckily, she was in advanced courses and I was fighting to stay out of remedial classes. What a blessing. I made it through the day without running into her in the halls, which was rare, unless we were avoiding each other, which we were, or at least I was. I even ate lunch in the cafeteria that day, which I never did because you know the type of kids that eat in there. I scanned the room and assessed which kid would accept me despite the soon-to-be common knowledge that I was a queer. I sat down next to the kid with teeth jutting straight out of his mouth, his lips unable to conceal them. I imagined that he could see them without the use of a mirror. I tried not to stare and hoped he wouldn't stare at me.

At the end of the day, I emerged victorious and closeted, for one day at least. Even on the way home, no sign of Ruby. I was able to walk a little slower. I was able to focus on whether the light was red or green at the intersection of Soto and First Streets, which I was unable to do that morning, sending Mr. Nash into a tizzy. I wanted to call him a faggot under my breath but then remembered something about throwing rocks at the house you live at or something like that.

My stride was right as I turned the corner onto the street that I lived on. Home free. My house was in the middle of the block; Ruby's was two before. I had to pass it before reaching mine. I considered going around the other way but I was confident because although I strolled at a leisurely pace I had been let out of school fifteen minutes earlier by Sister Margarite for looking nervous and pale. I didn't even have to ask.

A couple of steps into the street that led me home I realized something was terribly and most definitely wrong. The surreal took over. Everything slowed to a glide. The motion of my leg taking one step filled an eternity. My sweating palms turned the notebook I held to pulp. From the end of the block where I stood motionless I could study the scene like a photograph too vivid to be real. Little things were brought from the background into painfully clear focus. The Puentes' house, so blue and simple, demanded attention. The blooms of the bougainvillea climbing up the side of Ruby's white house cast a fuchsia glow on the gray sidewalk. From five houses with five lawns away I could clearly see my mother on our porch. Standing. Holding another woman.

I knew it. I was about to be confronted. I was a poor liar. Like a bad comic with bad jokes I would try to cover one bad lie with another, persisting and grimacing to punctuate my need to believe my own lies.

On Ruby's lawn were two men and a woman with a child clinging to her thick leg. The most astounding sight was that of Aunt Sarah. She was sitting on the steps leading to the porch. She was wrapped in a blanket or a sheet. My ears went deaf as I forced myself to step forward to the memory of my home and not back. I had to squeeze to keep from peeing myself, which made it harder to walk. I moved slowly, like a long confession. I felt betrayed. In twenty-four hours the trust I had given over to her, so completely, had faltered.

As I approached Ruby's house, I recognized that one of the men standing there was Ruby's father. He and the other man turned and vaulted over the five or so steps that Sarah buried in her size. They entered the house. The woman picked up the child, defeated in that her legs were not long enough to step over onto the porch. The child thrashed in her arms to be released back onto the grass. The woman held tight and turned to face Sarah. Sarah's skin was translucent and pale. In the sun I finally noticed a resemblence to her sister. It was the eyes. She looked at me. She lifted a part of the sheet she was in and covered her face, crying.

I forced myself to look beyond her onto my porch, where my mother, home early from work, was rocking the woman in her arms. Side to side, as she used to do me when I'd run home crying if I skinned my knees or got stung by a bee. The woman was Ruby's mother. Her head was in my mother's shoulder. I could see the wetness of her tears on my mother's uniform. Blood rushed into my head and the sounds became sharp and deafening. My mother was crying. *"Oh señora, oh señora."*

My bladder let go. I ran across the lawn but before I could reach the porch I could feel the wetness that soaked through my thighs, then my socks. With my books in front of me I lunged up the steps, whipped open the screen door, and raced into the bathroom. I slammed the door and threw my body against it. I covered my face with a towel and cried quietly, trying to suck air through it. I was crying because I didn't know why I was crying. I was fourteen, gay, and felt out of control because I couldn't figure out what was going on. Had I really caused all of this?

I heard the screen door bang. My mother tapped on the door, waited, then tapped again and said: *"Mijo,* change your pants and come out into the living room. We need to talk. Okay, *mijo?* This is important so I need you to be a man right now. *Un hombre fuerte como tu papá."*

"Okay, wait a minute, Ma," I called out. I pulled off my pants and underwear. I dug through the hamper for the shorts I'd worn all weekend. I felt the silkiness of the liner and yanked them out and put them on. With reluctant purpose my legs led me out of the bathroom to the hallway, to the living room, where my mom and Ruby's mom were seated next to each other on the sofa. For the first time I noticed that my father was home. He was seated at the table with my sisters and my cousin Freddy who had his head down on the table. My father had tears in his eyes. I had never, ever seen him cry. The makeup on my sisters' faces was streaked down to their cheeks. They looked at my wrinkled shorts, my knobby knees and my wet socks. One black, one blue.

My mother patted the seat next to her. "Sit down, *mijo*, I have some terrible news for you," she said softly. Her voice trembled. "Ruby had an accident last night, baby, she slipped in the shower and bumped her head on the side of the tub." My mother was choking up, almost unable to continue. "Her hair blocked the drain and she drowned. Oh baby I'm so sorry." Ruby's mom doubled over and wailed. My sisters echoed her. My father moaned. My mother covered her face with her apron.

My own tears blinded and disoriented me. I stood to flee but ended up on the floor next to the sofa, engulfed in blackness. I awoke with all of them standing over me, bent at the waist, dripping tears on me. Pleading for me to get up but I wanted nothing more than to go deeper in the dark, to wake up in bed on some other day and go to school and come home to laugh at the way Ruby's hair frizzed out when I'd undo her tight braids. To say anything to her in confidence. To know that secrets and trust are sacred, private, and glorious privileges.

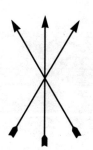

Photo: Giselle Chamma

ALEX R. SILVA left Rio de Janeiro for Manhattan when he was fifteen years old, a mere Corioca boy. He was inspired to become a writer out of his love for the works of Gabriel García Márquez. The story in this anthology marks his debut as a writer.

MARA'S MARVELOUS MATCH

Alex R. Silva

Mara woke up with the same feeling of emptiness that had been trailing her for months. She drew the velvet curtain and, as the orange light of sunset gusted into the room, she had to hold on to the window frame to not lose her balance. The ocean, all melted copper and gold, was an astonishing vision, and its immensity amplified her feelings. On the avenue below, the line of tiny cars was endless and uproarious, as usual. Mara turned around and began to sing, *El día que me quieras*. She loved tango; after samba, it was her favorite music: so romantic it helped to keep away melancholy.

Mara walked into the bathroom, stared at herself in its mirrored walls, and the same thought of every day flashed through her mind, "I'm getting old." This was basically a money concern, for she had given up on finding a man and she didn't care about growing old, not much, anyway. But she would have to find a new way of making money, since the oldest profession is unsympathetic to the older ones. Especially in Rio de Janeiro, where young girls sprout on the streets every few seconds. "The socio-economic conditions act like a fertilizer on the weak flowers, a powerful one," Mara scoffed. "But don't worry, darling. You'll find a way. God will provide…" With these words, and a kiss on the mirror, she reassured herself.

Mara was her own biggest fan. She was still a beautiful woman. Inspecting her body in the mirrors made her feel proud of herself. It took many years, lots of money and courage, to transform herself into the enigmatic object of desire she was. With pleasure she touched her breasts. They were still firmly in place, not too big. She wanted them to look natural, she had told the doctor. The hormones she began taking when she was fifteen worked miracles—her voice was smooth, and the hairs on her body didn't grow much. Two years of painful electrolysis had eliminated the undesirable remnants of her maleness, as well as the curse of all transvestites: her beard.

Going down her body with her manicured, delicate hands, she arrived at the forbidden place. With both hands between her legs, smiling, she said, "If it were not for this, only this, I'd be a real woman…but a penniless one."

She was right. Beautiful transvestites like Mara were rare, and when she was young, men would pay high amounts for the moments of exquisite pleasures she provided. Besides, most of her clients—many of them married men—did not want a woman, or a fake one, but a woman with a very peculiar mystery between her legs.

Around midnight she was ready to go to work. The heavy makeup had the opposite effect of what she wanted to achieve. The blush on her cheeks made them look musty, and the fake eyelashes were so thick the wrinkles around her eyes became more visible. But her African lips, thanks to her grandmother, were still beautiful, and the cherry-red lipstick made her mouth very desirable. She was finishing drawing her eyebrows when she heard Ladybug cry.

"Okay, okay. I'll take you for a walk," Mara snorted.

Ladybug was a sensitive, scared, and nervous miniature Chihuahua. She had narrowly escaped death many times when she was sat on or stepped on by Mara or her drunken guests. Mara picked up the dog and smothered him with kisses. Then she set him down again. "Later, darling."

Mara lived and made her living on Avenida Atlántica, the best address in Copacabana Beach. She stopped at a bar, ordered a scotch, and nibbled on codfish cakes. A second scotch gave her time to gather strength for another night of work. She heard Desiree calling her.

"Maaaara, baby! I've been looking for you. I passed by your corner and saw a chick there. Have you leased your office, darling?"

"Who's at my corner?" snapped Mara.

"I've never seen her before. I guess she's new."

Mara gulped her drink. "Carlos, put this on my tab," she told the bartender, and she left like a hurricane.

Desiree followed her, excited by her own malice.

Mara screamed at the skinny girl. "What are you doing here? This is my place."

"The streets are public, and I stand where I want," replied the arrogant girl.

Mara, her territory invaded, was a furious lioness. Yet she

controlled herself, and held her attack.

"Listen, you little faggot. I pay good money for my office."

"Money? To who? To the mayor?" The girl laughed.

Mara looked at Desiree incredulously. "Besides breastless, she's also brainless," Mara hissed. She turned to face the girl and screamed in her face, "To the police, stupid! To the police!"

Sensing the girl's inexperience, Mara decided to frighten her. Quicker than a cowboy draws his gun, she produced a razor from her bag. Holding it very close to the girl's face, she said, "How would you like a big centipede on your pretty face for the rest of your life?"

The horrified girl ran away.

Mara and Desiree laughed and laughed and only stopped for fearing of ruining their makeup.

Desiree wandered off to meet a client in a club nearby. Mara stood on the corner, alone. The night was warm, even for winter, too warm for the black Givenchy raincoat she was wearing, which she opened to show herself dressed only in red panties and a garter belt to the cars that slowed as they passed her. She opened the coat many times that night, to no avail. Mara had standards: she wouldn't go with weird types, and she wouldn't take less than her price.

"I guess I'll have to stop being so choosy," she admitted to herself, fighting her pride.

The girls on the nearby corners had already gone off with johns. Mara was there for over two hours, opening and closing the raincoat. Hope finally abandoned her when she saw a blue Mercedes stop for a young girl two blocks away. There was only one blue

Mercedes in all of Rio that was interested in transvestites. Mara knew that. It belonged to one of her oldest clients, an ambassador, a gentleman who had told her many times, "I like you very much, Mara." He brought her Godiva chocolates and called her "my flamboyant girl." Now she had lost him. Mara felt humiliated; for a moment she wanted to cry. But she also knew that men are not attracted to girls who cry. She held her sadness in her heart.

Feeling lonely, depressed, she crossed the avenue, bought a beer at a *barraca* on the sidewalk and walked along the wide-sanded beach for a while. She sat down and searched the clear sky, hoping to see a falling star. At moments like this a falling star can be of great help to a girl who has faith. She studied the sky for a long time. But no stars fell.

Lucky stars, however, can come from other places, like the sea, or wherever; and from the darkness of the moonless night came Mara's.

A tall man with gleaming silver hair and skin like brown sugar approached her. "What's a lady like you doing all alone at the beach at night? You seem troubled. Is there anything I can do to help?" If Valentino had a voice in the movies, he would have sounded like this. He was respectful, not leering. He seemed genuinely concerned.

Mara was a little scared, she knew that God's world was full of weirdos of all kinds. But without betraying her fear she said, "I came here to talk to Yemenjá."

"Oh, I see. You're a woman of faith," he said.

"Faith is what carries me through life."

The man sat down beside her. "What a beautiful way of living," he said more to the starless night than to her.

"I don't see what's so beautiful about it."

"Life is a simple thing…"

"It is not! Not my life, anyway."

"But you are simple. I can see your heart. Your eyes are green, and people with green eyes have simple hearts."

I can't take off the contacts as long as I live, Mara thought to herself.

They talked about life, about God, about Yemenjá, and about the magical moments in life. Faith, love, loneliness—all these were discussed. Yet they didn't have time to talk about themselves. There was an urgency to their conversation, as if the fate of all things depended upon their conclusions.

The metallic darkness of the sky had begun to give way to the blush of dawn when Mara, awakening from her trance, not wanting to spoil the magic of the last hours, said, "I have to go."

"Why?"

"I have to walk my dog." That seemed as good an excuse as any.

"Another good quality," he said, mesmerized. "Love of animals."

Right then and there Mara swore she would never again spank Ladybug, even if she shat upon her Persian carpet.

They walked together to Mara's building. She walked fast, not wanting him to see her in full daylight. When they reached the entrance, he didn't ask to go upstairs, but offered to wait for her until she brought down Ladybug.

"Please go," she said.

"I'll leave, but not before you tell me your name." Then he blushed. "May I have…your phone number?"

"My name is Mara Miranda. I'm listed."

"Marco Marcial." He kissed her hand and walked away.

Startled, looking at the hand he had kissed, Mara thought: "So many M's. Could this be Mara's marvelous match?"

Upstairs, Ladybug was waiting by the door, anxious to go out. Mara didn't want to take the chance of running into Marco in full daylight. "It's okay, Ladybug," she said. "You can use the Oriental today."

The doorbell rang many times before Mara woke up. A delivery boy arrived with a beautiful bouquet of yellow roses with a card that said,

> *I hope one night will not be enough for you.*
> *Can we meet tonight for dinner at Antiquarius?*
> *My heart waits singing the melody of your voice.*
> *Marco*
> *P.S. I am also listed.*

Mara pinched herself. Was she still dreaming? If she was, this was a long dream, and the feelings were intense and real. Mara smelled the roses and, as she crossed the living room, stepped on Ladybug's shit. She screamed. Ladybug jumped on the sofa, shaking more than customarily. Mara, remembering Marco's words, said, "It's okay, Ladybug. Don't worry. I'll never spank you again. I promise."

She dialed some digits. "Desiree, I need to talk...answer the fucking phone. Desireeee!"

"I hope this is an emergency," said a sullen Desiree. "How dare you wake me up at three in the afternoon?"

"Desiree, listen. It's important. I think...I'm in love."

"You in love? This is indeed an emergency."

"Forget everything I've said before about not falling in love again. You know one cannot control one's heart."

"Of course I know. I'm the one who's always saying that," said Desiree with some annoyance in her voice.

"Shut up, Desiree. I met this man last night. A wonderful man…"

"How old?"

"I don't know. Fifty? Fifty-two?"

"You mean you met your grandfather?"

"Bitch. You're jealous."

They laughed. Then, after a pause, Mara said, "Desiree, he doesn't know."

"Didn't you tell him?"

"He's not a trick. We didn't do anything. He walked me to my door downstairs. He's a gentleman."

"I bet he can't get it up!"

"Be serious. What should I do? He wants to take me to Antiquarius tonight. Can you believe it?"

"He must have money."

"Looks that way. But that's not it. What should I do? Tell me, girl. Should I tell him the truth?"

"You have to. You know how bad things can get if you don't tell them up front. But tell him after dinner and dessert, darling. Don't miss the passion fruit mousse!"

"You're pathetic," Mara said and hung up.

Desiree was right. Not telling him meant things could only get worse. If she fell in love, she would get hurt at the end of love. And Marco would hate her forever. She'd been there before. She didn't tell one guy and she ended up with a broken nose that cost her two months' work to pay for the plastic surgery. The second time, she told the man after a week of dates and dinners—he jumped out of his second floor apartment window. Mara spent a week in jail: the man was a lieutenant in the Federal Police.

"I'm creating a tempest in a glass of water," Mara said to Ladybug. "I'm not in love…and he won't fall in love with me. Why should he? Ten, twenty years ago, maybe. But now, no way!"

Mara was wrong, for she was in love. If she was not in love with him—Mara had a complicated heart—she was at least in love with the man who sent her flowers, and who treated her as a lady. "Let's get real," she told Ladybug. "A man like that could be the answer to our uncertain future." She knew he could love her. She was a beautiful woman with many good qualities: her delightful and intelligent conversation, and a charming personality. And for the most important reason: love is not a reasonable emotion. When it happens, there's no escape.

At Antiquarius, the finest Portuguese restaurant in Rio, they dined on roast baby goat and red wine. They talked with even more fervor than the night before, passion singing in their eyes. Marco told her about his life, his loneliness. His wife had died two years before. Without children or relatives he was left alone with his ninety-five-year-old blind mother, who was just waiting for death to rescue her from her misery.

"I haven't been with a woman since my wife died," he said softly. "Actually, I haven't been with another woman since I got married."

His sincerity and innocence touched Mara. Men like this didn't exist anymore (probably never had!). Nothing touched her more than innocence. Hers had been lost a long, long time ago. She wanted to envelop Marco in her arms (and legs) and never let go of him. But she also knew the best thing for her would be to disappear before it was too late. But it was too late already—they were in love. She could feel the ropes of love tying knots around her, knots impossible to unmake. She sipped her wine. "Marco, I have to tell you…I'm not the woman you think I am."

"Please, Mara," he said, placing two fingers on her lips. "I know who you are."

"You do?"

"Of course. I told you last night. I can see your heart. It's true. Believe me."

"And…?" Mara felt her heart stop beating.

"I know what kind of woman you are. And believe me, that's not what I want from you. I just don't want one night in a motel room…I want you for the rest of my life. I want to marry you."

His hands trembled as he took from a pocket of his jacket a little box. He presented it to her.

Mara opened the box. Inside she saw an obscenely extravagant emerald engagement ring. Mara gasped. She looked at Marco, then at the stone, repeatedly.

He smiled, pleased that she liked it. To Mara it was the most innocent smile she had seen since her little brother, Duda, had died of meningitis at age five. The memory brought tears to her eyes. She cried loudly and shamelessly. Marco didn't say a word, his eyes becoming very shiny and deep.

Suddenly Mara stopped crying. She dabbed her eyes with her napkin and her mood changed. "Why do you make fun of me like this? What kind of sadist are you?"

Marco looked surprised, but he kept his composure. "I don't know what you mean. I love you, Mara."

"No, you don't." Anger rose in her throat. "You don't know anything about me. You just met me. This is not fiction! This is real life."

Undeterred he said, "I was sure of my love when we parted this morning. I want you like I've never wanted anyone in my life. I want you to be my source of happiness and pain for the rest of my life."

"Enough!" she blurted out. As she dried her eyes again, a contact fell out. Mara removed her eyelashes and stashed them in a cigarette box. Walking with the dignity of a lady, Mara left the restaurant with only one green eye.

He sent yellow roses everyday. Yellow was Oshum's color, the goddess of sweet water, Mara's protector. Marco sent her long letters listing all the reasons why they were meant for each other. He serenaded her with guitar players under her balcony, though she lived on the twelfth floor. He stood guard outside her building, just to catch a glimpse of her. He sent her beautiful jewelry and fine dresses made in Italy and France. He called her machine many times a day just to hear her voice on the tape.

In the beginning, Mara enjoyed it; she was flattered. But when he continued his attention day after day, her love for him grew until it was no longer pleasurable, until it turned into a new kind of pain. Mara tried to hate him; she returned all his gifts and the flowers, too. But the delivery man got tired of taking things back and forth, and refused to take back anything from her. She sent the flowers to a friend who was in the hospital. Soon, the whole floor for infectious diseases looked yellow from the perfume of the roses. She gave the dresses to a friend. The jewelry, she sold—

with the exception of a pink diamond bracelet that she kept on Ladybug's neck. Mara stopped working. With the money from the sale of the jewels, she planned to open a small cosmetic shop.

Contempt was her new approach. But the more she refused and ignored him, the more she fueled his love.

Mara asked the gods for guidance. But neither the chickens sacrificed to Exu nor the flowers and food presented to Iansa helped to free her from the vortex of love.

One night she called the police. Marco was taken away by two rude men who respected no one's rights. Desiree was at Mara's house that night.

"Girl, you can't go on like this," she said, full of pity for Marco. "You will kill this man or he'll go crazy. Why don't you tell him the truth?"

"Are you nuts? If I tell him the truth now, he'll kill me!"

Marco disappeared for three days. The feeling of emptiness returned, and only when the feeling returned did she realize that it had been gone for a while. Mara worried about Marco. What if he was still in jail? She felt guilty. She removed the bracelet from Ladybug's neck and put it on her wrist. She was about to cry, when the intercom rang.

"Your friend is here," the doorman said, his voice dripping with irony.

"What friend?"

"The man with the yellow roses."

For a brief moment, she was happy. Then anger and despair took over. Mara had only one way out of the insanity of her present situation. "Tell him to come up," she said.

Mara opened the door and let him in. "Sit down and keep quiet," she told him. She held a small revolver in one hand. With the other hand she began to unbutton her negligee. It fell on the floor. Then she said, "Look. Are you happy now? Here, take this gun. Kill me if you want. But do it now because I'm not the kind of woman who can live fearing death every time I go out."

Marco stared at her nakedness with his usual placid expression.

"Aren't you shocked?" Mara asked.

"Shocked? No. Not at all. Surprised, yes!" He laughed merrily.

"This is no laughing matter. Are you insane?"

"If that is the reason you refused me for so long," he said, still chuckling, "then I have to laugh."

Stupefied, Mara dropped the gun on the rug. "Did you know all along?"

"No, of course not."

"So you see now? I can't accept your love. It's not real. You don't love me. You love the woman I'm not."

Marco sighed. "You never understood me, Mara. When I said that I saw your heart, I didn't mean your sex, or your intellect, but your soul. Anyone who thinks he falls in love with a person is a fool. Love is not about a form or an idea, but only about the essence that precedes it. Only the soul is deserving of love, this noble expression of respect and recognition. Don't you know the expression 'soulmates'? It comes from the Greek myth of love." He extended his hand and she took it. "Come sit here near me," he said. "I'm going to tell you that story."

AFTERWORD

➤───────────➤

Jesse Dorris

In the liner notes of his 1998 LP *Fabrication Defect: Com Defeito De Frabricação*, Brazilian tropicalist Tom Zé compares his music to *arrastão*, a robbery technique in which a group disperses silently into a crowd and then runs furiously through it, snatching and grabbing whatever it can. It's an idea that fits his music perfectly, but also points to directions beyond the confines of the record sleeve.

The idea of *arrastão* kept running through my mind as we put this anthology together. Not out of ties to crime—though there's plenty of it in these stories, both against society and of the heart—but because it seems to me that the authors included here could well be that group. They are here, they are suddenly visible, filling their pockets and stories with things society has tried to deny them: love, power, identities, and all the rest of life's valuables. They appear when society recognizes what they possess. And of course they have always been here, mingling in the crowd; but the action provides a spotlight, a focus. The group names itself or is named—here are the Latinos, the gays, the men—and perhaps the energy disperses as crowds form and are themselves infiltrated and appropriated. Zé writes of "an esthetic of *arrastão* that ambushes the universe of the well-known and traditional." New traditions are formed and torn down; it's a continual process. We are lucky to have documentation of it happening before our very eyes.

So let's hope that the group of authors here, and others like them, will continue their robberies and invention. They've grabbed some inspiring stuff from the crowd of modern society. May this book continue the *arrastão*.

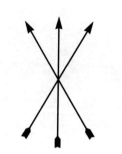

OTHER BOOKS

→

from Painted Leaf Press

Poetry

Blood & Tears: Poems for Matthew Shepard
Edited by Scott Gibson   1-891305-15-8

Balefire
Star Black   1-891305-16-6

Other Selves
Rosanne Wasserman   1-891305-04-2

The Sentence that Ends with a Comma
Dean Kostos   1-891305-05-0

My Night With ▪ Mi Noche Con Federico García Lorca
Jaime Manrique   0-9651558-3-8   Bilingual Edition

Night Life
Paul Schmidt   0-9651558-0-3

Winter Solstice
Paul Schmidt   0-9651558-2-X

October for Idas
Star Black   0-9651558-1-1

Cold River
Joan Larkin   0-9651558-5-4

Desire
Tom Carey   0-9651558-4-6

Sor Juana's Love Poems
Sor Juana Inéz de la Cruz   0-9651-558-6-2   Bilingual Edition
Translated By Jaime Manrique and Joan Larkin

In the Open
Beatrix Gates   0-9651558-7-0

Island Light
Eugene Richie   0-9651558-8-9

A Flame for the Touch That Matters
Michael Lassell   0-9651558-9-7

Fiction

Christ-like
Emanuel Xavier   1-891305-14-X

Bad Sex Is Good
Jane DeLynn   1-891305-00-X

Colombian Gold
Jaime Manrique   1-891305-01-8

New York Sex: Stories
Edited by Jane DeLynn   1-891305-03-4

Non-Fiction

The Queer Press Guide
Edited by Paul Harris   1-891305-17-4

Latin Lovers
Edited by Erasmo Guerra   1-891305-13-1

Men Seeking Men: Adventures in Gay Personals
Edited by Michael Lassell   1-891305-02-6